Dennis McCort - **The Golden Pot**

Dennis McCort

The Golden Pot

A Fairy Tale for Our Time

PalmArtPress
Berlin

Bibliografische Information der Deutschen Nationalbibliothek
Die Deutsche Nationalbibliothek verzeichnet diese Publikation in der Deutschen
Nationalbibliografie; detaillierte bibliografische Daten sind
im Internet über http://www.dnb.de abrufbar.

ISBN: 978-3-96258-109-1

First Edition, 2022, PalmArtPress, Berlin

Cover Design: Catharine J. Nicely
Layout: NicelyMedia
Druck:
Printed in Europe

PalmArtPress
Pfalzburger Str. 69, 10719 Berlin
Publisher: Catharine J. Nicely
www.palmartpress.com

Table of Contents

VIGIL 1

A Close Encounter

At three in the afternoon on a recent July 4th holiday in Journal Square, Jersey City, young graduate student Anselm MacGregor ran smack into a chestnut pushcart as he rounded the curvilinear walkway of the strip mall. The old peddler, who looked like a fugitive from a 1930's gangster movie in his suspendered tweed pants, stood there casting an evil eye on the young man, who sat woozily on the ground taking stock of his bodily integrity. Chestnuts were strewn everywhere and the pedestrians, coming and going, were doing a little egg dance to avoid crushing them underfoot. Street urchins on the run grabbed many of them up and kept running.

"Your ass behind glass! Your ass behind glass! ... Soon!" the peddler's wife screeched at poor Anselm, pointing her crone's arthritic finger at him as he struggled to get to his feet. Her straggly hair was up in a limp bun and she was clad entirely in black, as though in mourning, despite the summer heat. The young man, his fair face flushed with embarrassment, pulled a thin wad of cash out of his wallet and paid the man a hastily agreed-upon sum, returning the two or three bills left him to their now-roomy leather slot.

Then, looking to bolt, he found himself crowded in by curiosity seekers mouthing comments about equally divided in sympathy: "Poor kid, he didn't see the cart." "What's he doing running in a strip mall anyway" "Those old farts had no business crowding the pedestrian space." "He should give them everything he has …" Anselm pushed his way through the small throng and headed for the PATH station to catch the train for Liberty Park, the new raised green in Lower Manhattan built on the site of the World Trade Center. Finally he was going to have a day of fun and spend some money, seeing the Oculus for the first time, this being the hub of the area in the shape of a great, white bird with clipped wings, a bird housing a labyrinthine system of subway connections, an interior plaza as large as a football field and an appallingly elaborate mall that had to be nirvana to compulsive shoppers. He was going to join the patriotic celebration in the plaza, have a few beers and sit among the revelers at one of the flag-bedecked tables, listening to the Sousa marches being bleated out by a military brass band and, who knows, maybe even catching the eye of one or two of the many Manhattan, and tourist, beauties sitting nearby.

But, suddenly realizing he now had no more than two fives to rub together, he stopped in the middle of the PATH plaza, slouched over to a nearby hatbox seat, wearily lowered himself onto it and, feeling moved to bemoan his fate, began muttering to himself: "What a fuck-up I am. F-U-C-K-U-P! Could I have sabotaged this day any more brilliantly? My first real break from the books in more than a month and I go and squander it, running into that old witch's pushcart. Now I can barely afford to *get to* Manhattan, much less enjoy its pleasures. And boy was I going to enjoy. *Boy … enjoy!* There! I'm a poet and I *do* know it! – Anyway … bellying up to the Oculus bar for a few drinks, maybe buying one for some sexy senorita. Regaling her with stories about Byron and Shelley (assuming she's a literary type; yeah, lots of luck with that)—it's a good time for it, right in the middle of preps as I am for doctoral prelims on the Romantic poets. I'll never know more about them than I do now, Professor Holman says … Anyway, I'd tell her about Lord Byron wandering through the Alps, plagued by guilt-ridden love. Or is it his hero Manfred who's plagued? Or both of them? Jeez, I'd better get straightened out on that one when I get home. – I don't know, things just never seem to work out for me. Last week I go bowling on couple's night. Nice girl, Jenny. Wouldn't you know it, the guy on the next lane gets a little too close and drops his fucking ball right on my big toe. I can't bowl, I can only keep score, and I mess that up too, pissing everybody off. – Reminds me of when I was little, serving as an altar boy. Different year, same shit.

Six-thirty Mass on a weekday, a school day. Father Fitzpatrick hates saying six-thirty Mass. He needs a little jolt to get himself going. Asks me to go back to the sacristy and get the big—*really* big—wine cruet, fill it up and bring it to him. The one I brought must hold at least half a bottle of that cheap rotgut they use for Mass. He fills the chalice to the brim, emptying the thing, then goes to hand it back to me and—still half stupid with sleep myself—I drop it right into the chalice, I go to grab it, too late of course, but overzealous me winds up giving Father Fitz a karate chop to the chest and he drops the chalice with the cruet in it onto the altar floor, wine splashing all over the place, then falls down on top of it himself, and now we've got a real circus show going, for shit's sake. Not surprisingly, I never served Mass with him again. – Or the time I was working as a graduate assistant in the department for Professor Hillis and accidently pressed the delete button on his bibliography of rare Baroque books, something he'd been working on for five years. What, didn't he have a back-up file, a flash drive? Of course. Didn't it open up? Of course not. That almost got me thrown out of grad school. – If I'm introduced to someone important, like that Dante scholar at the MLA conference last year, I can't get the words out straight: 'Hell is just … well, *hell* in the *Inferno*, don't you think?' Duh, well, yeah, I suppose it is, he says. Hell is hell? Hell is *hell*? Really? Is that the best you can do, MacGregor? – Or the year I ripped up twenty-five or thirty parking tickets in Baltimore, figuring because I had Jersey plates, the cops couldn't touch me. Not only did they touch me, they frisked me on campus in front of some of my own students and threw me into the paddy wagon for a ride downtown to city court. Thank God the Dean lent me the money for the fine, or I would've sat in a cell. – How many girls have I lost for being tongue-tied, how many wallets on the bus or the subway, how many jackets, books, phones for being just generally out to lunch? – Who was that guy in the L'il Abner comics that went around with a dark cloud always over his head? Joe something or other …"

And as he sat there muttering despondently, his elbows on his shorts-clad knees, holding his head up with his hands, a sustained, high-pitched sound came within his earshot from within the bowels of the station. At first he thought it must be the squeal of a wheel on a breaking train, but he soon realized the sound was much too beautiful for that. It was the strain of a violin, its volume low, its tone sweet and delicate, then loudening slowly and gently, slicing right through his dark mood, causing it to evaporate. It evolved into an exquisite melody, unlike any he had ever heard before, yet not so much a melody as a phrase, a phrase that kept repeating itself, over and over, building upon itself, climbing the registers and swelling as it burgeoned. *Must be some panhandling fiddler down the corridor,* Anselm thought to himself in a reflex attempt to rationalize what was happening. But it really didn't matter; he was utterly caught up in the music and swept away to an aural paradise. Other sounds in the corridor, ordinarily tedious or irritating, seemed to transform themselves into musical lines in harmony with the violin: the hum of the fluorescent lights, the syncopation of turnstiles, the gabbling echoes of commuters. The lights seemed to be singing, "We are your vision, clear, deep and true"; the turnstiles chimed in with, "We are your movement, the turning of your world in place"; and the gabbling commuters with, "We are your words, the meaningful sounds binding us all together." It all ebbed and flowed and then suddenly surged up ecstatically into some vast, supernal symphony of the angels, and the student Anselm no longer knew where or even who he was. At some point lost to time and space, there was nothing but the music itself and the music was enough, and more than enough.

Then, at some indeterminate point, a train pulled into the stop below ground with its characteristic cacophony—a thunderous roar capped off by the aurally painful screech of steel wheels on steel track. A more than sufficient intrusion from the world to bring Anselm back from his brief otherworldly sojourn. For a moment everything was still around him as the shuffling exchange of passengers took place on the level below. Then the train pulled out, next stop Hoboken, slowly accelerating in both speed and noise, though the noise never reached the shattering pitch it had on arrival. It was, however, enough of a nuisance to allow Anselm to begin to appreciate what had just been lost. *What the hell was that? What just happened? I just went someplace without moving! Where did I go?* Where, indeed? But as he looked around him searchingly, it was obvious that the fluorescent lights were again merely fluorescent lights, their hum again just a hum; the turnstiles were again mere turnstiles, rotating harshly each time a card was swiped; and the gabbling commuters resumed their gabbling. Too, the violin that had started it all was nowhere to be heard. Just then a profound weariness came over Anselm and he leaned back against the curved hub of the seat, momentarily closing his eyes to collect himself.

VIGIL 2

Mai Tais with Kafka

It was an island, South Sea perhaps. He couldn't tell. It seemed deserted and was entirely covered by close-cropped monkey ladder vines, such that, except for within a ten-yard radius from where he stood, at no point could he see ground. His only advantage, if advantage it was, was that he stood at its very apex and could survey all around him. It was a kind of natural panopticon, yet there was nothing in particular to watch except the burgeoning green. Farther off, the ocean, under a brilliant sun, was a mesmerizing deep blue, utterly serene, which gave the island by contrast a tinge of anxiety.

He turned around, counterclockwise, expecting to confirm the total greenness to himself, then swiftly swung halfway back, for something had caught his eye:

"Hi there! Or should I say, "Sup, man!' … You Americans with your outrageous elisions."

Anselm just stood there, speechless, only half-catching what the fellow had said. He was a young man, or youngish at least, no more than forty, and was lying in a hammock suspended between two sturdy vines, his hands cupped behind his head and smiling broadly. Dressed in shorts and a Polynesian shirt, untucked and unbuttoned, he had his bare feet propped up against the hammock's bottom knot, perhaps a foot higher than his head. He was thin, almost gaunt, with high cheekbones and close-cropped, pitch-black hair. His eyes seemed even blacker, though his gaze was soft and caressing, and, despite his smile, a tad sad, rather than invasive or challenging.

"Whew! What a relief," Anselm said, slowly shaking his head. "I thought I was stuck here alone."

"'Stuck,' you say. You mean 'marooned?'" the man replied cheerfully, switching foot positions.

"Yes, of course. There doesn't seem to be anyone else around. Looks like we're alone," Anselm insisted, a bit testily. What else could he possibly have meant?

"No, not at all," the man contradicted. "On the contrary. You're actually much closer to home now than you were before you got here." He picked up a glass, heretofore hidden under the hammock, removed the tiny umbrella, tossing it into the brush, and sipped from a pineapple Mai Tai.

This made Anselm a bit *more* testy. However, not wanting to seem ungrateful to his putative host, he kept his counsel and decided to limit himself to fact-finding questions. *Where did that drink come from?* he wondered.

"Closer to home? Here? That makes no sense. I've never been south of Baltimore," Anselm replied, as much to himself as his interlocutor, as he made a slow panoptical scan, which failed to discern anything but 360 degrees of undifferentiated green and blue.

"Well, you'll know what I mean soon enough," the man said somewhat ominously (or did Anselm just hear it that way), taking another sip of his Mai Tai. "Meanwhile, why don't you join me over here on this twin hammock and sip one of these tropical drinks yourself. You've been standing there for quite a while; you must be parched."

Anselm saw the second hammock but had no idea how it had gotten there. Throwing caution to the winds (what was the point?), he shuffled over to it and carefully lowered his tall frame down onto it, whereupon his companion handed him another Mai Tai, replete with straw, ice cubes and toy umbrella, this time green not pink. No longer curious as to its origin, Anselm accepted the drink with a nod and, ignoring the straw, took a long, grateful swig from it, emptying the glass about a third. Expelling a long, satisfied "Aah," he felt ready, eager, to pick this fellow's brain:

"So, tell me, what are you doing here? How did you get here?"

"I'm not sure myself how I got here. Probably the same way you did," the man speculated, seemingly incurious. "As for what I'm doing here, I should think it's obvious I'm here for you, for your benefit. By the way, my name is Franz, ... Franz Kafka."

"For *my* benefit! How could—Wait, wait a minute ..." Anselm interrupted himself, in his astonishment not sure which tack to pursue, the man's purpose or identity, both irresistible, both compelling. But he could only pursue one at a time, so he chose the latter: "Did you say Kafka, *Franz* Kafka, the Czech writer, possibly the twentieth century's greatest writer," inserting the "possibly" as a hedge, since, as a serious student of literature, he didn't want to sound absolutist in an age of dreary relativism.

"None other than," the man answered, swatting a mosquito with a baseball cap he suddenly pulled from his back pocket. Anselm could see the superimposed orange "N" and "Y" sewn into it, identifying it as a Mets cap. *At least he's not a Yankees fan.*

"Although, the accolade is up for debate," he added with an air of modesty, but it was only an air. "There's Proust and Joyce and Virginia Woolf, and one or two others, I suppose. Elite company," he sniffed. "Of course, they relied heavily on the tedious stream of consciousness technique. For me, a sentence or two of third-person inner monologue was always enough to give the gist of a character's thought process," he ended with a self-satisfied smile.

"You know," Anselm enthused, almost breathlessly, "I did sort of recognize you at first glance, even in that exotic beach outfit, even without the iconic bowler hat or high collar or gilded walking stick. I'm a big fan, you know. I'm in literature myself," Anselm rushed to add, embarrassing himself with the presumptuous self-reference, as if he and the great man could possibly be in the same club.

"Yes, I know. You're a graduate student in English literature— the Romantic poets, isn't it?" Kafka asked, seeming to perk up a bit.

"That's right, but how would you know that?" Anselm asked in turn, in an almost accusatory tone. "And didn't you say a moment ago you were here on this island for me, for my benefit? That doesn't make any sense; would you mind explaining it?" But without waiting for a response, Anselm turned away from the man and began muttering to himself, almost as if he were alone on the island and having an imaginary conversation with himself. *He knows me and I know him. Of course, it's not the same, not the same at all. I know him by reputation, but he seems to know me personally. So odd.* Anselm had the sinking feeling that the logic he was using to try to make sense of his situation was futile, like applying a wet band-aid to an abrasion. No matter what angle he tried, it wouldn't stick.

"Think of it this way," Kafka suggested, swinging his legs over the side of the hammock and sitting up, "right now you're in a special place, a solipsistic sort of world where everyone and everything in your field of consciousness is a part of you, as though by some miracle you had been turned inside out and all the thoughts, feelings and images that normally arise *inside* you, the stuff of your inner life, were now arising *outside* instead, and you could see it all clear as day."

"But that would mean *you* were part of me too, wouldn't it? Which would mean you're not really Kafka at all, just my subjective image of him," Anselm asked, hoping for an answer that would contradict him. He wanted the man to be Kafka.

"A very astute question, very astute indeed," Kafka replied, looking pleased that Anselm was paying attention. "I could answer it, but right now the answer wouldn't help you, so I'm going to put it aside for a later time."

Anselm wasn't sure how he felt about that: He liked the prospect of an answer but not the passage of time it might require. How long was he going to be stuck here?

"I've read your story about the insect … *The Metamorphosis*, and the other one, about the father and son, 'The ah …'"

"'Judgment,' 'The Judgment,'" the writer prompted, brushing some imaginary sand from his shorts. "Yes, actually that's my favorite, the latter I mean. I wrote it in one night at my desk, sitting like a stone even with the incessant family traffic coming and going through my room, which, alas, was centrally located in the railroad apartment. But I was so concentrated, so focused, so one-pointed, I didn't hear a thing. It came out of me like an unimpeded fetus, all bloody and slimy, but all the purer for that. My instincts told me not to edit it, not to 'correct' or 'polish' it in any way. It was pure writing, warts and all. Leave it exactly as it is and let future critics interpret it to death. Which, of course, they have—and *do*. In due course, I'll tell *you*, a probable future critic yourself, something about them—the critics, that is – By the way, you'll recall the end of the story when Georg Bendemann falls from the bridge from which he's dangling into the Prague river in an act of self-execution. I was going to end the story precisely there, but I experienced such a rush of bliss—just between us, to the point of orgasm—over Georg's release that I added a tag sentence about the vehicular traffic crossing the bridge in that moment. The word for traffic in German, *Verkehr*, is the same as the word for sexual intercourse. Do you think that makes the story too autobiographical, too self-absorbed per-haps?" And with that Kafka let out a hyena-like bray that both astonished and delighted Anselm.

They both got up and stood side by side gazing out east-ward over the sea, the sinking sun at their backs, the healthy, well-fed American almost a head taller than his tubercular Czech companion.

From the first, Anselm had noticed Kafka's somewhat ema-ciated look, more apparent now that he was standing, rail-thin and of slightly stooped posture as he was. Though feeling awk-ward about it, Anselm felt compelled to acknowledge it: "Are you all right? You seem a bit unsteady there. I assume it's the ravages of that dread disease of your time."

"Very good, very good, Anselm. You know something about me," Kafka smiled approvingly. He knows my name, Anselm thought. Funnily enough I'm not surprised. "And you're quite right," Kafka continued, "the illness consumes me, no pun intended, as it has half of Europe. But that's no concern of yours in present circumstances. For that matter, it's no concern of mine either, for reasons you're not ready to appreciate." As he said this, he laid a gentle, reassuring hand on Anselm's left shoulder. Anselm allowed it and, in fact, rather enjoyed the gesture of familiarity. It leavened a bit the profoundly uncanny nature of the situation.

Yet one thing bothered him about the remark: "You keep saying things like 'not ready yet' and other futuristic expressions. Does that mean I'm—or rather we—are in for the long haul on this island? Am I looking at some sort of challenging course, an ordeal of some kind?" As he said this, Anselm looked down at his own feet. He noticed they were sandaled, noticed also he was wearing a sleeveless basketball jersey and white spandex shorts, as if about to begin an intense workout.

"That, my friend, depends entirely on you and your degree of personal evolution. But I won't sugarcoat it; even those who come to this island in an advanced state undergo deep suffering. There's no avoiding it. It's never easy to 'leave home,' as an ancient master once put it: He lamented that 'No one has ever come before me having left his home entirely behind.'" *So there have been others*, Anselm thought, then barked, "Aha! I've got you there!", believing he had caught this smug, self-styled Solomon in a contradiction: "You said earlier that I was closer to home here on the island than before I got here. Please explain!"

"Excellent, my boy, excellent!" Kafka beamed. "You have a sharp, incisive mind, and you pay attention. Attention is good. I will say only that I've been using the word 'home' paradoxically. It meant one thing earlier and means quite another here. To say more would be to push you beyond your present limits."

This really pissed Anselm off. *There he goes again with the grand, uncertain future. He's got to be half a sadist with that smug, all-knowing bullshit.* Kafka, of course, instantly read Anselm's consternation and proceeded to walk him gently by the elbow to the edge of the precipice. Anselm was wary and pulled back, as the descent was sudden and steep.

"Oh, don't worry about slipping. You're in safe hands," Kafka encouraged, now placing one arm around Anselm's shoulder and passing the hand of the other over the vast, dense wilderness below.

"Behold," he declared grandly, "your Más a Tierra!"

"My what?" Anselm asked, at a loss.

"Your Más a Tierra. Your Robinson Crusoe Island."

Anselm gazed away in thought for a moment, then responded with, "Crusoe, of course!", sighing and rolling his eyes slightly. "Something in me 'inkled' we might be getting around to him sooner or later."

"Ah, so you're familiar with the story, eh?" Kafka asked, delighted.

"Familiar with it? That's an understatement. Like any American kid, I grew up knowing the tale, playing survival games with my pals and seeing a few movie versions. (Buñuel's is the only one worth watching.) And I've read the novel twice, once in college and then again just recently as I was plowing through the reading list for the doctoral qualifying exams. So, yeah, you could say I'm 'familiar' with the story," Anselm explained, not without a note of smugness.

"Wonderful. Wonderful!" Kafka exclaimed loudly, though Anselm could barely hear the sound of his words, catching their meaning mainly through lip reading. It suddenly struck him that the waves pounding the shore below—was it high tide?—were making a thunderous racket that was absorbing all other sounds, including their conversation. Anselm stepped a bit closer to his companion to hear better.

"And what do you think of it," asked Kafka, seeming genuinely curious.

"What do I think …?" Anselm repeated, as much to confirm his dim hearing as to express his guardedness over the question. *Is this a quiz? An ordeal of intellectual as well as physical survival? Just what I need with qualifyings coming up, right?*

"Yes, what's your take on Defoe's hero? How do you read him?"

"Well," Anselm began, shuffling his feet and softly clearing his throat, "obviously he's a man of great resourcefulness. Isn't that the whole point of it, to show that a man—or woman, of course—brought up in a modern, civilized Christian society is equipped with all the skills, all the tools necessary to not only survive, but thrive in just about any environment? Isn't it Western man's paean to himself … A bit narcissistic if you ask me. Edward Said would have had a field day with such vainglory," Anselm added by way of footnoting his own précis. He was mustering the heavy intellectual artillery, less to impress his literary companion than just to show strength on some level, any level, in a situation in which he felt totally helpless.

"That's certainly an interesting, and no doubt important, way to read the novel," Kafka responded, "… as a document of self-indictment against the arrogant superiority of Western culture." Having thus favorably acknowledged Anselm's argument, Kafka could easily have gone on to refute it, but he had no interest in a duel of interpretations. What did interest him was contained as a germ in his next question:

"But aren't you overlooking the obvious appeal of the novel as a sheer adventure story? You know, man—whatever his cultural provenance—against the elements, wrestling with nature in a sustained effort to subdue her, tame her, and finally, live in harmony with her? Isn't the exuberant adventure of it, the heady danger to life and limb, the reason young boys even today are attracted to a book they've never heard of, a book they don't even know exists? It's the adventure trope, the archetype, that grabs them—grabs all of us. Life without adventure is like soup without salt."

"Well, sure," Anselm said. "Who could argue with that? I was just offering a postmodern sort of take on the book, viewing it as a cultural document, as you yourself put it, and not as an example of a special category called 'literature,' implying some sort of transcendent function, some sort of ontological or metaphysical superiority to all other documents and kinds of documents that make up the great pool of a culture's written expression." Hearing himself speak such derivative professorial jargon to the great writer, Anselm was astonished and thought he had better get off his academic high horse. Besides, something in him told him that all his deconstructive rhapsodizing was beside the point for Kafka, that Kafka's responses were subtly, and solely, intended to keep him on point. But *what* point? Just what *was* the point? What the hell was he doing here anyway?

Anselm watched Kafka for a moment as the latter gazed out over the infinity of blue that surrounded them. "Tell me, Anselm," he began finally, "what do you think it is that enables Robinson Crusoe to survive?"

Sensing that his companion's question was, finally, close to the point of this little inquisition, and hence to the point of the entire experience, Anselm thought for a moment and said, "Well, as I've mentioned, Robinson is a very resourceful man—"

"—Ah, yes. Falling naturally into the present tense. Very good! He *is* a resourceful man. Yanked out of the dustbin of history back into life. I like that very much," Kafka effused and applauded, which totally befuddled Anselm. What was the big deal? Equally befuddling was the fact that the crashing of the waves below was no longer a hindrance to hearing his companion's speech. Had he made some aural adjustment?

"But, please, forgive the interruption. Go on, my boy, go on. A resourceful man, you were saying," Kafka prompted, rubbing his hands together in anticipation. Anselm thought Kafka seemed to be enjoying the exchange, but wasn't sure how to feel about that. Was it honest enjoyment over an exchange of views or was he being lured into some intellectual or psychological trap? Wasn't he already trapped enough?

"That's right," he ventured. "He had brought some vital skills with him to the island, like farming and crop rotation and carpentry, while he developed others during his long years there, particularly the higher, spiritual functions such as contemplation and his relationship to the divine, this latter enjoined on him, of course, by his total isolation. Even in this, though, he didn't arrive on the island a blank slate, having been brought up with a solid grounding in his Protestant faith." As he said this, Anselm watched Kafka's face minutely, hoping to glean something, anything, that might indicate how he was being received. But the man wasn't giving anything away, it seemed, merely standing there leaning on his ear-high staff, eyeing him with a kind of poker face that suggested the barest hint of a Mona Lisa smile. *Staff! A walking stick. Where did he find that?*

"Yes, yes, all that goes without saying," Kafka granted, jabbing his staff forcefully into the sod and grinding it. Did this signal approval, Anselm wondered, or impaling the pig for roasting on a spit. "All of these skills and abilities contributed to the establishment of a viable life for Robinson on the island. No question about that. But my question is after something subtler, some event happening deep within the crucible of Robinson's heart, a *sine qua non* event enabling—no, un*leash*ing—his successful development and deployment of these 'survival tools.'"

Anselm sensed the time for Q and A was over, that Kafka, having entered upon the dark and slippery terrain of Robinson's mind and heart—the terrain of consciousness—would take it from here and reveal at last what all the fuss and nonsense over this supremely uncanny moment of his existence were about. For by now he was convinced that R.C. was a literary effigy of none other than himself, which conviction, in turn, moved him to give Kafka the benefit of the doubt.

"Consider this," the scion of Prague urged, lowering his voice and taking a step closer to Anselm, as if to intimate the confidential nature of what he was about to say. "You may recall that the shipwrecked and, no doubt, desperate Robinson Crusoe spent his first days on the island right here on top, on this very sod on which you and I now stand, obviously in hopes of being seen and rescued by a passing ship. But consider: Had Robinson never left this highest, or, more correctly, this most visible point of his island, from a need for comfort, or faintheartedness, or fear, or ignorance, or longing, he would soon have perished. But since, without paying any attention to passing ships and their feeble telescopes, he began to explore the whole island and take pleasure in it, he managed to keep himself alive and finally was found after all by a chain of causality that was, of course, logically inevitable." Kafka continued to fiddle with his staff as he spoke, but gently now, more in order to balance it than to dig a hole with it.

"This sounds a lot like what you were saying earlier about leaving home, or being ready to leave home," Anselm said, as much in the tone of a question as a statement.

"Exactly, my boy!" Kafka almost shouted. (Geez, you wouldn't think someone with TB could vocalize so robustly, Anselm thought.) "So now the question becomes, What inner event must take place that makes it possible to leave home, leave it entirely behind, shed it like a dead skin? And, to give you a clue, I'll admit something personal here and tell you that I myself never succeeded in this. Oh, I tried! I lived on my own at several different addresses in Prague, but you could say—and the biographers certainly have, ad nauseam—that I never really left the Minuta House of my parents on the Old Town Square."

Anselm was sinking into the question of the inner event. Kafka had succeeded in seducing his intellectual—or rather, existential—curiosity. One metaphor used by this most unmetaphorical of writers (according to critic Stanley Corngold, at least) in posing the question caught Anselm's fancy and he went with it: "Hmm. You spoke of 'shedding home like a dead skin.' I use that metaphor myself when I tell people how I abandoned the religion of my upbringing, which was Catholicism. I usually say the Church peeled off me 'like a dead skin' the day I got on that Delta airplane and headed to England for a year of foreign study and travel around Europe during graduate school. So I guess it has something to do with death. Something has to die."

"Bravo, Anselm! You nailed it! (I'll overlook the contradiction of your earlier remark that you've never left the northeastern United States.) But you're quite right, a death must take place. A total letting-go. Not, of course, biological death, which is forced upon us all, like it or not, but a voluntary death, a death before death, which, precisely because it is voluntary, is much harder to realize. This death had to happen to Robinson Crusoe before he could feel free to explore the island. He had to give up all hope of rescue, all hope of returning to his old life, in order to make room for the new."

"So what you're saying is, Robinson is found because he is willing to be lost. A neat paradox," Anselm mused, shaking his head in wonder.

"Yes, isn't it though … But paradox is, after all, at the heart of dialectical logic, a higher logic, as Hegel has demonstrated, than the ordinary yes-or-no binary kind. It's yes-and-yes and therefore opens the world up to infinite possibilities. Isn't that fantastic!"

"I guess, if you say so. Who am I to contradict a master of language such as yourself?" Anselm answered, a tad obsequiously. "But tell me, will you, in this lost-and-found scenario of yours, what do you mean by 'found?'"

At that Kafka reared back and let out a peal of ludic laughter that seemed to Anselm to be swallowed up by the, again, suddenly intrusive cacophony of crashing waves, as if the laughter were morphing into that roar and becoming one with the sea itself, which could no longer hold back. At the same time, Kafka's physical appearance suddenly foreshortened itself to a laughing head, a head that swiftly zoomed away from him there on the apex and flew up into the cloudless, boundless blue sky. Strangely, yet unmistakably, when the head had receded to the size of a dot in the blue, some rhythmic verses seemed to swoop down from its mouth and straight into Anselm's ear:

> Still I stay close to the teat of the heat
> And even when I'm close to defeat
> I get a move on and rise to my feet
> My life's like a soundtrack I write to the beat
> Wake up in the A.M., compose a new suite
> I bring the fire 'til you're soakin' in your seat
> Yippy yo yippy ki yay …

VIGIL 3

A Boat Ride and a Duet

"Hey, fella, you all right?" asked the PATH station janitor, poking Anselm in the ribs a few times for signs of consciousness. The poor lad was sprawled over his seat, arms and legs fully splayed, mumbling incoherently in his sleep. "Lots of people have one too many, and then some, on the 4th," the janitor pronounced. "There's no shame in it. But this is no place to be sleepin' it off. This spot right here is muggers' heaven. It's best you get home and hit the sheets, sleep it off in your own bed, huh? Whaddya say … ," the man urged as he bent over to help Anselm up, intending to walk him outside and hail him a cab. Anselm, however, upon being thus rousted, came fully awake and, in his confusion, waved his left arm wildly, knocking the man's official PATH baseball cap to the ground.

"Whoa! Whoa!" the man reproved, as if he'd been mortally insulted. "There's no call for that sorta behavior. I was just issued that cap. It's brand new, and now it's sittin' there on the greasy floor."

"Uh—I'm sorry …Where the hell am I anyway?" the young man asked, more to himself than the janitor, as he looked around the cavernous concourse.

"You're in the PATH sta—" the latter began to inform him when they were sharply interrupted by a powerful basso-profundo voice that drew all attention to itself: "Anselm! Is that you? Are you all right? What's going on?" Anselm looked up through the haze of his brain fart to see his good friend Paul

Manheim standing right behind the janitor, who himself leapt up from his crouching position like a terrified frog at the booming greeting and, assuming the young man was now in good hands, pulled his PATH cap down hard onto his head and shuffled off.

Manheim was an assistant principal at a local high school, Sts. Peter and Paul, and knew Anselm through a mutual friend who had graduated from there, the three of them having attended several alumni celebrations in common. (More about this friend later.) Still blinking away mental cobwebs, Anselm stood up. However, in an effort to appear sober and alert, he did too much too quickly, propelling himself headlong into the schoolmaster's chest, who involuntarily put his arms around him and tried to minimize everyone's embarrassment by quipping, "Ah … I like you too, Anselm, but this is ridiculous!" For, alas, the schoolman was not alone: With him were his two daughters, Veronica or "Ronnie," age eighteen, and Sally, age twelve. Rounding out the small party was Harold Branden, a family friend, who was the registrar at nearby Empyrean University where Anselm was studying for his doctorate.

The Manheim daughters were both precious, but only Ronnie had been significantly blessed with physical beauty. Which was the reason Anselm was especially mortified by his own clumsiness of the moment. "Ah, Paul, … please … excuse me!" he stammered, straightening himself up. "I don't know what got in my way there …"

"Good thing it wasn't the third rail, huh?" Branden quipped with a little subway humor (very little), further easing the general discomfiture.

"Right … Exactly!" Anselm added, again rather clumsily, in a vain effort to show he was "with it." "Well, nice to see you," he continued, "nice to see you all … How odd that we should run into each other here; then again, maybe not so odd. It *is* the 4th after all, and I'm guessing you're taking the train to some fun place where they're making merry. Am I right?" Anselm brushed his dark hair back with his hand and marveled at his friend's height and girth. Manheim was a huge, portly man, to whom Anselm had to look up, even though he was himself a good six-foot-two. Feeling at this point almost himself again, he was finally relaxed enough to allow himself a lingering gaze at the comely Ronnie, stunning today in her magenta summer outfit with matching tank top, shorts and pink sneakers, all beneath long, lustrous blond hair neatly parted on the right and full, pouty lips.

"Sharp as ever, my friend," Manheim answered, not without irony as he threw Branden a quick conspiratorial glance. "Of course, you'll join us?" he offered with a smile. "We're on our way to the Hoboken ferry, gonna take a nice boat ride across the Hudson to the Wall Street Seaport and back. It's a cheap way to go sailing and cool off on a hot afternoon. Welcome aboard!"

Anselm considered for a brief instant whether he really wanted to tag along—he wasn't exactly having his best day—then took another look at Ronnie in her snug magenta outfit and said, "Count me in!" She gave him a big smile as she tugged on one of her blond locks. Clearly, she was pleased with his decision.

The little party took the subway three stops to Hoboken and made their way up and over to the old historic Lackawanna Terminal, which had recently managed to survive both Hurricane Sandy and a devastating train crash. Passing through the lobby, they moved out onto the dock in the rear in time to see the South Waterway Ferry pulling in.

As they waited for the passengers to debark, Anselm inconspicuously inched over to Ronnie, who gently rotated her right shoulder to indicate she had noticed the maneuver. The air was sultry, heavy with the smells of sweating wood and polluted water and engine fumes. The smell that had moved Anselm, however, was emanating from Ronnie, an intoxicating mix of shampoo, deodorant and perspiration, which together formed a fragrance somewhat redolent of fresh crumb cake, of all things, the crumb cake whose aroma Anselm would breathe in on Sunday mornings in his boyhood while he stood in line at Dino's bakery after Mass waiting to buy sesame-seed Kaiser rolls for the family's breakfast.

When it came time for the party to board, Anselm, walking close behind Ronnie in order to sustain the olfactory spell as long as possible, tripped over the unequal seam between boat and dock and barely managed to avoid decking both of them. He recovered just in time to avoid being seen by the others who had boarded ahead of him.

"Everything all right, Anselm?" Ronnie asked, noticing his flushed cheeks and taking his arm.

"Oh sure ..." he said, fanning himself with his free hand. "It's just so damned hot, don't you think?"

"Poor boy! Maybe you should take your shirt off," she said smiling, with just a hint of a suggestive tone, as she eyed his well-proportioned chest and shoulders. This flustered him, such fluster his default reaction whenever a girl remarked favorably on any aspect of his altogether pleasing good looks.

"Let's catch up to the others," he said, changing the subject and leading Ronnie by the hand to the upper deck, to which he had seen the party repair. The two joined them at the fore end, squeezing in on the bench lining the bow and turning their flushed faces thirstily towards the gentle winds of the Hudson, behind which loomed the brilliant, sun-drenched skyline of Manhattan. The water was dead calm, more foamless ripples then wavelets, as if the heat had baked the river into submission.

"Anselm," Manheim said after a while, leaning towards his friend from his seat on the bow, the better to be heard over the boat's engine and the bifurcated swells of water below, "we're heading over to my place later for drinks and snacks. You'll come along, won't you?"

"Yes, thanks, sounds like fun," Anselm answered, relishing in his thoughts the chance to remain near the alluring and flirty Ronnie into the evening, perhaps even carving out some alone time with her somewhere in the Manheim apartment, which he knew from countless visits to be vast, with many nooks, alcoves and even closets the size of small rooms sequestered in larger spare rooms.

"Excellent! That's excellent," approved Manheim, looking to Branden to corroborate his judgment, which was immediately, and obsequiously, forthcoming: "Yes, that's fine, Anselm. It's been a while since we've had a chance to chat. I've been wanting to pick your brain for insight into the English Department's current line-up of courses," the registrar droned. "You know, so many of the professors seem to have an ax to grind, especially the younger ones, ... all these leftist-propaganda courses about social oppression and identity politics and plutocracy and oligarchy and our evil colonial past. You'd think literature was no more than a source of documentation of man's inhumanity to man, a sort of radical wing of the poli sci department ..." And on he went in that doleful vein, while Anselm pretended to listen though keeping his gaze firmly fixed on the fetching Ronnie as her radiant blonde hair streamed artlessly in the breeze.

Maybe I should make up an excuse and get out of this, he thought. *If this gasbag buttonholes me at Paul's, Ronnie'll get bored and disappear on me.* A low-grade struggle commenced within Anselm over the issue of whether to stay with the party or break away. An opportunity to get physical was in the offing—God, how long had it been—but only at the risk of being trapped within four walls by a double dose of academic Ambien.

As Branden droned on, tweaking his near-Hitlerian moustache every now and then, and Anselm mentally dropped out, the empty space of the latter's consciousness began to be slowly impinged on by the rhythms of the surrounding sounds. As his intellect snoozed, his auditory sense awakened. Most prominent was the sudden short blast of the ship's horn signaling its mid-river change of course ninety degrees starboard as it headed down to the Battery. For most passengers the horn was just the usual mild jolt, but for Anselm it marked a strange opening into yet another auditory utopia, an Eden of sound that caressed his ears like the cooling breeze. He noticed the croaking cries of a dozen or so gulls circling the boat overhead, perhaps accompanying it to its destination. A nuisance for most, for him the croaks sounded like the plaintive notes of a trumpeter in love, and the deep growl of the boat's engine like the low roll of a bass drum, and the swoosh of the water as it hit the prow and cleaved itself in two like the rhythm section of a cool jazz combo, or even those swirling strings lifting Wagner's Valkyries into Valhalla. It was all music and no music, the gist or essence of music, the spirit of euphony—as though Euphony were a god or goddess torn from the pages of Bulfinch's mythology and delivered to the Hudson, here and now, holding young Anselm in utter thrall.

At some indeterminate point, the panoply of sound distilled itself down to the lingering trumpet cries of the gulls, and then these, too, morphed in turn into the yearning strains of a cello, and it was to Anselm as if that instrument's climactic chord, long sustained, were giving form to some sweet, abruptly released ache within his own heart. For a nanosecond he flashed back to the celestial symphony that had filled the cavern of the PATH terminal, which, oddly, he had completely forgotten about, and suddenly felt moved to pursue the music and take possession of it, here and now, as if it were a discrete physical entity and therefore subject to capture. It was a mad impulse, though a pure one, that drove the young man to jump up from his seat on the bow, climb over the guard rail and lean out over the deck below while holding onto the railing with one hand as he frantically searched for a safe surface below on which to land. He was going to dive into the river, that, to his mind, being the most likely location of the being he was seeking, especially in view of the fact that the ambient air above was inaccessible to his wingless body. The main thing was to abandon ship and enter one of these two boundless elements. Of course, the illogic of pursuing a finite being within an infinite sphere did not occur to him.

Naturally, the others were aghast at such bizarre behavior on Anselm's part, rising as one to grab onto him and prevent a nasty fall. "Anselm, what the hell do you think you're doing …"

Manheim shouted furiously as he extended a little umbrella he'd hurriedly taken from a beach bag he was carrying outward, latching onto the young man's neck with the curved handle and tugging, fearful of pulling too hard and risking a choke hold that might cause Anselm to collapse and fall to the deck below anyway. At first Anselm resisted, flexing his neck in opposition, so much so that he wound up pulling Manheim with all his girth towards the railing, forcing him to let go of the umbrella, which promptly fell below, barely missing an elderly lady who looked up in astonishment, along with the rest of the passengers gathering around her.

Branden, much shorter than Manheim, reached through the vertical pickets and grabbed onto Anselm's lower left leg, the one flailing loosely in the air, and, in a desperate move to pull Anselm to the railing, ended up merely pulling his left sneaker off, which on its way down missed the same old lady below deck, landing beside the errant umbrella. There was obviously no room for the girls to pitch in in this rescue effort, which in any case depended much more on brute strength than agility or finesse, so they simply stood aside, Ronnie alternately squealing and covering her mouth with her hands in shock, Sally just standing next to her, somehow oddly unruffled, even throwing the occasional glance around to note the attention the incident was attracting on both decks.

Finally, Anselm all at once seemed to come to, his whole body going slack, including his right hand holding onto the rail, which almost led to disaster, but by now the two men had him securely in tow and were pulling him back over the railing to safety. Manheim, whose friendship with Anselm had lasted nearly a decade and who therefore felt free to speak his mind, let go with a fury: "My God, Anselm, I always regarded you as a stable fellow, but the stunt you just pulled was the behavior of either a schizo or a fool! What in God's name is wrong with you?" Anselm, as befuddled as his friends were over the incident, could think of nothing to say and kept his eyes riveted on the deck.

Ronnie, who had a vested interest in "rehabilitating" the young man, spoke up: "Daddy, please don't be too harsh on Anselm. It's just possible he was dreaming when we found him asleep in the subway station and that some of the ... 'dream stuff' ... was still clouding his mind when we got on board here."

Then Branden, who had a vested interest in Ronnie, came to her support, which helped to lift the dark cloud hanging over Anselm and lighten the general mood: "Paul, don't you think it's possible for someone to slip into a kind of trance or reverie even in waking hours? Why, I did so myself, to be honest, just yesterday. I was sitting in my usual café over afternoon coffee and pastry when I drifted into a kind of deep brooding state during the digestion process. Don't ask me how, but I believe that my activated metabolism and my strange mood somehow 'colluded,' if you will, in bringing to mind the location of a student transcript I had spent the whole morning searching for in vain."

"Well, Harold, I'm not so surprised," Manheim said obligingly, by now somewhat mollified by the generous, benefit-of-the-doubt perspective on Anselm's weird antics taken by his companions. "You've always had a weakness for the poets, which makes you vulnerable, I'm afraid, to tricks of the imagination—aberrations, fantasies, visions and other such nonsense."

Meanwhile, it did Anselm a world of good to listen to all the exculpatory dialogue going on around him, though, oddly, also excluding him, as though he were a lab subject under dissection. Fortunately, he didn't notice this and so continued to brighten unhindered, once again completely forgetting the sublime music that had triggered the fantastic incident in the first place. Aiding and abetting this forgetting, however unwittingly, were the wide-open blue eyes and excitement-flushed cheeks of the nubile Ronnie, who proceeded to squeeze her way in on the bench to sit next to Anselm, forcing her father aside with her supple left hip, then taking the young man's left hand in her own and asking most tenderly and solicitously, "Anselm, are you sure you're all right? Is there anything I can do?"

At this Branden barely managed to keep from rolling his eyes, while Manheim, happy for his own private reasons over having his doubts about Anselm's sanity assuaged, broke into a warm smile and, reaching across his daughter's lap, patted Anselm on the shoulder, who, for his own part, was happy just to be back in everyone's good graces, especially Ronnie's. Basking in her attention and tiny ministrations, especially the ones requiring touch, such as feeling his forehead and taking his pulse (did she know how?), he was soon feeling himself again. In fact, he was feeling more than himself, he was feeling his best self, his body humming with energy and a relaxed joy that he attributed to Ronnie's ardent concern, now completely oblivious to the music of the spheres that had visited him twice that day and was still coursing through some subterranean cavern of his consciousness. The more his senses opened up, the more relaxed and focused he became. He began to feel intimately plugged in to the moment, to the scene around him, the boat, the gulls, the bracing river breezes, his companions, even the baking sun and his own perspiration. Whatever he focused on lavished delight. How could he have failed to notice how alive, how vibrant, everything was, as if he had heretofore merely been reading about a holiday boat ride in some slick magazine in a dentist's waiting room? Damn it, he was happy! And from this happiness new confidence was born. He engaged Manheim and Branden in lively conversation on various and sundry topics—current events, academic politics, good undiscovered restaurants in Hoboken—now powering the discourse, shaping it, instead of just seconding others as was his usual way. Every now and then, he would notice one of the men throwing the other a furtive glance, as if to question, not his oddness or eccentricity, no longer that, but this sudden new fluency of his, this nascent power of articulation, and he let himself bask in their covert, yet discernible, admiration.

He also managed to exchange several secretive glances with the winsome Ronnie, who seemed utterly beguiled by his new-found charisma and nuzzled up to him there on the bow seat, totally unconcerned with her father's watchful eye. "I'm so glad you'll be joining us at the apartment later, Anselm," she exuded. "It'll be oodles of fun! I've got a new Coldplay CD we can listen to—in my room."

"Does your room have a door?" he asked.

"You bet it does, with the key on the inside," she answered, brushing some imaginary debris from his shoulder.

Swimming in visions of erotic privacy, the young man briefly wondered how he could possibly have been seduced by those earlier auditory aberrations. I've got to cut back on the beer and booze, he scolded himself. Ronnie is all the sensory stimulation I need.

The return trip to Hoboken harbor passed pleasantly and uneventfully. When the party arrived back at Manheim's apartment, a posh high-rise condo on Kennedy Boulevard near St. Peter's U., everyone was in high spirits, both tired out and energized by an afternoon spent outdoors and thirsting for a bit of the grape. Manheim fancied himself a patron of the arts, a collector and connoisseur, so naturally his walls were hung with excellent copies of the Impressionists, in particular Degas's ballet-dancer series; also his Bose stereo table was strewn with just the right kind of music CDs—Bach, Buxtehude, Scarlatti—and one wall was lined floor to ceiling with books commensurate with such impeccable taste, including the collected works of Nietzsche, Proust and a Norwegian novelist who was at the time all the rage in effete literary circles, Karl Ove Knausgaard. When Anselm, who had been browsing, naively asked his friend if he had read all these books, Manheim, his mental acuity belied by his physical heft, feinted deftly and answered, "No, but I know what's in them."

They all relaxed in the high-ceilinged living room and chatted for a while, the wine, both red and white, flowing freely, glasses frequently raised and clinked on all sides. Anselm was still in a mood of utter delight, now with the added satisfaction of having managed to finish the day with no further faux pas, especially vis-à-vis the lovely Ronnie, the sole exception being his stepping on her left Achilles tendon in his rush to debark the ferry in Hoboken and scraping it bloody. No matter though. It gave him the opportunity to caress the aggrieved foot and wrap it tenderly in his (thank God!) fresh, unused handkerchief and support her with his arm wrapped firmly around her waist for the rest of the return trip. She, of course, showed her appreciation for his solicitude with numerous adoring glances.

After a while, Ronnie and Sally brought in two large trays from the kitchen displaying hors d'oeuvres of various kinds, including cheese, puff pastries and bruschetta, and they all drained their glasses (Sally included, whom Manheim, after his wife's death giving birth to her, had raised in the continental fashion, which included early education in the prudent consumption of wine and beer) in eager anticipation of the impending noshes, for which a day on the river had powerfully whetted their appetites. As they happily ate and drank, the music on the stereo, Bach's *Goldberg Variations*, Glenn Gould on piano, finished. This inspired Manheim to leap up and suggest with great verve that Ronnie play a selection for the group on the Steinway grand in the corner. Over the years Daddy had dropped a ton on expensive piano lessons for her and was eager to display his daughter's fine breeding and therefore also her attractiveness as an elite "catch" for some young man, present company included. The girl, who secretly suffered from performance anxiety, tried to beg off, citing her injured foot as an impediment to effective peddling, but Dad was having none of it and spirited her over to the piano, getting there a step ahead of her to place a cushion on the seat, thereby saving her the nuisance of raising it. Anselm, somewhat dismayed by what had struck him as his friend's bullying behavior, got up and padded over to the piano, offering to sing a duet with her, ostensibly to be sociable but in truth to lighten the pressure on the poor girl for whose lame foot he was, after all, responsible.

Anselm's training in various school glee clubs and choruses had made him into a passable tenor, at the very least a confident one, always ready to belt out a tune or two at parties, especially after three or more glasses of *vino bianco*, and so together the charming couple successfully navigated a few standard show tunes, such as "Memory," "The Music of the Night" and, for the older generation, "If I Loved You." Anselm was less than rock solid on some of the *Phantom's* high notes, but he did hit every one of them. In fact he had never sung better, doubtless held aloft by the intoxicating, yet subtle and elusive, spirit of music that had hovered over him all day. As the final note died away, Ronnie rose from the piano and curtsied graciously during the light but enthusiastic applause; Anselm, however, remained rooted to the piano bench, stock-still and mouth half open. To the others he seemed to stare into space, as though in thrall to a force or power whose presence only he could sense. Again as earlier, Manheim and Branden glanced at each other in furtive concern, Manheim finally getting up out of his easy chair in hopes of nudging the young man back to the moment.

"What is it, Anselm?" he said, laying a hand on his knee. "Has the music left you in a state of reverie? Perhaps the wine and the music together have transported you to some exalted plane whose rarefied air only true poets can breathe." Tongue firmly in cheek, he was putting the best face on the situation, but he briefly stuttered and the company was flustered by the suddenly obvious rationalizing intent of his words. Everyone sensed that there was something uncanny going on in the young man, including the young man himself, but no one had a clue as to what it might be.

But, with the further flow of wine and resumption of chit chat, it wasn't long before all "eccentricity" was once again smoothed out of Anselm and he was back to his new-found garrulous self, matching Manheim and Branden quip for quip and aperçu for aperçu on the arts, politics and the evils of academic life. All three men were academics, so it almost goes without saying that their politics were liberal, though they did cover pretty much the entire spectrum left of center, from Manheim's centrism ("Steve Bannon has read Ayn Rand who read Nietzsche, you know"), to Branden's progressivism ("If the Democrats could only find their voice, they'd be dangerous") to Anselm, who, to the extent he was political at all, entertained youthful pipe dreams of small-scale revolution ("If the students at Empyrean U. ever get around to a sit-in in the administration building, I'll be there with my lunch").

After a while, Ronnie, who had just rejoined the party from her room where she had gone to straighten up, both the room and her lovely tresses, that is, and was now dallying at the entrance to the living room in a suggestively languid pose, began sending subtle signals to Anselm to extract himself from the small loquacious circle and retire with her to her room so that they could pursue the extraterrestrial rhythms of Coldplay as well as possibly other, more chthonic, rhythms not necessarily related to recorded music. Alas, however, just as the couple had one foot outside the room, Anselm was stopped short by the voice of his friend in its most strident register: "Oh, by the way, Anselm, Harold here has something he'd like to bring up that might be of interest to you … Isn't that right, Harold?" At first Branden seemed nonplussed, drawing a blank on his friend's reference. "You know," Manheim prompted him, "that business about the Archivist we were talking about earlier … hm?"

"Oh yes, of course," Branden said with a snort, tapping his temple and shaking his head over his own absentmindedness, "Archivist Lindhurst over at Stoneham. Yes, yes."

Anselm let go of the lovely Ronnie's hand as he turned around, a bit tentatively, and walked back to the coffee table where the two men were refilling their glasses. He was not at all sure this tidbit would be "of interest" to him, though he was sure it would pale in interest next to a chance to slip into Ronnie's room with her for maybe half an hour. Alas, it was not to be.

"Sit, Anselm, sit," Branden urged, patting the couch cushion next to him. "Last week I was passing the jobs bulletin board outside my office and a notice beautifully done up in some medieval Gothic font caught my eye. It seems an old friend of mine, Lindhurst by name, who is a retired archivist for the Stoneham Institute of Technology—you know, the engineering school on the Hudson bluffs in Hoboken—well, anyway, he's looking for a copy editor to transcribe the texts of some rare ancient and medieval manuscripts onto the computer. Knowing as I do your extensive background in the classical languages, Latin and Greek and so on, and your punctilious work habits, I immediately thought of you for the job. What do you think? Would you be interested?"

Instantly Anselm brightened, all thoughts of Ronnie and Ronnie's room withering away. *Would I be interested? Just try and keep me away!* He was in desperate need of funds to help finance his last year of graduate study at Empyrean, the so-called dissertation year and the final step towards the Ph.D. His menial teaching assistantship barely covered his room rent and two jars of peanut butter a week. Besides, he was a good typist and had romantic fantasies about the arcane knowledge contained in old manuscripts. Who knows, maybe he'd stumble onto something worth writing a dissertation about, say, "William Blake and the Emerald Tablet" or "Yeats's Secret Alchemical Sources."

After thus pleasantly zoning out for a moment, Anselm mentally rejoined the conversation as he heard Branden broach the subject of money: " … and the notice specifies a salary of $400 dollars per week, for 30 hours of work, each weekday from 12 noon till 6. That's not bad money for part-time work, not bad at all," he opined. Anselm could not have agreed more, but he was reluctant to show any unseemly eagerness and so limited himself to a smile and the question, "When do I start?"

"Well, let's not assume anything, my friend. I'm sure Dr. Lindhurst will want to interview you first," Branden cautioned. "Besides, there will certainly be other candidates applying for the job, in which case it'll be competitive. That goes without saying. But a good word from Paul and yours truly whispered in my friend's ear is sure to give you an edge," he added airily, obviously much impressed with his own power of influence. "Just show up at Dr. Lindhurst's mansion behind the backwoods of the Stoneham campus tomorrow at high noon and ring the bell … Oh, yes, there is one caution, my friend. Dr. L. has a reputation for being a demanding taskmaster. From personal acquaintance I know this reputation to be well deserved—he's an irascible man. If you make more than the occasional typing error you will experience his wrath. And if you mishandle a manuscript—say, put an errant mark on one or 'fold, spindle or mutilate,' as they say—God help you! He's been known to put delinquent student assistants through a window, and not always a *ground-floor* window."

Anselm laughed, sure that Branden was exaggerating, his mind filled with visions of a sky raining greenbacks and jars of Smucker's Strawberry Jam, the latter magically making their way to the shelf next to his two jars of Skippy Peanut Butter. When he climbed out of bed the next morning in his rented room in the West Side section of Jersey City, he put on his best—his only—suit and even forced himself into the noose of a tie, this for the first time in well over a year. He hated ties with a passion, and wearing one was a measure of how seriously he wanted this job. For "references," he stuffed four or five of his best academic papers into a handsome leather satchel—a gift from his Aunt Mabel for getting his Master's—slung the bag strap diagonally across his chest and headed down to Il Vento's Bar on West Side Avenue for a double shot of Jack Daniels before taking the PATH train to Hoboken. From the Hoboken terminal he hoofed it the few blocks up Hudson St. to the Stoneham campus and planted himself in front of Dr. Lindhurst's doorbell at exactly twelve minutes to noon.

He was glad to have made it there early and without a mishap. He took a look around an area that was new to him. Since the campus was perched on a bluff above the river, most entrances were on its west border facing the city and easily secured, giving the Institute a high degree of natural privacy. Lindhurst's manor house itself was tucked away behind a copse of deciduous trees on the far-east side of campus and enjoyed a panoramic view of the Hudson and the breathtaking skyline of Manhattan. Anselm stood there astonished by the grand prospect even though the sky was heavily overcast and a thick mist shrouded the tops of the skyscrapers across the river. Then he turned back to the house and looked at his watch. It was still too early to ring so he surveyed the premises. The house itself was a large two-story brick structure in Georgian style with handsome gabled wings jutting out from a central block and a white portico entranceway framing a huge, formidable oaken door. A manor worthy of the name—grand, solid and stately.

Just then the campus chapel bells commenced their noontime toll: a snatch of "Onward Christian Soldiers," followed by twelve resounding strokes. With each stroke the air seemed to quiver. This pleased Anselm as he thought to make a good impression by ringing the house bell in synchrony with the chapel bell's stroke of twelve. Perfect promptness! What could go wrong? Nothing—and everything! As Anselm pressed the round, white bell button, the thing receded into its cast-iron mount creating a hole. This set off a deafening cacophony of bells and whistles as bell mount and hole twisted themselves into a hideous gargoyle face which, horror of horrors, bore an uncanny resemblance to that of the old hag whose chestnut cart Anselm had upended at the Journal Square mall. "Your ass behind glass! Your ass behind glass!" bleated the crone's toothless maw of a mouth in a frightful gravelly tone. Anselm reeled back in shock, slamming into one of the heavy posts supporting the portico; this, in turn, propelled him forward. He would have crashed headlong into the door had the witch-faced doorbell assembly and the electric wire to which it was attached not immediately come flying out of the doorframe and turned into a gigantic basilisk, a serpent heretofore believed to exist only in ancient myth. In one of its enormous spirals the gargantuan creature caught Anselm just in time, but only to wrap itself around him in a suffocating grip that pressed tighter and tighter, in short order expelling all breath, breaking bones and spilling blood. "Kill me! Kill me!" Anselm struggled to cry out, managing, however, only a weak rasp in the throes of impending death.

When he came to, he found himself in his room lying on his dilapidated single bed. At its foot stood his friend Paul Manheim, hands clasped behind his back and head wagging as it hissed the question, "For Christ's sake, Anselm, what the hell is going on with you?"

VIGIL 4

The Only Game You Win by Losing

Off in the distance he sees a man in uniform standing guard in front of a large open doorway with a Gothic arch. Through the doorway shines a brilliant light from within. Having traveled here a great distance from the country, Anselm is overjoyed to see this fine figure of a man protecting the entrance, for the pomp and circumstance of a doorkeeper tells him he has finally reached his goal. He approaches the guard gingerly, cautiously, the latter being quite tall and imposing. He looks to Anselm like those fierce Tartar warriors he has seen in illustrated histories of the Middle East: big, black, bushy hat, thin neatly twirled moustache and goatee, red uniform jacket with gold buttons and black diagonal chest belt. He stands motionless and looks straight ahead, even when Anselm slowly draws near to him, dropping his backpack gently to the ground maybe twelve feet away. He can glean nothing from the doorkeeper as to his approachability, since the man stands still as a statue, not even blinking, which, moreover, arouses in Anselm an uncertainty, this in turn causing a wave of anxiety. *Do not tell me I have come this far only to be turned away!* he thinks.

"Is this the doorway to the Law?" Anselm asks, trying to sound neither stupid nor impertinent.

"It is," the doorkeeper answers in a neutral tone, but at least answering.

"I would like to be admitted, please."

"I cannot grant you admittance now."

Anselm considers this, finding a ray of hope in the word 'now.'

"Perhaps later?"

"Possibly, but not now."

Slowly, thoughtfully, Anselm nods his head and looks around, at nothing in particular. Then he steps cautiously over to about the middle of the open doorway and peers inside to see what he can see. His eyes now somewhat used to the light, he makes out a blurry sequence of receding open doorways, one behind the other, each an exact replica of the one in front of it. The light shines out through all of them from within as a continuous beacon, finally flooding out to and beyond himself—its source shrouded in the mystery of its own brilliance.

"Go ahead, try your luck, if you're so inclined," the doorkeeper says smugly. "But know this: Each door has its own keeper, and, while I am powerful, all those behind me are more powerful still, in an ascending order of power. Sometimes I can't even bear to look at the third doorkeeper myself."

Anselm shifts his feet and remains standing there, deflated. He had not expected anything like this. Of course, he had an anxious inkling but he kept it in the back of his mind, in a remote corner, lest he lose heart on the long, treacherous journey. Then suddenly a wave of anger surges up in him as he remembers that the Law is supposed to be totally accessible to all on an equal basis, its door permanently open to anyone seeking its wisdom and compassion. But discretion bids him hold his tongue and consider other strategies. Whereupon it soon becomes obvious that there are no other strategies beyond the obvious one—to park his carcass there and wait.

So he picks up his backpack and steps over to the side so as not to appear impertinent. Sitting down on his backpack, he folds his hands and stares straight ahead, careful to take only occasional glances at the doorkeeper, again to avoid the appearance of impertinence. He sits and waits, and sits and waits, and sits and waits some more. Days, weeks and months pass. All the while, his mind is as chaotic and craving as his body is still. Finally he decides patient waiting is not the way and he changes tack to Q and A, hoping he can somehow verbally massage the doorkeeper into some sort of concession, some favor, however small. The doorkeeper fully cooperates in these exchanges, answering all questions politely to the best of his ability, still, however, without giving even the slightest sign of encouragement. Months turn into years, years into decades. His life seems at once agonizingly slow and turned up to fast-forward. The fast-forward aspect sends him reeling through the mature and declining phases of his life at the speed of astronaut Bowman's journey, "Beyond the Infinite," in Stanley Kubrick's *2001*.

Finally, a decrepit Anselm, who by now is intimately acquainted with every feature of the doorkeeper's appearance, not excluding even the tiny fleas in his beard, considers asking the fleas to intercede for him with their host. But even in his semi-senility, he fast dismisses this idea as absurd. At last, on a day like all others, his backpack and the ground adjacent to it now a kind of deathbed, Anselm gets up on one elbow from his supine position and waves the doorkeeper over to him for one last question he feels compelled by all his years of experience here to put to the man. The doorkeeper, taking pity on poor Anselm for a futile and wasted life, comes over and bends down close to his mouth so as to hear the question clearly, for Anselm's voice is now no more than a faint croak.

"How come," he rasps, "in all my years here before the gateway to the Law, which we are told is open to all comers, no one besides me has come seeking admittance?"

"You are insatiable with your questions," the doorkeeper snickers, shaking his head. "But, as you've become feeble, I will keep my patience and answer this one too. No one else has come here seeking admittance because this door is intended only for you. I'll go now and close it."

"Hold on there," Anselm wheezes, limply raising his left arm to the doorkeeper whose back is turned as he steps toward the door to close it. Yet something in the old man's voice, some quirk, some new wrinkle in its ragged timbre, gets to him, stopping him in his tracks.

"Yes, what is it?" he asks, affecting an impatient tone as he turns to face the old man, who is still down on the ground leaning on his elbow. "We need to get on with this. I'm scheduled for orientation on my next assignment later today and I need some downtime. So let's make this quick."

"You say this door is meant only for me, yet you've barred me from stepping through it from the beginning. This is unfair, to say the least, an outrage really. It's like giving a starving man a meal after sewing his lips together. It's sadistic."

"All I can say is, what looks to our limited viewpoint like unfairness, cruelty, or even sadism, is, from the all-seeing vantage point of the Law, perfectly just and in order, and, in fact, could not be any other way."

"So let me get this straight," retorts geezer Anselm, bracing himself more firmly on his elbow and clearing his throat. "What you're telling me is, there is salvation, just not for us?"

"Precisely."

"Well, then, for whom? For what?" Anselm asks insistently. He was getting his dander up, and, being near his end, no longer saw any point in suppressing it. He might as well just let it all hang out.

"Why, for the Law itself, of course. Although, it is probably technically inaccurate to speak of the Law as 'needing' anything, even salvation, since it is sufficient unto itself and needs nothing beyond itself. It is, rather, salvation that needs the Law." The doorkeeper says this last in a desultory tone, nevertheless chuckling at his own verbal cleverness, then lowering his rifle and scraping some tiny—likely imaginary—debris from its muzzle. He obviously wants Anselm to get on with his dying.

Anselm, however, who only a moment ago was about to give up the ghost, now has no intention of doing so. On the contrary, he suddenly feels new life, angry life, coursing into his veins and sinews and muscles, not enough to get him to his feet certainly, but enough to clear the rasp out of his voice and make it sufficiently commanding to hold the doorkeeper's attention.

"My ... friend," he begins, with an ironic hesitation on the word, "for someone who has spent his whole life guarding the door to the Law, you don't seem to know very much about your superior. No matter what I ask you, you offer me only paradoxes, word games and puns—and bad puns at that, like the time you said a paradox was the most efficient way to the Law because anyone making a serious effort to reach the Law would need at least a *pair of docs* to accompany him on that treacherous journey."

"Ha, ha, ha!" guffaws the doorkeeper, bending over, obviously deeply enamored of his own wit. "I beg to differ. That was certainly one of my better ones—don't you think, really?"

But Anselm, feeling anything but agreeable, merely waves a dismissive hand at his antagonist and looks away.

The doorkeeper, seeing the old man's frustration and admiring his dogged persistence even at death's doorstep, suddenly, and again, takes pity on him—for he is not at base cold and unfeeling, not a monster—and feels moved to try to clarify things for the old fellow using language he will understand, that is, rational, logical speech, no subterfuge, no trickery, no duplicity, even knowing that his effort is bound to fail.

"Okay," the doorkeeper says, "I'm going to try to help you. Tell me, when does a person resort to paradox, irony and other tricks of language to make a point. In what sort of situation?"

"When he wants to torture his interlocutor and, ultimately, drive him insane with frustration?" answers Anselm with a wickedly snarky question of his own, now sitting up and wrapping his arms around his knees. His anger is a warm current of nourishment, slowly lifting him out of moribund decrepitude.

"Now, now, Anselm, we're talking here in good faith. Please respect me with a straight answer to a straight question. In what sort of situation?"

Anselm is shocked to hear the doorkeeper actually use his personal name. He's never spoken his name before, or, if he has, it was too long ago to remember. He regards it as a genuine friendly gesture and is moved to give a sincere answer to the question put to him. "Well, I suppose the bag of language tricks is opened when there's no other way to make yourself clear (which is itself ironic, you know, using mystification to achieve clarity), ... when rational discourse falls short. For example, instead of saying roses are beautiful, which might elicit a yawn, a poet says, 'A rose is a rose is a rose,' which catches most people's attention." He was feeling it now, straightening his legs out on the ground before him and leaning back on his arms to brace himself. He wiggled his torso a little, just to regain the feel of his body. What was he thinking of doing next?

"Excellent," the doorkeeper enthuses, jamming the butt of his rifle into the ground. "It's a nonsense statement that, through repetition of the word 'rose,' thrusts the red beauty right before your eyes, doesn't it?"

"Sure, sure, point granted," a rejuvenating Anselm answers with a slight swagger of impatience. "But what does all this have to do with anything? How is this supposed to help me? You're just carrying on with your old tricks!"

"No, no, my friend, not at all. Please bear with me," the doorkeeper pleaded. "The point I'm trying to make is subtle, and beyond my powers of speech—beyond anyone's for that matter, which is ... oddly ... precisely ... the point. So it's going to take patience on both our parts. The impossible can take a while."

"*My friend?*" *Where is this coming from?* Anselm thought in astonishment. *Just a minute ago he couldn't wait to get out of here, and now it's almost as if* he's *holding* me *up.* As he puzzles over this, Anselm, quite without realizing it, gets up onto one knee and leans down on it with his elbow. "Patience for what?" he demands, flinging his free arm into the air in a gesture of disgust. "Everything with you is just around the corner, always about to arrive, yet never quite getting here, or I'm never quite getting *there*," he corrects himself, pointing to the open doorway. "I'm up to here with your stalling tactics and strategies. Enough already!"

As he says this, looking through the doorway, Anselm suddenly remembers the long series of doorkeepers in the inner chambers and realizes he has forgotten all about them over the years, having come to think of the man in front of him as his only obstacle. As the full realization of his own stupidity sinks in, he snickers, then chuckles, then bursts into a howling fit of laughter, loud enough to penetrate the doorway to the Law and echo throughout its inner chambers. At the same time, something inside him is released and goes soft, giving him a sense of almost dizzying ease and flexibility. All at once, his body feels like water, soft yet powerful in its own way, able to accommodate itself to any shape, any circumstance—in a word, free. Dazed, he looks down at his hands and holds his arms out in front of him, rising to his feet in unthinking astonishment, checking various bodily parts and joints and finding, to his absurd delight, that absolutely everything is in tiptop condition, looking and feeling better than it did when he first arrived here so many years ago as a young man from the country. "What the hell is going on *now*, you devious bastard! What did you do?" he roars at the doorkeeper, unable to suppress another peal of laughter sufficiently booming to shake the inner chambers to the rafters.

"Believe me, it's nothing *I've* done," the doorkeeper answers sheepishly, laying his rifle down at his side and kicking it away, aware that it is now just useless weight. "Whatever's happening is entirely *your* doing. The question is, I think, what did *you* do?"

"*Do*? What did I *do*?" asks Anselm. "I did nothing. Absolutely nothing. I think it's more a matter of what I didn't do, or, more precisely, what I *stopped* doing."

"What did you stop doing?"

"Anything. Anything at all. I even stopped waiting, if that makes any sense. When I suddenly remembered all those doorkeepers behind you, each more powerful than the last, in an infinite series for all I know, well, I guess I just caved in, crushed by the futility of it all. Without wanting to, and just for a moment, I faced the sheer impossibility of my whole quest, its utter futility, and it all just fell off me, fell away, like a dead skin … In fact, right now I can't even remember exactly what I'm doing here, why I came here in the first place. It's something to do with the Law—that much I know. But what? And what is the Law anyway? … It all seems so silly."

"Of course it does!" shouts the doorkeeper with glee. "And let me congratulate you, my boy." *My boy?!* "When the quest to be admitted to the Law turns silly, as it clearly has in your case, then you are indeed admitted. The truth is, as you now can see, you have never *not* been admitted, or, put round the other way, you are always *already* admitted."

"I see," says Anselm amazed, reeling with delight. "Would you even go so far as to say, there *is* no Law that is not I myself?"

"Indeed, there is not!" affirms the doorkeeper, smiling from ear to ear.

"And so it follows that there is nothing for you, dear doorkeeper, to keep, is there?" adds Anselm with a little good-natured teasing.

"NO, THANK GOD, THERE IS NOT! NOTHING FOR ME TO KEEP, NOTHING FOR YOU TO REACH!" roars the ex-doorkeeper in an excess of high spirits, turning around as he does to raise his arms to … nothing. Nothing at all. Door gone, inner doors and doorkeepers gone, light in its brilliance now equally distributed everywhere.

When an astonished Anselm finally returns his gaze to the ex-doorkeeper, he is again stunned, delightfully so, to see his lifelong companion transformed: Tartar headdress gone, uniform gone, twirled moustache and rifle gone. He is several inches shorter and dressed in a tweed jacket and cravat, his dark hair parted in the middle. He is carrying what looks like a Czech walking stick with a carved dragon's head for a handle. Anselm recognizes him at once, but only vaguely, and hasn't a clue from where.

"It's me—Franz!" the fellow says. "I see you don't remember. Well, not to worry. It's a temporary problem at most." They both laugh, step toward each other and embrace.

VIGIL 5

An Evening at Mitzi's

"Then the spirit emptied itself out and the earth came into being. It was mostly waste and void until the waters separated from it and the overflow plunged down into the abyss. Then the sun appeared and there was light, some of it beaming down as rays to create an idyllic Romantic garden in the center. The nurturing warmth brought forth a myriad of life forms, animal and vegetable, all living together in a community of perfect harmony. There were all manner of flowers, of stunningly beautiful colors, to please the eye and vegetables to sustain the various animals, which were mostly reptilian and amphibian. Life in the garden was an endless round of festive activity by day and restful tranquility at night. A true Eden.

"Then one day the salamander came upon a beautiful lily blooming in a part of the garden he had never visited before. Her petals were a luminous white and her inner stems an enchanting purple-rose. He immediately fell in love with her and decided he could not live without her. So he made his home by her side and they lived together in bliss … for a time. Until, that is, the ferocious fire-breathing dragon, rising up from the abyss for his once-per-century inspection of the garden, noticed the beautiful lily and decided to move her to a more prominent, more visible, location. Pulling her up by the roots, the dragon transplanted her to a mound that lay dead center in the garden. The lily struggled to get free and return to her home with the salamander, but the dragon pinned her down on top of the mound with his massive lethal claw.

"Upon waking from his slumber, the salamander saw instantly that he was alone. After a moment of shock, he flew into a violent rage, running helter-skelter all around the garden, breathing fire, and thus singeing and setting aflame many of his floral friends and neighbors. (In the garden, salamanders had the power of fire, along with dragons.) When he finally came to the mound in the center and sized up the situation, he proceeded to breathe his most powerful jet of fire up towards the dragon holding the lily on top. But he undershot the mark, reaching only up to the dragon's claw, which the latter easily lifted, exposing the helpless lily to the fatal blast. The dragon, seeing the ash beneath his claw and the path of scorched death and destruction the salamander had left in his wake, closed his massive claw tight and pointed one accusing toe down towards this final victim of the salamander's rage. At this the salamander went slack and wept; life as he knew it was at an end, and he knew it was by his own hand—or, should I say, breath?

"As if to pour salt into the wound, the pronouncement came from on high: 'For your thoughtless and unbridled expression of anger, you are herewith banished from the garden, condemned to inhabit the outer world and to earn your keep by the sweat of your brow. You will marry and have three daughters. Not until you have married off all three to young men of a genuinely poetic disposition will you be welcomed back into the garden—'"

"—Tell me, John, just what leaves have you been smoking lately in that greenhouse of yours?" Harold Branden asked his old friend amiably. "John" was Professor John Lindhurst, retired Archivist Emeritus at the Stoneham Institute, who was also an avid amateur botanist and a host of other things as well, probably the closest approximation to a Renaissance Man in the tri-state area. He also owned a small library of old manuscripts, which his discerning eye had spotted and purchased dirt-cheap at various antiquarian bookshops and estate sales all over the world. These manuscripts, which he kept in his house on campus, were in various ancient languages from Old High German to Attic Greek to Cairene Arabic. They comprised the precious trove that Lindhurst wanted transcribed onto the computer as a hedge against their perishing or being lost. He told people he respected that his purpose on earth was to preserve the written word.

"I assure you, my friend, that I am stone-cold sober," he replied with a mock air of having being deeply insulted. Huffily he brushed some imaginary lint from the sleeve of a threadbare green suit jacket, worn over a darker, equally threadbare green vest. He had a great mane of bushy white hair that, alas, covered only the rear half of his gargantuan head, along with tufted sideburns that extended a good inch below his fleshy ears and looked as if they hadn't felt the blade of a razor in ten years.

He was holding court at a round table in Mitzi's Pub, his preferred Hoboken watering hole near the Stoneham campus, over an after-dinner mug of beer with two colleagues from the Philosophy Department. At the table were also Harold Branden and Anselm. In the wake of Anselm's disaster at Lindhurst's door, Branden had decided to take the young man with him to Mitzi's to introduce him to Lindhurst personally. He knew that the Archivist had his own round table there, which he shared with friends several evenings a week. As for

Anselm, he was basically intact but still somewhat traumatized from recent events and therefore less than an enthusiastic participant in the conversation. Moreover, something about the Archivist's steady gaze and slightly metallic voice, with its almost undetectable German accent, held his senses in thrall and kept him almost mute for the duration of the visit. Fortunately for Anselm, a student passing by had seen him lying at Lindhurst's doorstep, apparently being tended to by an old hag, and called 911, which sent an ambulance that took him to the ER at St. Mary's Hospital in the city. Following a cursory examination ending with the diagnosis of a panic attack, he was sent home with a Xanax prescription.

He certainly could have used a Xanax right now after hearing Lindhurst's rafter-ringing burst of laughter in reaction to his friends' round of friendly teasing. "Come now, John, what are we to make of your little Paradise Lost story?" asked Marshall Bergman, specialist in theories of consciousness and the philosophy of mind.

„Is it some sort of allegory or symbolic rendering of your life history— say, a mythical curriculum vitae?"

"Believe me, esteemed colleague," Lindhurst replied with a snarky curl of the lip, "when I say that it is anything but an allegory. Those events took place *exactly* as I recounted them. I should know. The esoteric history of the garden, as contained in several ancient palimpsests which I now hold in my personal archives, reveals that the salamander was my great- great- great- great- great-grandfather and was of a princely lineage in the garden, that is, up to the moment of his banishment. So technically, at least, that would make me a prince as well," the Archivist sniffed, raising his mug for another long draught.

At this the entire table erupted in gales of laughter, everyone, that is, except for Anselm, who felt cold shivers running up and down his spine and couldn't keep his eyes off the storyteller.

"Herr Archivar, " teased Professor Bergman, a small, slender man with a perfectly coiffed goatee who fancied turtlenecks, believing, irrationally, that they made him look taller. He was sitting on Lindhurst's left, next to Branden and Anselm who sat directly across from the Archivist. He loved needling his friend by addressing him with his German title. "Herr Archivar, that's certainly one of the tallest tales I've heard in quite some time. However, if you were to insist on its literal truth, I would be sorely concerned for your sanity. Of course, in a sense, we're all part of the creation story, bearing the brunt of the consequences that befell man when he evolved into a rational animal, though, oddly, just then commencing to behave as anything but. Surely, that's the gist of what you're telling us, *nicht wahr*, Herr Professor?"

"*Nein*, Herr Professor, that is precisely what I am *not* telling you," Lindhurst shouted, slamming his mug down onto the table with enough force to inadvertently spray bits of foam onto his antagonist's turtleneck. "You must take what I say as, in your own words, 'literal truth,' details included, and not a whit less. My great grandfather, five-times-removed, which would indicate … oh, let me see, some three-hundred-sixty-five years ago, was in fact that very salamander who unintentionally destroyed the love of his life, the exquisite lily, and suffered exile in this world as punishment. His burden in this valley of tears, the command to see three daughters married to men of a poetic nature in order to gain re-admittance to the garden, has been passed down from generation to generation and now, alas, hangs like an albatross around my own neck. Thank the powers that be that I've succeeded in getting rid of two of the three, but the third one lingers and lingers. It's not that she is not beautiful; quite the contrary, she practically has to beat her suitors off with a stick. It's just that we live in a society that, sadly, has grown tone-deaf to the world of the unseen, the spiritual, the symbolic—in a word, the poetic—with the result that suitable candidates for marriage have become scarcer than … well, scarcer than honorable men in politics … I wonder if any of the present company has an eligible son he'd like to see married and out of the house … Hmm?"

Once again the beer mugs hanging from the ceiling rack tinkled with the roar of laughter. And when the laughter subsided, the other member of the academy, seated to Lindhurst's right, spoke up. This was Professor Glenn Hunsucker, an aging, hulking graybeard who came across as a bit shy and laconic, odd traits, some might say, for an authority in the philosophy of language. He had also spent several years researching the life and work of philosopher Martin Heidegger, in an effort to rescue the great man's philosophy from the taint of National Socialism. His line of argument was the venerable one of conceding the man's personal flaws while insisting that these had no substantive effect on his thought. The man was one thing, his work another. This was an argument more often used in defense of "instinctual" artists than "rational" philosophers. In any case, Hunsucker now offered his one comment of the evening, and, as is common in men of few words, it was a gem: "My son is eligible. The trouble is, he's been eligible three times already, with three alimony payments to show for it. I'd love to recommend him to you, John, if only in the selfish hope of some degree of financial relief for myself, but, in all good conscience, I cannot."

Another collective guffaw. Anselm, however, continued to be the odd man out, staring at the floor as if lost in reverie.

"Well, in that case, gentlemen," Lindhurst said, resuming command of the conversation, "perhaps we had better switch subjects. But before we do, let me forestall any skepticism you might have regarding my descent from a lineage of salamanders. Let's just say it was a matter of accelerated evolution ... And don't be so arrogant as to think that the so-called reptilian, or 'lower,' species, are inferior in intelligence to ourselves. You'd be astonished to know the truth of the matter. Remember, the garden is an Eden, and exile from it a profound loss. That is something to conjure with. — Now, I wonder if you wouldn't enjoy hearing about my brother Dieter, a mining engineer living in the Tabassah mountains of Tunisia."

A general stir all around the table. "What's that? ... Dieter?" asked Professor Bergman, taking the lead. "John, you never mentioned having a brother, much less a brother living way off in the Middle East. I suppose you don't see him very often."

"On the contrary, my dear Bergman, I see him almost every day. You see, he is also an amateur astrophysicist, and with his advanced instruments, mostly self-invented, he has discovered this peculiar black hole that connects the mountain tunnel he is presently surveying for silver and barite deposits with my office here on campus. A real time-saver that. It's a marvelous convenience that the hole can be entered from either end, so I visit him as often as he does me. Saves a small fortune in airfares. – At the moment, however, my brother is incommunicado: You see, he recently came across this magnificent carbuncle while doing some exploratory digging. Hacked it right out of the damned cavern wall with his pick-ax. He told me that, even in its unrefined state, just lying there on the ground, its vermillion rays were blinding. And it may be the biggest one ever discovered. Priceless!

"In any case, he is currently in the process of selling it to Father Christmas, who is a sort of unofficial patriarch of Lapland and owns a herd of thoroughbred reindeer. Very delicate negotiations, you know, presently being conducted in Rovaniemi, the capital city. Even the Finnish government has got itself involved. Anyway, I don't expect him back in his mountain lair for another two weeks at least."

At this the company just looked at each other sheepishly, totally flummoxed. They hadn't a clue as to how much of the Archivist's little tale was to be taken at face value and how much was metaphorical. Lindhurst, who was, of course, quite accustomed to such reactions, read this one instantly, and repeated his disclaimer of earlier: "As I said a moment ago, gentlemen, every word I've spoken to you here is to be taken in its strict literal sense. I don't use metaphors or figures of speech of any kind. They are the tools of poets, not scientists."

Beyond two seconds of respectful silence, the company could not contain themselves and again burst into raucous laughter, this time bordering on pandemonium as customers at nearby tables, lured by the stentorian tones of the Archivist's voice, chimed in to enhance the general ridicule. As for Anselm, however, ridicule was the farthest thing from his mind, for the Archivist's words had entered his brain like hot ingots dropped into a tub of butter. It was all he could do to keep his composure at the table, internally tossed to and fro as he was by a myriad of conflicting emotions—awe, fascination, fear, doubt, and the spark of a longing he had never felt before.

Following his doorbell debacle, Anselm could not be persuaded to have another go at getting into Lindhurst's house. The day after, he had said to Branden at Manheim's apartment, "That was the most bizarre, the most horrifying experience of my life! Call me crazy, but I swear to you, that old hag from the mall was there! If I had woken up and found the witch there hovering over me, I would either have had a massive coronary or I would have gone totally psycho, funny farm, bananas ... Look at my hands," he said to Branden, holding them out, "They're still shaking." Branden looked sympathetically and then stole a glance at Manheim. Both did a quick roll of the eyes, reinforcing their mutual judgment of Anselm's instability. What had, in spite of everything, kept both men in the grad student's corner was that they knew he was highly intelligent and had great potential, enough at least to persuade them to give him the benefit of the doubt and assign him to the more socially acceptable category of "eccentric"—the "mad genius" type—rather than to some disqualifying entry in the *DSM-5*. Ronnie, by contrast, required no such mental gymnastics to find favor with this exceptional boy toy. She could not care less what category the two men assigned him to. He had her full support, and then some.

It was then that Branden came up with the idea of a personal introduction at Mitzi's. For which the moment was now ripe: Lindhurst dropped a few bucks' tip on the table, got up and handed a ten-spot to Bergman, who usually kept the books for these meetings. Then he laid his brown elbow-patched sweater over his arm—he always had a sweater with him in the evening regardless of the season—and headed briskly for the door. The old man did not stand on ceremony; his departure was quick, without a wasted word or move, leaving Anselm and Branden sitting there, mouths agape. Finally, Anselm jumps up, almost upending his chair, and bolts for the door, getting there a step ahead of Lindhurst, who stopped abruptly and gave the young man a grimace that would have curdled a young mother's milk.

"Uh, ex- ... excuse me, sir ..." Anselm stammered, but that was all he could manage, becoming totally petrified by the old man's furious dark eyes. Branden, who was a step behind, finally got there and set to work mediating the teapot tempest. " ... John, this is the young man I called you about ... Anselm MacGregor, meet Dr. John Lindhurst, Archivist Emeritus at the Stoneham Institute ... John, Anselm is most interested in transcribing your rare manuscripts to the computer. And in my judgment he is more than able. He is a highly thought-of doctoral candidate presently preparing to take his qualifying exams at Empyrean—"

Without waiting to hear more, the Archivist declared dismissively, "How nice for him," pushed both Branden and Anselm rudely aside, and disappeared through the glass door. Nor did he look back as he crossed the heavily trafficked Washington St., while both men stood there gawking at him.

"That is one strange bird, the Archivist," Branden muttered, continuing to gawk as he slowly shook his head.

"Oh, you mustn't take the Archivist's brusque manner too seriously," Professor Bergman said with a laugh. "He's just in one of his moods—surly, cantankerous—you know, the downside of his particular brand of bipolarity. He's a rapid cycler, though. Just watch, tomorrow evening he'll be his old sweet laconic self again, sitting around, reading newspapers and smiling at everybody who comes in." *Certainly, the Archivist is really a fine old gent,* thought Anselm, *a brilliant and complicated man, a man of many parts, not to be trifled with, a man who doesn't suffer fools gladly. Branden had no business getting in his way when he wanted to leave, probably to check on some vital experiment in his private arborium.* Anselm was putting a euphemistic spin on the old man's gruff personality, needing as he did to see him in a positive light in order to rouse himself to have another go at securing the job and increasing his cash flow to at least a trickle. Of course, there were other motives in play as well, mysterious inklings and stirrings evoked in Anselm by Lindhurst's odd charisma, but these were too obscure, too inchoate, to figure in the young man's conscious consideration. Nevertheless, they had their effect: *I'll be there at that fucking doorbell at noon sharp tomorrow, even if an army of serpents and witches show up to keep me out!*

Once roused to action by a pressing need, be that need material or psychological—and this need was both—Anselm could be as courageous as a lion. The anger stoked in him by being denied something he believed to be his, whether by right or by nature, could make him fearless. This leonine passion was belied by the placid, amiable manner with which he usually confronted the world and which, together with his good looks, easily endeared him to others. His father Archie, who had the same placid front but entirely lacked his son's latent ferocity, was fond of recalling the first time he had witnessed this shocking shadow side of his son's personality. In June of 2005, when Anselm was twelve, his father and he had driven down to Queens from Syracuse, the upstate city where the MacGregors lived, to take in a Mets baseball game. It was a "subway series" between the Mets and the Yankees at the old Shea Stadium and they were sitting in lower-deck seats on the first-base side. The cleanup hitter for the Yankees fouled off the first pitch. The ball climbed high into the air and drifted over towards father and son. Archie watched young Anselm punch the pocket of his outfielder's mitt several times in antic-ipation as the ball came down. He had no intention of trying to catch the ball for him. The kid had the glove; it was his to catch or miss. His the victory, his the defeat. The ball landed with a loud pop dead center in the pocket of Anselm's glove, setting off a modest though raucous celebration of applause and admiring whistles among the surrounding fans. Anselm was in baseball nirvana—for about a second. Even before he could secure the ball with his ungloved hand, a kid wearing a Mets cap and t-shirt sitting directly behind him reached over Anselm's shoulder into his glove and pulled the precious sou-venir out of it, holding it firmly to his chest, as if the ball were now rightfully his. Archie just smiled deferentially, as if to say, "Oh well, easy come, easy go, Anselm." But his son was having none of that.

"Hey, that's mine! Give it back!" he shouted, turning around. He saw that the kid had a couple of years, and inches, on him, but that mattered not one jot. "Give me back my ball," he growled, "or you'll be sorry." The kid began taunt-ing Anselm, holding the ball out to him and pulling it back as Anselm reached for it, then adding a little teasing jig and jeering tune for good measure. Anselm watched intensely—for a moment. Then he stretched his left, or throwing, arm back, like a pitcher winding up, and flung his glove as hard as he could right into the kid's face, producing a sort of extended slap. Instantly he jumped up over the back of his own seat to the kid's higher level and began pounding him with rights and lefts with a fury that stunned his father, awakening the senior MacGregor to an intensity of righteous indignation in his son that was nowhere to be found within himself, not even in his most aggressive insurance-claims-adjuster persona.

A somewhat muted degree of that same outrage seethed in Anselm now, blotting out his surface diffidence and spurring him to a devil-may-care bravado that now saw Lindhurst's doorbell as something to attack rather than dread.

VIGIL 6

Petrifaction

Anselm crawled out of the water onto the stony bank, then raised his head to see the imposing figure sitting there aslant on horseback in front of him. The man sat ramrod straight on his mount, a noble black steed. The animal seemed to Anselm to reflect its rider's own nobility, for the latter, judging by looks and bearing, could have been the son of a king and therefore a king himself, even in the first flush of youth. He looked hardly more than a boy, Anselm thought, his dark curly locks ringing his brow like an ancient bard's laurel wreath. Anselm was filled with awe and trepidation in equal measure. He realized he had come out of the water stark naked and now stood there in dripping contrast to the well-armored warrior who looked down at him with a faintly bemused smile.

The rider then reached behind him to a leather sack and pulled out a long collarless shirt, which he lobbed to Anselm underhanded. Anselm caught it, bowed in gratitude and quickly pulled the garment over his head, its hem reaching almost to his knees. Then he looked around to get his bearings. He half-turned to see the sun rising behind him and the water gently lapping the shore on which he stood. On the far-side shore were low-lying hills, drumlins perhaps, dotted with houses whose orange terracotta roofs shone brilliantly in the morning light. And before him, of course, sat rider and horse, the one holding a pole weapon straight up, the other, a massive black stallion, sporting a white star on its brow.

"I wasn't expecting to find anyone here," Anselm said almost apologetically, dabbing his face and neck with his baggy shirtsleeve.

"Obviously," replied the young rider in a mildly derisive tone. "Where are you coming from?"

Stunned by this simple question, Anselm put his hand to his forehead, as if trying to recall something, then looked around and replied shaking his head, "I … I don't know. I honestly don't know. I suppose I could've come from over there," he speculated nervously and without confidence, pointing vaguely towards the far shore roughly three miles across. "I *am* a strong swimmer, but I must admit I'm mystified."

"I doubt your speculation very much," the rider offered. "You're obviously a Westerner, so there's no reason for you to be coming from the eastern shore of the Hellespont, which is in Asia—"

"—Hellespont! Are you kidding me? That's the threshold connecting Europe and Asia, isn't it? What would I be doing anywhere near the Hellespont, or Europe or Asia Minor for that matter? I'm barely conversant with the Hudson, which links New York and New Jersey."

"The Hudson? New York? New Jer- … What was the name? They must be far west of here," the rider opined, patting his horse's neck.

Observing the rider's solicitous treatment of the animal, Anselm began to relax into the confidence of standing before a basically decent fellow, even if a tad haughty. And so he was suddenly moved to ask the fundamental question, the question whose answer he knew would determine the nature and outcome of this encounter. But even so, he couched the question in the least intrusive, most deferential grammatical style he could muster: the subjunctive: "I'm Anselm MacGregor, student of English literature. And who, might I ask, would you be?"

Silently studying Anselm with great intensity for a moment, the rider finally pronounced—for it had the hauteur of a pronouncement—"I am Alexander III, king of Macedonia."

"Alexander ... the Th- Third?" Anselm repeated, his mind reeling with the shards and fragments of his scant knowledge of the ancient world. "Alexander III is ..., I mean, aren't you ... 'the Great'; I mean, that would make you Alexander ... the Great, wouldn't it?" Anselm stammered, feeling like an utter dunce.

"Some call me that, it's true," the rider replied, nodding his head in modesty. Whether genuine or feigned, Anselm could not tell. "Please don't be put off by it. It's merely an honorific. So many rulers throughout history have been called 'Great' or 'Terrible' or 'Magnificent' that all such epithets become pale and vacuous, much like the superlative descriptions of fresh produce in the *agora*—er, that's 'marketplace' to you. In my own case, however, I do think I have a fighting chance to earn the 'Great' label in the coming days: I will be leading my army into battle against King Darius and the Persians. Like me, Darius is 'the Third', but he is not called 'Great'. I mean to see to it that he never is."

"A few things are confusing me," Anselm replied with understatement, scratching his head. He suddenly felt the air becoming heavy and humid, which made him uncomfortable, even though he was nearly naked and still dripping wet, whereas "his Majesty" sat stock-still in his saddle in a heavy suit of chainmail armor, apparently quite comfortable. "One is your translation of the Koiné Greek word 'agora,' as you put it, 'for my benefit.' Why would you use 'agora' in the first place since we're both speaking English here, a language, by the way, that doesn't—or didn't—even exist in your lifetime? I'm not even sure what I'm asking here—even the basic categories of thought like time and space that I rely on for asking ... well, basic questions, seem to be failing me—"

"—I can see that," Alexander said, not without a modicum of sympathy, "but I'm afraid there's nothing I can do about it. Let's hope that in time your confusion clears up."

Anselm did not know what to make of that. Was the king mocking him? Or was he sincere? But why should such a great leader, a man with the fate of the ancient world on his mind (yet how could it be the *ancient* world if he, Anselm, was in it?), have the slightest concern for his welfare? *For that matter, why would he linger here in casual conversation with me in the first place?*

It was all too much and threatened him with epistemological collapse, the worst psychological malady that could befall anyone who knew what the word "epistemology" meant. For it would be one thing to suffer such a fate in ignorance, but to suffer it knowing the exalted place the compasses of knowledge hold in human psychic life would be for a budding professor the ultimate shipwreck. Anselm sensed all this dimly and it gave rise in him to a mounting panic of claustrophobia right there on a beach from which one could see for miles in any direction, as if there weren't enough space in the world to comfort him. All he could do—and this by an act of sheer will—was push the epistemological leviathan aside (it *did* seem to have crawled out of the water with him) and focus the mental energy remaining to him on the matter that concerned him most: *How is it possible that I'm here on the Hellespont talking to a figure from ancient history I know very little about? How? By what magic of time travel?*

The air grew heavier, the open space around him seemed an illusion, and it began grating on him that, given these oppressive circumstances, neither the rider nor his horse made the slightest movement, the sole exception being Alexander's mouth, without which he would obviously be rendered mute. Their very stillness seemed to be complicit in the increasingly stationary quality of the moment.

Still standing at the edge of the water, Anselm began slowly pacing back and forth along the bank, occasionally stopping to dig his toes into the clayey soil, as if thereby to unearth the truth of his absurd predicament—philosophical truth, psychological truth, or some blend of both, whatever would relieve him of his bizarre disorientation. His other motive for pacing, more or less unconscious, was just to move, to feel his body in motion, for he was being affected, perhaps magnetically, by the deepening rootedness to the ground of the rider and horse in front of him. Or was the rootedness he was feeling his own, either wholly or in part?

Alexander's response raised more questions than it answered: "'Asia Minor,' as you call it, means nothing to me. I assume it's a place, but it's certainly not in my mental geography. Asia itself I know, but I see no reason to call it "minor." Also, you categorize me as a figure from ancient history, which would make me one of the early dynastic pharaohs of Egypt, which I obviously am not. The only other alternative is that you are from the distant future, making me 'ancient' from your standpoint. But that would mean you had traveled backward through time to be with me here and now—a phenomenon you yourself just described as 'magical.' While there are many myths in different cultures that envision the phenomenon of time travel, there is no evidence to believe they are more than myths … So, you leave me no other choice but to doubt your sanity, or, put less harshly, to agree with your own questioning of the proper functioning of your basic categories of thinking—you know, time, space, cause-and-effect. What you referred to earlier as your 'epistemological crisis'—"

"—Now wait just a minute," Anselm interrupted testily, forgetting the noble stature of the man before him. "I never mentioned the phrase 'epistemological crisis.' I may have *thought* something of the kind, but I never said it out loud … Oh yeah, by the same token, there's that business about the 'agora,' which you translated for me earlier as 'market place,' which, by the way, I already knew. Translating from Greek to English implies we're speaking English here, an historical impossibility in your case. But it does tally with my experience of this conversation. How about yours?"

Alexander continued to sit imperturbably on his mount, regarding Anselm with a wry smile. At length he pursed his lips and spoke words that might have issued from the mouth of the oracle at Delphi, for they were no less ambiguous: "Epistemological agoraphobia, epistemological claustrophobia: English or Greek?"

Momentarily flummoxed by the king's verbal dexterity, Anselm looked down at his own left foot and saw it digging furiously, if also somewhat stiffly, into the sandy soil, almost as if it had a mind and will of its own. He stopped digging and self-consciously began smoothing out his borrowed smock-like shirt, looking down to make sure it reached below his valuables. From the quick peek he allowed himself, however, he couldn't quite tell whether it did and tried pulling on its bottom hem to increase the shirt's length, but he couldn't pull hard enough to avoid calling attention to the act—something to be prevented at all costs. Also, the pulling was costing him some considerable effort: His arms and shoulders felt as if they had heavy weights attached to them. It was a curious predicament suddenly reminding him of a long series of shame dreams he had been having at least since puberty in which he would find himself naked or nearly so in a public setting and try to force whatever scrap of a garment he had on to cover more than it reasonably could, stealing glances at the onlookers the whole time and wondering whether he was "pulling it off." In fact, the irony of that very pun would often strike, if not amuse, him in such dreams. He would also experience the same heaviness of limb he was suffering now, arousing a depressing sense of the futility of all physical effort to help himself.

Then suddenly it occurred to him that changing the subject might work to deflect the king's attention from his "southern exposure." But what to bring up, where to turn? Ah, yes, people love to talk about themselves, how much more a king.

"So, your majesty," he began, the royal epithet feeling unwieldy on his American tongue, now itself growing unwieldy. "You stand on the brink of an invasion of the Persian empire. But I see only you. Where are your armies?"

"They are bivouacked about ten kilometers west of here, awaiting my return. I like to do my own advance scouting whenever feasible."

"I see," said Anselm, resuming his toe-digging. "I'm guess-ing that's very important in this particular campaign, since you have this body of water here to cross, with all those thousands of men and horses and equipment." He was proud of this casual display of savvy logistical thinking. Not bad for someone as totally unmilitary as I am, he thought, who couldn't tell a captain from a corporal.

"How do you plan to accomplish it?"

"Pontoon bridges," answered the king without missing a beat, though Anselm thought his words were slightly slurred, and so asked, "Come again?"

"Pontoon bridges," Alexander repeated more loudly, and not without a tone of slight annoyance, as though not accus-tomed to being asked to repeat his words.

"Forgive my ignorance. What is a pontoon?"

"It's a flat-bottomed barge or boat, or just about anything that floats. You place a hundred of them side by side, across a river or, as here, a strait, and then lay planks on top, to build a bridge. They work beautifully—it's a very old technology. The only thing you have to be careful about is not overloading them. The weight *on* the bridge must never exceed the weight of the water displaced *by* the bridge."

Anselm listened carefully, but more to the tone and cadence of the king's speech than to its content. He was sure now that his words were coming more slowly than earlier, at a pace approaching the slightly inebriated speech of a tippler and in the slurred basso tones of a decelerating recording. He decided not to mention the issue—not yet, at least.

" ... I usually bring about a hundred small skiffs with me on a campaign, just in case, but even that is not always enough," the king droned on, slowly rotating his head on its axis, as if to dissipate a growing stiffness in his neck. "A few years ago, in my battle against the Triballi tribe in Thrace, I laid one hundred boats across the Lyginus River and still came up short by about thirty. I immediately set my shipwrights to building the requisite extra boats so as not to lose my tactical advantage of surprise ..."

At this point, Anselm was intensely focused, and not just on the behavioral aspects of the king's speech but its content as well. He felt dazed from astonishment over the casual tone in which this colossus of ancient history spoke of events now (*now?*) considered to be of world-historical significance, almost as if they were routine, as if they were just another day at the office. Alexander discussed Thrace while swatting flies from his horse's mane and every so often gave a furious sniff to stem the heat-induced flow of mucus from the royal nostrils. Anselm could not mentally square these closely observed physical banalities, among the countless trivia that make up the moment-by-moment passage of even a great hero's life, with the mythical image he held of the great man, however vague, however broad-stroked. Myth in any shape or form was, after all, a higher order of life, with no room for flies or mucus, wasn't it?

In perhaps the strangest conflation of the brilliant and the banal, the sublime and the ridiculous, Anselm was suddenly reminded by the king's anecdote about "A Bridge Not Far Enough" of a similar bridge from his own childhood, the thought of which now made him laugh out loud, involuntarily, causing the royal left eyebrow to rise in curiosity. "I know you'll find this silly," he began, shaking his head, for he couldn't believe his own cheek in bringing up such a trifle to a man about to make military history. Nevertheless, he felt an inner compulsion to do so. "You'll think me mad for mentioning this, but there's a bridge in a town not far from where I grew up in upstate New York—that's about three hundred miles north of ... Oh, never mind. Where it is in relation to New York City is irrelevant here anyway ... This bridge crosses a river and links the townspeople to a major interstate, ... er, major road or highway that runs east-west through the entire territory. Anyway, the point I'm getting to is that the bridge itself is incomplete, just like your bridge across the ... what was it ... the Vagi— "

"Lyginus River," the king prompted. He seemed oddly attentive to Anselm's ostensibly trivial recollection. His gaze was riveted upon him as he sat straddling his mount, now perfectly still, all fussing having subsided. Was his stillness the result of his deep, almost hypnotic, attentiveness to the young man's words or was it a consequence of the bodily lethargy creeping over him? Or could these be two aspects of the same thing? Whatever the case, what significance could this random childhood memory, recalled by a stranger, a foreigner no less—yes, a *barbaros*—possibly hold for him at this time and in this place?

"Right, the Lyginus," Anselm said, nodding gratitude for the prompt. "But this bridge I'm talking about now is a very old bridge; we—that is, my family and I—would pass it every time we drove—er, traveled east. It looked to me like an old truss bridge, you know, the kind with an erector set built overhead, shaped sort of like a trapezoid." He knew the erector-set analogy would be lost on the king, but he had to let it go. He couldn't translate every modern reference he happened to drop, could he? "The whole structure is covered in rust and just worn out. The engineers must have condemned it years ago, and eventually, I suppose, they began deconstructing it, taking out the southernmost quarter of it. But here's the thing: That's as far as they ever got. For reasons unknown to me, possibly financial, they simply stopped and left the remaining three quarters of the bridge intact, just hanging there, spanning three quarters of the Mohawk River. So that now it looks like an absurdity, a bridge "not far enough," so to speak, and you just have to laugh your ass, er, your head, off when you see it. There it is, looking like a mechanical arm reaching out across the river, reaching towards drivers—wagoners, let's say—heading west or east to maybe pluck them out of their wagons and force them to join the captive population of Amsterdam. Sounds like a Stephen King novel … Oh yeah, he's this writer from a neighboring tribe who seems to churn out a novel—you'd call it an epic poem—every twenty minutes or so …"

Alexander continued to sit quietly, as if deep in thought, now looking past Anselm to the Hellespont, which he and his armies were soon to cross in the biggest campaign yet of his military career. Perhaps he was trying to envision the size and shape, to divine or at least infer the materials and structural principles, of the absurdly comic bridge Anselm had just described to him. When he finally spoke, it was as if his body were solidifying into a stone effigy of itself, his mouth the only part of it still flexible enough to move and therefore shape words. As for the words themselves, they came very slowly but with a touch more emphasis, a touch more gravitas, for that:

"I don't wonder at your recall of this ludicrous bridge in your native land, or even at your mention of it here and now on the eve of this momentous battle, one destined to change the geography of the known world. I know well why it occurs to you, why you bring it up, even risking my royal wrath over being annoyed by a buzzing fly—that being you—on the brink of a life-and-death moment."

As he listened, it never once occurred to Anselm to question the validity of this assertion on the king's part of superior knowledge, intimate knowledge, of the innermost recesses of his mind, bizarre as it was, just as he had not questioned the reality of this moment as a global event, bizarre as that was. Something about Alexander, something beyond even his historical stature, commanded docility, something possibly even aided and abetted by the creeping petrifaction of his form. Anselm sensed that he was meant to learn something from him, something important, something entirely new, possibly even transformative, and that it had, absurdly, to do with three quarters of a bridge.

This, however, did not mean that the young man wasn't roiling inside with conflicting emotions. Was he being vindicated or condemned? Again, he had no choice but to listen and hope to find out. "I too have known such a bridge," the king continued, "a bridge 'not far enough,' you might say, a bridge reaching high across a river with its mighty shafts of light. Yes, that's right—a bridge made of light! It was in a dream I had on the eve of an early campaign against the Thracians, a dream reflecting my anxiety over engaging an enemy army renowned for its savagery in battle. At first, the dream seemed to be reassuring me concerning my worry over a bridge we would have to cross, a bridge I had never seen before that crossed a river bordering enemy territory. However, as the dream progresses, to my horror, the shafts of light come to an abrupt end three quarters of the way across the river and I begin to panic that we will be stuck there and overwhelmed by the Thracians in midstream, so to speak. A dream of glory turns into a nightmare.

"But then, the strangest thing. In the dream, of course, I'd already given the signal for my troops to cross over. As I hang back on Bukephalos—that's "Oxhead," my faithful steed—closely overseeing the advance with my staff officers, we sit there watching with approval, marveling over the swift and easy mass movement. Surely no army has ever crossed a river on a wider, more beautiful, more magnificent bridge. Verily it shimmered with the colors of the rainbow, and even though its material structure was strangely hidden by a vaporous mist of mesmerizing pastel hues, no one had the slightest doubt of the bridge's structural integrity. It had to be indestructible.

"Except that it wasn't. And this is what makes my dream story so fabulous, more fabulous even than the fact of you and me, you an alien and me a Macedonian king, talking with one another here on the banks of the Hellespont. You see, as my officers and I finally began the crossing ourselves, after roughly four fifths of the army and animals and equipment had presumably reached the far shore, I abruptly stopped at about the midway point and signaled my staff to stop with me, ... because I seemed to discern something visually—and I say 'seem' because of the utter lunacy of it—something that could not possibly be: As I observed the soldiers ahead of me reaching what I thought was the shore, I noticed that *I could not see a single man jack of them actually standing on the shore.*

Through the haze on the bridge all I could make out was grass and rocks and dirt. Not one human shape, nor animal, nor man-made object. Where could they all have possibly gone to? Where in Hades were they?

"So I give the order to march and, riding Bukephalos, I proceed further across the bridge, but now slowly, with great caution and rising anxiety. At last I come close enough to the edge of this bridge 'not far enough' to see what is—or rather what *seems to be*—happening. And it's this: Everyone and everything in front of me, without slowing down one jot, is marching right off the edge of the bridge and … er, disappearing into the mist, into … nothingness. They all went from solid to porous to streaky to gone, row by row by row. All gone, poof! It was as if some massive invisible force had its mouth open right up against the edge and was insatiably swallowing up everything that marched into its immense maw. Naturally, I immediately ordered the men to halt, but it was as if my words were stolen by the wind. Everyone continued to move towards the invisible maw, including me. But here's the thing: The closer we got to it, the more my panic began to fade and, indeed, to transform itself into its own opposite. I became calmer and clearer and found myself being gradually overcome by a sense of delight—*delight*, of all things. Can you believe it? A delight that beggared description or explanation. It was as if I were being shown that the unbearable weight of the world that we all carry around with us like a sack of rocks day in and day out all our lives, kings and commoners alike, is a grand illusion and that it's possible to experience it as such, to see it as nothing more than a fata morgana, a trick of perception, if you will. I *was* experiencing just this, then and there. It was as if, as I approached the maw, all meaning, all significance, all gravity, were being sucked like dead weight out of me and everyone around me, as if the entire world were being voided, emptied of substance and significance. And it somehow seemed that all being and all be*ings* were destined to pass into this vacuum then and there. It was the death of all things human beings hold sacred—meaning, goals, purpose, continuity—and hence the death of humanity itself. And as you stepped off the bridge, you stepped into a vast emptiness wherein meaning became meaningless. But here's the surprise: At that point, you wanted nothing other than this—this glorious emptiness. As the poets say of death, its approach is terror, its arrival bliss. You *wanted* to be emptied out, to the depths, so that you could start over and, who knows, maybe this time get it right."

Anselm stood there perfectly still, all ears, enrapt.

"Of course, I would like to tell you," the king concluded, "that I surrendered to this marvelous epiphany right then and there; it would make a fitting ending to my little dream story. But honesty compels me to tell you that I did nothing of the sort. On the contrary, as I drew near to the edge, a tiny scintilla of doubt began to niggle at me, and the more I tried to suppress it, the more powerful it grew. Soon enough, just as I was about to step off the bridge, that doubt, and the fear accompanying it, drove me to awaken, thus ending my dream adventure in *mediis rebus*, so to speak. But that dream has stayed with me, and its afterglow has paid wonderful benefits in my military career. It has completely banished my fear of death and my fear of combat. My presence of mind before and during battle is now always calm, precise, unshakable. And this equanimity carries over to my officers and from them to the men. It has given me a power—call it a passive power—that I can rely on in all circumstances."

During the king's telling of his dream, both he and Anselm had almost lost awareness of the stiffening and hardening of their bodies, so absorbed had the one been in the telling and the other in the listening. Now it was as if their bodies were, at most, peripheral to the communication taking place, as if the communication were bordering on the telepathic. But, the telling now over, the earlier awareness resumed in both just at the point of imminent total petrifaction. They looked into each other's eyes, no longer able to speak, nor, finally, to move, each regarding the other as a mirror image of his ossified self.

"I do not have to go back again, the cell is burst open, I move, I feel my body."

Anselm heard the words but did not know their source, coming as they did from a profound, all-encompassing darkness. As the darkness slowly began to fade, he could make out the figure of a man, young and slender, in a dark overcoat and bowler hat, carrying a cane. The man was walking away from him, heading up the narrow sidewalk of what looked like an old-town European street, cobblestoned and lit by gas lamps. As Anselm's eyes focused, he watched the receding man suddenly stop and half turn towards him, lifting his cane. With its handle he gave Anselm a mock salute, then turned back and continued on his way.

VIGIL 7

Another Encounter, Not So close

D ear reader, may I be so bold as to address you directly?
Will you allow me a literary conceit that has been out
of fashion for a good two hundred years? I promise
to invoke it only this one time, only here, only now. (Well,
maybe a second time, later. But don't worry about it.) ... Let
me ask you, then, have you ever found yourself just generally
out of sorts, disconnected from people and events, at odds
with yourself, unable to find comfort in any of your customary
distractions and diversions, whether alcohol or drugs or sex or
reading or sleep? This malaise might go on for days, weeks, or
even months. Even your serious pursuits in life—work, or art,
or religion or intellectual contemplation—suddenly become
meaningless to you, like so many banal and insipid exercises,
no more stimulating than folding laundry or going to the
corner for a pack of smokes. Yet you sense there is something
momentous on your mind, though not directly or immediately
so; rather it sort of tugs at your awareness from below. (Below
what?) It's all intensely frustrating and you begin to feel that
you no longer belong entirely to this world. Its joys and sorrows are no longer your joys and sorrows: They have given
way to some quasi hidden Something for which you begin to
realize you are yearning, perhaps have always been yearning.

If, dear reader, you have ever felt this way, then you know
from your own experience the condition in which the student
Anselm found himself. The subway symphony, the dazzling
palette of sounds aboard the Hudson ferry, above all, Archivist

Lindhurst with his absurd tales of family history, obviously the allegory of an eccentric, yet one that held Anselm spellbound, shaking him to his core—these and other strange events were perturbing, poking and gently piercing his quotidian view of the world, making him, as a philosophical technician might put it, less ontologically sure of himself, less comfortable with his particular way of being in the world.

My friend, I only wish I could produce the student Anselm himself in the flesh, right here before your very eyes, so you could see for yourself what I've been trying to describe in these nightly narrative vigils of mine, sessions that have cost me a fair amount of sleep, I might add, which, the sleep studies tell us, can never be recovered, never made up. For I must admit to a fear that you may well become skeptical of anything I write, not just of the existence of Anselm himself, mind you, but of Assistant Principal Manheim and Registrar Branden and Archivist Lindhurst and even Manheim's comely daughter Ronnie. I assure you these individuals do exist and may this very day be found walking the streets of Jersey City or Hoboken.

So it seems that Anselm had fallen into a kind of melancholy brooding and had taken to walking over to the subway entrance at Journal Square, not to go anywhere, but just to sit down on that same hatbox-shaped seat in hopes of hearing once again a line, a phrase, even a bar, of those celestial strains of the violin that had recently enchanted him. Of its rich emotional sustenance he felt a deprivation that was almost physical. But over the next days and weeks, nothing happened. Trains screeched, turnstiles clicked incessantly, people jabbered as they came and went. It was the ordinary subway cacophony, which, with a dash of cynical irony, he took to be more or less the opposite of music. *God, what am I becoming? A man stranded in the desert, wandering around looking for an oasis I'm beginning to believe was a hallucination? The more I long for it, the farther away I feel from it. I absolutely must hear that music again. I don't know how I'll carry on without it. For that matter, I don't know how I'll carry on with it. It's ... what's the phrase ... total terra incognita. I have no appetite for study these days. I should be reading for my upcoming doctoral prelims, but the very thought revolts me. I seem to be stuck between two worlds, one refusing to die, the other to be born.*

And as Anselm sat there on the hatbox seat, deep down in the doldrums, elbows on knees, head in his hands, a sharp, ever so slightly metallic voice assailed his ears: "Hey there, young man! Weren't you supposed to be my manuscript copyist? What are you doing dawdling here in this black hole? Why haven't you shown up for work?"

The powerful voice shocked Anselm back to the here and now, for he recognized it instantly as belonging to the man who had so recently mesmerized him with tales of a family that had, in the telling, seemed both less and more than human. It belonged to none other than Archivist Lindhurst, who now stood there in front of him, dressed in suspendered summer slacks, a light sweater slung over his shoulder "just in case," and leaning on a gold-handled walking stick. "What's going on with you, young man? Why haven't you come by to begin work?"

The truth was that, since that fateful noontime on the Stoneham campus, Anselm had not been able to muster the courage to go back to that damned doorbell and ring it again, even though promising himself every evening that he would definitely do it the next day. Now, however, overcome by discouragement, he felt suddenly fueled by the anger of that discouragement, the anger born of despair, and broke into a rant that raised the Archivist's left eyebrow: "You'll probably think I'm crazy, Dr. Lindhurst, but frankly, I couldn't care less. I've been coming here almost every day lately, ever since the recent July 4th holiday, hoping to hear again the beautiful violin music I first heard that day, actually *twice* that day: The first time was right here in the subway entrance; it must have been some beggar of a fiddler with his hat upside down on the sidewalk—I didn't see him myself; and the second time later that afternoon on the Hudson ferry sailing over to Wall St. (I have no idea where *that* music came from!) I've never in my life heard anything so enchanting; it's as if my ears had been asleep till that day, as if some scintillating world of sound—a hidden world—were only then opening up to them ... Call me delusional, sir! Call me a basket case, an overworked grad student gone round the bend! Your opinion of me is of no concern...."

But the Archivist did no such thing, merely gazing attentively at the student for a long moment, then, in a calm, steady voice, replying, "Nothing of the sort, my lad, nothing of the sort. Please go on with your recounting of the events of that day."

Both mystified and buoyed by the Archivist's apparent receptiveness to this "madness," Anselm gathered himself to tell him the entire arc of events occurring on that fateful July 4th. He told of running into the old lady's pushcart in the strip mall, and of her curse upon him: "Your ass behind glass"; of falling asleep on the very same seat he now occupied; of the alluring Ronnie in her pretty magenta outfit and how she flirted with him on the ferry and even more so later on in the apartment she shared with her father. At the end of his story, feeling now a bit disburdened, he repeated his earlier assertions of indifference to the Archivist's opinion of him, thus demonstrating that he was anything *but* indifferent to it: "I know, I know, you're thinking I should be hauled off to the St. Mary's psych ward, right? … Well, think what you want. All I know is, I'm not long for this world if I don't get to hear that heavenly music again. I *must* hear it! It's non-negotiable! … I can see by your slight smirk that you think I'm pathetic, right?"

"Not at all, my boy. Not at all. What you took for a smirk was an expression of wonder, of astonishment—astonishment at running into a promising candidate like yourself in these benighted times."

Candidate? For what? Anselm wondered uneasily, though also feeling a slight tingle in the abdomen, about two inches below the navel. But he didn't quite have the courage to ask, rather contenting himself with the satisfaction of knowing that Lindhurst apparently did not consider him daft.

"You see," the Archivist continued, "the fact is that it was my daughter who produced the music you found so enchanting. I was working in my lab at home at the time and her fiddling was interfering with my concentration, so I asked her to stop—which is why your subway symphony so suddenly morphed back into those screeching wheels and clacking turnstiles. But not to worry, my boy. If you come to work for me, you'll have ample opportunity to hear her play the violin, and even to make her acquaintance. You see, she practices every day, and the room you'll be working in is on the same floor, almost within earshot of hers."

Strangely, rather than thinking the Archivist, at best, an eccentric, and, at worst, a raving maniac only too ready to buy into his own fantasy to create some grotesque *folie a deux*, Anselm was feeling himself swept up in a nimbus of fascination, of mystery. His sense of the Archivist as somehow a kindred spirit simply outweighed the skepticism he would otherwise have felt. But before he could begin to put his thousand breathless questions to the man, the latter pulled his iPhone out of his pants pocket and blew on the little black screen; then, holding the phone up to his ear, he smiled and handed it to an astonished Anselm, saying as he did, "Here, my boy, listen and enjoy."

Anselm took the phone and held it up, at first cautiously, not quite letting it touch his ear, as though it might bite him. But it was close enough to let him hear, as it were, a tiny, tinny replica of those haunting strains of the violin for which he longed. Now quickly warming to the instrument, he held it close, listening intently, hungrily, gratefully, and, as he did, the quality of the sound seemed to deepen and bourgeon beyond the tiny confines of its electronic container, spreading out and filling the vast reaches of that echo chamber of a subway station. Soon he found the phone was no longer even necessary and absently handed it back to the Archivist, who beamed at him with satisfaction, delighted to have found, after a long, barren period of waiting, a viable "candidate." Anselm was so lost in the music, it didn't even occur to him to wonder where the phoneless fiddling was coming from. Where indeed! Could it even be said to flow through the air, its waves to jostle space? Did others hear it? He was oblivious to such matters.

The Archivist sat down on the hatbox seat next to the student, careful not to disturb the moment. As Anselm sat there entirely absorbed in listening, he thought he could hear, entwining itself with the strains of the violin, a lilting female voice. It seemed to be intoning wisps of words, phrases, questions. "Anselm ... do you believe in me? ... Do you have faith? ... Only in faith is there love. ... Can you love, Anselm? ... Can you love?" Anselm seemed now to be gripped by a paroxysm of longing, and, finally unable to contain himself, surrendered to a spontaneous expression of emotion, as if responding to a call from nature itself: "Yes! Yes! I can! I want to! I must! ... Please hear me, lovely one!"

Noticing that Anselm was drawing the attention of passing commuters, a few of whom had stopped to observe the strange scene, the Archivist waved his hand in the air and broke the spell. "That's enough for now," he said, pocketing his phone, as the rubberneckers dispersed and went their way. "Tell me, lad, did you hear my daughter? Did you hear my Tina playing? Isn't she wonderful?"

"Oh, yes! Oh, yes! But how? ... What was ...?"

"Now, now, don't trouble yourself over it," Lindhurst admonished. "If you come to work for me, you'll see my daughter often enough. What's more, if your job performance is up to snuff, you'll hear her divine playing on a regular basis. But—and mark my words, lad!—by 'up to snuff' I mean copying the manuscripts I entrust to you with the greatest precision, with complete and total accuracy ... Think you're up to it?"

Anselm could only give a tentative nod, for the haughty aspect of the Archivist's personality was reasserting itself, and Anselm now felt thrust back into the same intimidation in the man's presence he had felt in Mitzi's tavern on their first encounter.

"At Mitzi's," Lindhurst went on, "Harold Branden told me to expect you to call on the following day, but you didn't show up. Nor have you since then, and I've been waiting. What's the problem? Have you changed your mind?"

The mention of Branden's name enabled Anselm to feel his two feet once again planted solidly on the ground in front of him. But the intimidation factor was still very much there, and as Lindhurst then stood up from the hatbox seat and resumed his earlier stance, hands placed on top of his walking stick as he gazed down upon the hapless student, Anselm had to summon more than a little courage to tell the man what had happened the day he tried to visit.

By the time he finished his tale of woe, the Archivist's face had softened its expression once again and he was, in fact, able to offer the student some words of consolation: "My dear boy, I know the chestnut lady who instigated the mayhem that befell you at my doorbell. She's always playing all sorts of mean-spirited tricks on me. The basilisk is her calling card, and I'm so sorry you had to be traumatized by this dastardly illusion. She's an outrageous old hag and it is simply unacceptable that she should continuously scare away visitors to my house, particularly the rare able applicant for the copyist job … Look, Anselm, if she shows herself the next time you call on me—shall we say, tomorrow at high noon, hmm?—dab a drop or two of this solution on the old girl's nose, and I think that will straighten everything out." As he said this, he handed Anselm a tiny vial containing a liquid of yellowish gold. Anselm hadn't a clue as to how the Archivist had produced the little bottle, as he had not seen him reach into any pocket. "And now I must bid you adieu," Lindhurst said, extending his hand to the student. "I'm late for an appointment with a colleague who lives just off the square. I need to hurry so I won't trouble you to walk with me. See you at noon tomorrow." He smiled and turned away, walking briskly out the subway entrance and turning left towards Journal Square. Following the man outside then lingering at the entrance, Anselm watched him walk away, noticing how with each stride he gently bounced his walking stick against the pavement, half catching it as it came back up on the rebound. Anselm thought how little the hearty old fellow really needed a walking stick. *Must be some kind of fashion statement,* he thought. *He's a strange bird—the Archivist.* And just as the student pronounced the word "bird" silently to himself, he saw how the sleeves of the receding Archivist's sweater, which he now had tied around his neck, had gotten caught up in the wind, making them look like the wings of a large bird—perhaps a herring gull—primed for take-off. And it so happened that a bird did in fact take off from the spot where the old man appeared to be, lost as he now was to Anselm's view in the crush of rush hour commuter traffic. *Maybe he turned into a bird. Who the hell knows? All I do know is, I can't trust my senses anymore. All sorts of weird creatures and events keep popping up all around me. It's as if all the ghastly things I see only in my worst nightmares are now entering my waking life and having their way with me. But I don't care! If that's the price I have to pay to gain access to that music and the angel who makes it, bring 'em on! Tina, my Tina, I'm coming to you. Please wait for me!"

These last of Anselm's thoughts, impetuous as they were, had burst into a loud, plaintive wail, loud enough to draw the attention of some passing homeward-bound commuters. One of these, a man in greasy mechanic's overalls with a basso profundo voice, expressed an equally loud rejoinder, delivered in a singsong tone intended to elicit the support of the crowd in mockery of the star-crossed student: "Oh, Tina, Tina, don't be mean-a! Don't be mean-a, please, to me!" Passers-by roared in merriment. Coming to his senses, Anselm shuddered at the thought, *Wouldn't it be just my luck if Paul or Harold—or Ronnie, oh God, Ronnie!—walked by just now?* But neither the one, nor the other, nor the third, walked by.

VIGIL 8

The Sirens

It was a dark and stormy night. Fierce winds howled and the rain lashed the faces of the men on deck, who worked furiously to secure the hatches and reef the sails. In all his years at sea, Anselm could not remember a time when the Mediterranean was as rocked by waves as it was now. Every few minutes a terrifying mini-tsunami would wash over the ship's bow, leveling anyone or anything standing. Anselm stood astern on a raised deck overseeing his men's efforts. Every now and then he would bark an order or shout encouragement, but the wind seemed only to hurl his words back into his face.

The storm lasted through most of the night. Then finally the clouds parted and a rosy-fingered dawn came up, which seemed to have a calming effect on the raging sea, gradually settling it down into a sunlit lambent rhythm. The crew, along with their leader, were exhausted and longed only for time in their bunks. But Anselm knew that most of them would have to remain on deck, alert and ready for action at least a while longer. For his maps had told him that their ship was approaching the enchanted isle of the sirens, located south of Scheria, the land of the Phaeacians. Anselm had heard of these strange creatures from stories repeated to him since childhood. Some said that they were half woman and half bird. Others that only their legs were birdlike. Still others said they had huge wings and could fly. While there was little agreement on their appearance in these tales, there was one aspect of the sirens—a fascinating aspect—that was common to all of them. This was the beauty and power of their singing. It was said that the song of the sirens was so beautiful, so seductive, so captivating, that it became irresistible to any man who chanced to hear it. Passing ships coming within earshot of their music would sail too close to their island banks and come a cropper on the rocks in the shallow water. Sailors would dive overboard and swim frantically to get closer to the source of this elixir of the ear. Legend had it that the grassy shore of their island was covered twice over with the bones of sailors who had attempted to reach it and been thereby lured to their death. So the sirens gained a reputation for being musical *femmes fatales*.

All this had been known to Anselm since the earliest stirrings of personal memory. But, being a curious fellow and a music lover, he knew he would not be able to resist the opportunity to listen to such sublime singing; and, being a clever, resourceful fellow, he felt confident of his ability to devise a method that would allow him to do this without harm. As the boat neared the island of the sirens, Anselm could make out its shoreline, clouded though it was in morning mist. He could see wisps of the branches of the lovely olive and oleander trees that crowded the shore, squatting there all gnarled and twisted like friendly old hosts awaiting their guests. But he was immediately disabused of this amicable impression by the long strand of bones that slowly came into view, abutting the interior forest and seeming to encircle the entire island. The sun was now getting strong, its mounting brilliance already turning that macabre necklace of white into a blinding graveyard, from which Anselm had to shield his eyes. Nowhere could he see a path up the beach through those bones. *Well, that's one part of the legend that checks out,* he thought, shaken but undaunted.

Putting his plan into action, he ordered his men to bind him securely to the boat's mast with rope and then had them all stuff their ears with wax to protect themselves from aural danger. Naturally he had considered the possibility of incurring serious physical and—what would be worse—psychic damage from the legendary sirenic voices, not to mention the danger of immediate addiction that countless sailors had bewailed—an addiction bound to be made even more lethal by the fact that his fettered condition would make it physically impossible for him to even attempt to satisfy his craving. But these risks only intensified his immense curiosity, which, ironically, was itself probably at least as addicting as any external stimulus could be. What amounted to his greatest intellectual virtue was also, potentially, his tragic flaw. *Just let me hear that music! To hell with the consequences, I'll deal with them later.*

As the boat approached the bone-blanketed shore close enough to pierce the morning mist, Anselm ordered the helmsmen to heave to starboard in order to avoid some protruding rocks that lay straight ahead. And just as he felt relief from avoiding this peril, he watched, aghast, as three of his oarsmen dove overboard and commenced to swim furiously towards shore. *They unstopped their ears, unable to resist temptation!* thought Anselm, then suddenly realizing that he too was now in earshot of what had lured his men into the water.

Almost before he became aware of the enchantresses' lovely strains, he felt something deep inside him go soft, a melting-away of all inner restraint. It was a lovely sensation, this, like casting off a burden so long borne, so habitual, he had hardly known it was there until now. But it was also this very feeling of airy lightness, so unaccustomed, that caused his instinct for self-preservation to kick in all the harder in the next instant. Where was discernment, where was caution, he demanded of himself to know! Where was common sense? Already he found himself pulling hard against the rope ties, squirming furiously to slip his already chafed hands through the loops, as if in mockery of his own calls for rational thought. He tried deliberately to stop this, but it was as if his hands had a will of their own. He could do no more than feel them behind his back as they went on writhing and pulling against their bonds, oblivious to the blood they were already shedding.

Then, as if suddenly curious, above all, to know the cause of this profound division within himself, he began deliberately to take in the lilting tones of what sounded like three female voices entwined in song. The air itself seemed to quiver as a trio of spellbinding vocal vines wove into and out of each other, producing an exquisitely fine intoxicant for the ear. Then it was as if his conscious awareness of the music activated that last remnant of self-control hidden beneath the nascent emotional surrender. He tried hard to listen critically, to, in some sense, understand what he was hearing, to master its profound allure with some mental map of logical causation, however roughly and hastily drawn. But something in him sensed it was no use. The sublime soprano trio had already ensnared him in the tentacles of their sweet harmonies, an indescribable blend, it seemed to him, of the erotic devotion of "I Do It for You" with the lavender mysticism of "Claire de lune." Still, Anselm persisted frantically in his effort to define and, therefore in some measure, control an experience that had rocked his heretofore stable sense of self. But he abruptly found himself rocked a second time by his flash of awareness on the very reference points he was drawing on for the comparison, the unlikely duo of Bryan Adams and Claude Debussey. Obviously he knew who these musicians were, but he didn't know how he knew this, nor did he know what their music, products of two different cultures utterly foreign to this one, had to do with this present world of sailing, sea and sirens? He hadn't a clue. He had at most a vague inkling that there must be worlds, other worlds, other realms of existence, that were located in some dimension not far from his own, perhaps juxtaposed to it, possibly even pressing in on it, parted from it by only "the filmiest of screens"—and yet utterly, wholly *other*.

Then suddenly Anselm saw those bones of dead sailors covering the beach begin to shuffle, as if by the power of the wind. That wind, or whatever it was, seemed purposive, seemed to be assembling the bones into some definite form, clearing that section of sodden beach as it did. At the same time Anselm felt the ship come to rest in the water, as if on cue from the wind. It must have been the wind, he thought, as the oarsmen were struggling in vain to row and the anchor had not been thrown. Anselm watched as the bones literally threw themselves upward, gradually forming two opposed walls connected by a slightly arched roof. The ghastly, sepulchral structure stood there with apparent solidity, as though the wind were keeping it erect, even though the bones continued to dance in place, all ajiggle. Anselm sensed immediately that the passageway onto the island formed by the jiggling structure was meant specifically for him, since he stood there at the stern directly facing it.

Quickly overcome by tunnel vision, having eyes now only for the forbidding passageway, he was at this point half forgetful of his identity in this maritime scenario: No longer a seaman, no longer a captain of men, no longer homeward bound, he was bound only to set foot on this strange, legendary isle of the sirens, those lethal seductresses, as he well knew, of so many men before him. At last wriggling free of his bonds and diving overboard despite himself, he swam directly towards the sepulchral passageway. As he reached the shore, he found that the eerie racket made by the rattling bones was more than offset by the lush strains of the female trio. But, although the sublime voices commenced to hold his senses in thrall, he was no more reassured for that, for he knew he was entering upon a world of unknowns, the only "known" being that men who entered here did not return.

He moved briskly through the passageway, trying hard not to appear in a hurry, not to show his claustrophobic fear of having the tunnel of bones collapse in on him. Just who it was he was hiding his fear from was a mystery, as the sirens themselves were farther off somewhere in the interior of the island. Finally coming out the far end of the tunnel, he waded his way through thick, almost suffocating trees and thickets. There was no path and most likely never had been one; the tunnel, a structure of obvious intelligent design, a thing of culture, had expelled him into raw nature, a dense, suffocating phantasmagoria of shifting shapes and shades of green. Undaunted, Anselm forged on, bulling his way through the choking claustrum of vegetation, his only compass those enchanting voices.

And just as the first, barely perceptible twinge of discouragement made its way up into his lower abdomen, he saw an opening as though beckoning to him from a few feet ahead. Slashing his way through the final, slightly thinning green, Anselm stepped out onto the fringe of a large, magnificent garden, enhanced at its center by a tiny lagoon shimmering in the Mediterranean sun and dotted with little groves of lemon and olive trees, with limestone crags jutting up through the grassy ground here and there. Many of the crags housed small grottoes just large enough for a human figure to enter upright. But it was the lagoon that immediately caught his attention, lying serenely in the middle of the garden, its elongated shape parallel to the coastline. For it was from there that the beguiling strains sweetly accosted him. Looking down on the lagoon from his slightly elevated position on the fringe, he tried to locate female forms that would account for what he was hearing. But the only movement he could discern was being made by two or three birds cavorting about the surface of a large boulder partially sunk in the middle of the lagoon. These he ignored as he continued to search the lagoon and its immediately surrounding area, at the same time striding down the gentle garden slope towards it to get a closer view. As he drew near to the water, he was staggered a second time, almost as profoundly as at the moment those divine harmonies first touched his ear. For he realized that he was misdirecting his search, that it was the birds themselves that were singing. It was a kind of birdsong! The sweet, lilting call and response of song thrushes. But these were no ordinary thrushes, this no ordinary song. As he saw upon examining the trio closely, each of them had the shapely head of a young maiden, and were fair of face, with close-cropped hair held in place by floral garlands.

Both stunned and strangely delighted by these "bird maidens," Anselm stepped to the bank of the lagoon to assure himself of what he already knew but could not process, that the seductive melody was indeed coming from these half-human songbirds. But there they were, the three of them, padding back and forth on tiny claws across the surface of the boulder, each going her own way without regard for the others' movement or position but all three in perfect vocal harmony in a song without words that seemed to be, as the cliché would have it, an endless melody. He stood there looking at them, literally unable to look away, as they carried on their little patterns of movement, continuous circlings, figure-eights, turns and such, for the longer he watched, the firmer did his sense grow that there was some governing pattern, some dance-like ritual, to it all, though he hadn't a clue as to what that pattern might be or that ritual mean.

He admired the almost seamless plumage of the avian bodies, the rich, effulgent colors—reds, purples, yellows, greens, and blues—hues more appropriate to a bird of paradise, and a male bird at that, than an ordinary female thrush, but, again, these were no ordinary thrushes. Least ordinary of all, of course, were the heads – youthful, comely heads of young maidens, framed by hair arranged in soft, silken wavelets, resting on slender necks that gave way smoothly, imperceptibly, to the avian bodies beneath.

Such tiny, cuddly things they were. Adorable to the point of inanity, their classical facial features and noble heads mounted on these tiny hopping bodies, bodies moved along by unsightly three-toed claws. The beauty/beast fusion delighted him. He wanted to sweep them up into his arms and play with them.

But their song, which never wavered and retained a hypnotic power that was not diminished one jot by the creatures' visual fascination, kept this impulse of his in check, protecting the trio from any untoward advances.

At one point, one of the trio stepped onto a flat spot on the lip of the rock surface close to Anselm and stopped singing. She hung her shapely head for a moment as if in prayer or meditation. The other two voices continued undisturbed, as if two singers, or perhaps even one, were enough to fulfill the mysterious function of their music. As long as melody was audible, all was well, it seemed. (It never occurred to Anselm to wonder how it was that the voices issuing from these tiny bodies could come within earshot of passing sailors beset by the whooshing sounds of sea and wind.)

After a moment, the silent siren standing before him raised her head, looked Anselm steadily in the eye and introduced herself. "I am Ligeia … And these," she said, extending a wing, "are my sisters, Leukaia and Loreleia. You are the first seaman to get this close to us in countless eons. Almost all either perish on the rocks with their ships or jump overboard and drown in their frantic attempts to swim to shore. Our song seems to have a bewildering effect on men's rational powers. It renders them helpless—or should I say, 'all at sea,'" she added with just the barest trace of a smile, again lowering her head, this time as if in embarrassment over this most innocuous of puns.

How mannerly, how utterly decorous, thought Anselm, now finding the strange little creatures more irresistible than ever. *Are their powers of attraction limited to their song*, he wondered, a little uneasily. "Permit me to introduce myself," he began, with a nod to what struck him as the curiously genteel quality of the encounter, "I am Anselm, a sea captain and soldier, and am travelling home from … well, I suppose it must be … Troy," he mused, more to himself than to the bird-maiden. "On my way to … Ithaca, I guess … Yes, yes, it *must* be Ithaca." He chuckled a bit at his own obtuseness, but strangely did not wonder any further about the why or wherefore of it.

"I grew up fascinated by the tales of the sirens and the reputed lethal powers of their song over the minds and hearts of men," Anselm continued. In saying this, he noticed that the voices of the two singing sisters, who continued to cavort about the rock surface behind the third, had diminished in volume. Was it to avoid interfering with the conversation their sister was having with this rare visitor? Was it so they could better hear the exchange themselves even as they sang? "Being a lifelong lover of the musical arts myself, and a devotee of Euterpe, the muse of music," Anselm explained, "I have always nourished a deep desire to hear your enchanting song, to hear for myself, so to speak, whether that song was as potent as the legends say, or just another popular exaggeration. And I must say, standing here listening as I now am, the legends do not exaggerate."

"And yet you stand there listening with impunity. You seem in no danger," Ligeia said. "On the contrary, you seem to be enjoying our melody as you would any ordinary tune."

"Yes, so it seems," Anselm replied. "I must admit I am perplexed by the fact."

"Perhaps," Ligeia conjectured, "because your curiosity is genuine, and grounded in a true love of the art, and is not in any sense a form of audible voyeurism, you are naturally protected from the lethal quality of the beauty of our song."

As she uttered these words, her sisters' melody suddenly modulated into a sort of sweet and gentle background fanfare, as if to underline, to make "official," their sister's speculation. Apparently it was their way of agreeing. *Are they always of one mind*, Anselm wondered.

"To voyeurs, of course," Ligeia continued, "beauty—above all musical beauty— is always potentially lethal, just like any intoxicant. The pleasure-seekers can't help overindulging themselves and eventually lose their way. Yet those Eastern mariners unfortunate enough to encounter our Indian counterparts, who are, by the way, much, much larger than we are, suffer an even more hideous fate than do Western men, for they are torn to pieces and eaten up by our sister sirens. The shipwreck suffered in these parts is a far more merciful fate, don't you think?"

"Well, I guess I'm not sure what to think," Anselm stammered, and, indeed, he was only being honest, for he was having a devil of a time keeping track of the discussion while his heart and his senses were longing to surrender themselves to the music in the background, which continued unabated and, for all he knew, was never-ending, a true endless melody. Even though he was protected from total seduction by his genuine love of music, still Anselm was almost riven in two by his conflicting desires to attend to both the discussion and the song framing it. Casting about in his mind for relief, he thought to blend the two and thereby ease his inner tension by focusing the one upon the other, the discussion upon the very music being performed.

"As I listen to your song," Anselm said, speaking slowly, thoughtfully, "it strikes me that, although it is exquisitely beautiful, it is also mostly in a minor mode, which is to say, sad—almost to the point of melancholy. I'd have thought that such a divine gift as yours could never fail to buoy your own spirits, to lift you into exalted realms of emotional affirmation of life. Yet I'm afraid there is much more of the nihilistic finale of Tchaikovsky's *Pathetique Symphony* in your melody than of the gay finale of, say, Rachmaninoff's *Second Symphony*, or the Beatles' 'Hey, Jude.' Why is that?" (Curiously, it occurred to no one on the scene to ask what world these musical icons belonged to.)

"You ask a very astute question," Ligeia replied, "but I must tell you—and please do not reproach me for saying this—that it comes out of ignorance. Ignorance of what my sisters and I are doing here, what we are about, ignorance of our function and purpose in the grand scheme of things. Yet your ignorance is balm to my soul, for it is grounded in a primordial need to know, to see, to raise consciousness, which is light years in advance of the greed and cupidity of the vast majority of those who approach these shores. Your ignorance is learned ignorance, *docta ignorantia* … Please, allow me to explain."

As she gathered herself to enlighten Anselm, Ligeia also gathered her sisters around her, one on either side, perhaps so as to rely on their moral support for what, so Anselm thought, promised to be a fascinating revelation. As the three of them clung to each other facing Anselm, the two outside sisters continued their song in a low hum, in support of the third's words that were about to come forth, language for the moment superseding tones in what was for the sirens a rare opportunity, indeed, for communication with an Other found worthy. (And yet it would be wrong to think of Anselm in this moment as experiencing any friction, any opposition, at all between the two expressive media. For he was by now already well into a rarefied state in which he was receiving the words Ligeia spoke to him as a sort of distillation, a precipitate, of the music being made by the other two. Words and music formed a continuum rather than a coupling, the latter "thickening" into the former, the whole an intrinsically unitary process. It even occurred to Anselm to recall what he had learned in a language class about the meaning of the German word for poet, which was *Dichter*. [The *German* word? Who were the Germans?] The German adjective *dicht* meant "thick," which meant a poet was in some strange sense a "thickener." He "thickened" things. But what things did he thicken? Things of the spirit, light, airy things, things that existed only in or as flow, like music. A poet, which in the German tradition meant an artist of any stripe, took spiritual truth such as music and "thickened it down" into a precipitate such as words. There simply was no duality there, and that non-dual nature of things ordinarily thought of as distinct and separate was precisely what Anselm was enjoying in this moment. It was a "no boundary" moment.)

Ligeia now proceeded to address Anselm's question: "Your description of our song as 'sad,' 'melancholy,' even 'tragic,' is accurate, but it is only half the truth. After all, are we not uplifted by the emotional catharsis of tragedy on the stage? Do we not feel purged and refreshed after listening to even the saddest song? Does not a good cry help to relieve our anguish, even over the death of a loved one? ... Feelings, too, are airy things, things that flow, sometimes violently, yet their free expression—short of acting out, which is not necessary—allows us to return to that condition of inner balance necessary for persevering in life." Anselm felt a slight twinge of anachronism upon hearing the expression "acting out," which struck him as oddly out of place then and there.

"If you watch yourself closely," Ligeia continued, "and are honest with yourself, you will observe within yourself a moment of the profoundest affirmation of life even in the depths of despair, over the death of a spouse or even your own child. This is precisely the moment our song evokes in those rare ones, like you, who have ears to hear. It is a moment that celebrates the indestructible joy of life, a joy, as one sage put it, that is 'deeper yet than agony.' In our own case, this joy is deeper than the agony we suffer over having claws for feet and sterile wombs. But our own 'thickener' saw fit to create us this way, and our song, sad as it is, celebrates the fact.

"That is why I say your truth is a half-truth. It fails to leave room for this joy, which is the other side of the coin—better yet, another coin entirely. In fact, truth be told, this joy is more, so much more, infinitely more, than the mere resultant sum of itself and its opposite. It is a joy that beggars all description. For us as sirens, it gives our song its divine stature, and when a rare worthy such as yourself chances to hear it, it confers divinity upon him as well—at least for a time. The vast number of others who hear it 'prematurely,' so to speak, pay dearly, for who can safely attend to the song of God without long and diligent preparation?" Once again, Anselm felt the tiny sting of anachronism, though without consciously recognizing it as such: here upon hearing the word "God." Then, freely associating, he thought of the depressing words of some writer, who pronounced, on what must have been a bad day, that "There is plenty of hope, no end of hope—for God—only not for us," and smiled.

At that point, Ligeia began to de-precipitate her words, dissolving them back into the dulcet tones from which they came. Anselm watched, transfixed, as the three bird-maidens continued to sing without words, standing side by side on their rock in the lagoon, treating the boundaries of ordinary reality as if these did not apply to them.

VIGIL 9

Going Over to the Dark Side

"I mean, I *like* the guy, I'm very fond of him," Paul Manheim said, taking a sip of his iced tea. He was sitting on his apartment balcony on a warm Saturday afternoon in early September, opposite his friend Harold Branden, who was nursing a half-full glass of beer on the little patio table next to him. "He's a good friend of the family," Mannhein continued, "but I have my doubts that he's husband material for my daughter. He's just a little too otherworldly for my taste." This, you must know, was a deliberate red herring on Mannheim's part, thrown into the conversation to elicit his friend's reaction to the prospect of a marriage between his daughter and Anselm MacGregor, a marriage he, Manheim, secretly coveted.

Branden took a long draft of his Heineken and carefully set the glass back down, exactly in the middle of its coaster. With the sole exception of his style of conversation, which was always effusive and excessive, he did everything carefully, thoughtfully. But in this case, he was subtly pursuing with Manheim a longstanding hidden agenda of his own, which was causing him to choose his words with unusual care. He was trying to turn his friend's favor gradually away from Anselm and towards himself in his secret quest to win the hand of the winsome Ronnie. He thought to do this on this occasion through the subtle strategy of damning his rival with faint praise, thereby implying his own superiority as "husband material." But in this the registrar made the fatal error of misreading his friend's expectations for his daughter, as the following exchange will illustrate.

"'Otherworldly,' you say," Branden replied, absently stroking his moustache. "That's an interesting word, not one you hear very often these days."

"Yes, that's certainly true," Manheim seconded. "We do live in an abysmally secular age, don't we, an age in which 'this world' is, more and more, the only one that counts. Church attendance is way down all over the Western world, even more in Europe than here, especially in the northern countries."

Branden didn't want the conversation spreading out into generalities, so he steered it back. "You call Anselm otherworldly, but, to my knowledge, he's no card-carrying Christian."

"No. Quite right, he isn't. I've been with him on many a Sunday morning in recent years and the subject of religion has never once come up. He's not a member of any church or sect, at least not an active member. But what I mean here by 'otherworldly' is something quite different. It's the sense I get in his presence that he's rarely all there with you in any given moment or situation. He's always a bit vaguely distracted, pre-occupied, as if he's got some sort of mental itch that he can't scratch. I'm certain this accounts for his frequent clumsiness. As you well know, if there's something to trip over, or knock over, Anselm will gravitate to it like a moth to flame. I noticed this about him first off when we met years ago at a St. Peter and Paul's alumni dinner and he accidently dumped a pitcher of beer into my lap. At first I chalked it up to ordinary absent-mindedness—you know, the distracted student—but soon enough it became clear to me that this ... this seeming subtle alienation of his from ... well, all things physical, I would say, was a constituent part of his personality."

Just then Manheim shifted in his skimpy beach chair, presumably to emphasize his next point, but in so doing popped the button above his fly loose from the puce Bermuda shorts he was wearing. The button, released at last from its chronic stress, fell to the concrete floor of the balcony and bounced briskly, as if it had a mind to, over the base railing and down to the street below. Manheim himself hadn't noticed a thing, but his friend had witnessed the entirety of the little drama and had to restrain himself with great force in order not to peer over the balcony to observe the runaway button's fate.

" ... I don't want to see my daughter married to a man who negotiates the world like a mine field," Manheim went on, "and who is, at times at least, socially inept ... Case in point, when I introduced him to Principal Smathers, my new superior at school last year, he said, 'Hello, Prince, nice to meet you.' And he wasn't joking! And just the other day, I let him drive us to lunch in my new Lexus; and every time he stopped for a light and started up again when it turned green, he would move his right hand as if to indicate he was shifting gears—and my car has an *automatic transmission*! When I asked him what he was doing, he said his father had taught him to drive on a manual, and he had never unlearned the shifting motion. Tell me, Harold, how can I marry Ronnie off to someone like that?"

Seeing this as the perfect opportunity to apply his strategy of damning Anselm with faint praise, Branden answered, "But you know, Paul, he *is* considered bright—at least in a "book smart" sort of way—by some of his fellow students and even by one professor in the English Department whom I know casually. This man said he was perfectly prepared to write the lad a letter of recommendation for a teaching position at, say, one of the local community colleges. Now that's—"

"—Oh my, really, Harold!" Manheim interrupted excitedly. "Well, I must say, that certainly puts a different light on the situation, doesn't it? A professor at a local college—hmm!" As the Assistant Principal sat there staring off into space in contemplation of a future family bathed in academic bliss, the registrar could only kick himself internally for overestimating his friend's paltry ambition for his daughter's future happiness.

Casually eavesdropping on the conversation was young Ronnie, who sat on the living room sofa just off the balcony pretending to be engrossed in her smartphone, her two thumbs poking a mile a minute all over the phone's tiny keyboard, repeatedly tapping out the name of the object of her affection—Anselm, Anselm, Anselm ... She was inspired to wax fanciful by the hopeful tone of the discussion on the balcony of the young man's professional prospects. She secretly hoped one day, not only to share these prospects, but indeed to enhance them through a career of her own in fashion design. She would be the admired wife of an English professor, and that was "yummy," to quote one of her favorite adjectives, but also a woman with her own claim to esteem for her modish hats and gowns and shoes. She was, in fact, one of the darlings in the current class of fashion design majors at a community college in lower Manhattan. She pictured herself and her rising-star of an English professor husband sitting over coffee and scones of a Sunday morning on a posh balcony of their own, greeting friends and neighbors passing by below on their way to the local bakery or church or ... anywhere. She could almost hear the admiring comments of the ladies below: "Such a splendid woman … I'll bet she's wearing one of her own creations. How incredibly chic! … Look at the two of them up there. Have you ever seen a more handsome couple? … "

Just then, speak of the devil, Anselm himself walked into the living room, let in by Ronnie's little sister Sally. After greeting Ronnie with a single long-stemmed red rose that he had purchased at a nearby flower shop on his way there, he stepped smartly to the balcony threshold and regaled the two men with a robust "Good morning, gentlemen! A fine day, isn't it?", proceeding to tell them all about the first week of his fascinating new job working for Archivist Lindhurst at Stoneham Tech, and how swimmingly it was all going. All were impressed by the obvious change in Anselm's manner. Indeed, he seemed transformed—bright, confident, extraverted, almost commanding, and not a single misstep between apartment door and balcony. Manheim, already encouraged by Harold Branden's estimation of Anselm's potential, however self-servingly modest, was set to such paroxysms of delight by the young man's new manner that he could hardly contain himself. And when the student announced that he must, alas, already take his leave as his services were urgently required at work—yes, occasionally even on a Sunday, the godless Archivist having no particular respect for the Sabbath—the Assistant Principle suddenly felt on the verge of a swoon. As Anselm said goodbye and turned to go, he could only mumble some incoherent syllables amounting more or less to "See you later."

Shortly thereafter, Registrar Branden also took his leave. Ronnie, still on the couch smelling her rose, was busy enjoying her own swoon. *Oh, it's for sure now! There can be no more doubt! Anselm does like me! And maybe more than that! But I mustn't go there, even in my thoughts. I don't want to jinx things.* But, of course, she couldn't help herself; everything was just so delightful, so exciting, so hopeful, and she let herself be seduced by a cascade of fantasies of the future Mrs. MacGregor, managing editor of the popular fashion magazine, *Tres Chic,* and most admirable wife of the esteemed professor of English literature, Anselm MacGregor, himself author of several learned volumes and even a budding celebrity of sorts for having appeared on *The Late Show* with Steven Colbert and exchanged quips with the talk show maestro extraordinaire.

Then, just as the besotted girl was about to sink even further down to a level of social self-regard bordering on the concupiscent, some strange hostile influence—was it from within herself, from the faintly fetid air outside, from some hitherto unknown provenance?—began to assail her. It invaded her fantasies, spoiling them, taking the forms of pessimism, cynicism, a deficit in confidence—in other words, the dark side of Ronnie's normally self-assured blithe spirit. "This is all nonsense, girl. Anselm is a mediocrity, a pathetic loser who's going nowhere fast. He will never be a professor, certainly not one of any distinction, and he'll never marry you. Let's face it, he doesn't love you; sure, he's got a little crush on you, but his heart's desire is for that infernal music of the spheres he's been hearing here, there and everywhere of late … Even with all your charms, girl, which are considerable, you don't stand a chance …" These and other, similar, maledictions tore into the poor girl's breast, clutching her heart, squeezing the joy out of it and replacing it with so many stabs of icy horror. Holding her head in her hands, she rocked back and forth and side to side on the sofa, letting out a half-suppressed wail, an "oh, ooh, oooh," that caught her father's attention. He, still out on the balcony, mistook her expression for an adolescent reaction to some bombastic headphone rock music (she wasn't wearing headphones) and huffed at her to " ... please, Veronica, take that drivel with you into your room or even further away if possible. I'm trying to read last Sunday's *Times Book Review*!" But she heard nothing, totally embroiled as she was in this freakish emotional attack "out of the blue." Still holding her head, trying mightily to regain some wisp of composure, she chanced to look down at her gift rose, which she had laid on the coffee table in front of her, and was again sent reeling, for the flower was all wilted and withered, sallow and colorless, looking as if someone had microwaved it for a full minute. Her panic mounted and suddenly she was feeling at odds with everything around her: The walls turned dark gray; the rug looked like a bed of ashes; the cat, heretofore napping peacefully on the easy chair across from her, now looked sinister and ready to pounce.

"Sally, does Cuddles look all right to you?" she said, a tad frantically, to her sister, who had just walked in.

"She's sleeping. How's she supposed to look?" the girl replied laconically. "What's the matter with you anyway? You look like you've seen a ghost."

"Oh, nothing. I didn't sleep well last night, that's all," she dissembled, and, taking another look at Cuddles, saw that the cat was indeed fast asleep on its favorite chair, and that the walls were their ordinary blue again and the rug its ordinary pattern. Then, turning to the rose, she saw that it was as fresh and as red and, just generally, as rosy as could be.

What on earth was all that! she wondered, flummoxed. But there was no time to pursue the matter as her good friends, the Strump sisters, Annette and Marsha, were due to arrive in a few minutes for a visit. There was no time to waste and she set about sprucing the place up a bit and making a pitcher of lemonade for her guests, who were sure to arrive parched from the heat. Manheim, seeing his daughter suddenly busy, assumed there would soon be two or more young chatterboxes in the apartment and made a beeline for his favorite bench in nearby Lincoln Park, taking his folded *Times Book Review* with him.

Minutes later the doorbell rang and in pranced the two Strump sisters, Annette, the sandy-haired younger and shorter one, extraverted, loquacious, always ready to laugh, and Marsha, tall, blond and a tad reserved, her hair pulled back in a ponytail, giving her pretty face a somewhat severe expression. They waltzed in in their minimalist summer outfits all giggly and gossiping about some acquaintances, who happened to be of the male persuasion, but, immediately noticing Ronnie's expression of anguished confusion, which hadn't yet left her face, they began importuning her, almost demanding that she tell them what the matter was.

After unburdening herself of her little trauma involving the walls, the rug and Cuddles the cat, Ronnie tried to laugh it off, calling herself a "silly thing," but it was too late. Ronnie's psycho-virus had already infected the Strump sisters, who were anxiously scanning walls and rug and wondering, nervously, where Cuddles was. Finally, Ronnie burst out laughing at the ridiculousness of the moment, which instantly drained all tension from the room, and the three girls had a good and hearty laugh together. But soon enough, Marsha's face again took a serious turn as she let drop that she herself did believe in the paranormal, and in evil influences, and in the ability of certain "gifted individuals" to foretell, if not indeed to shape, future events. As a matter of fact, she said with an odd mixture of pride and embarrassment, she herself was personally acquainted with just such a "seer," a "remarkable woman" who lived on the outskirts of Hoboken and who, for a fee, gave "readings" to anyone interested in "optimizing their own future prospects." With eyes cast sheepishly down at the rug, she confessed that she had in fact recently visited the old woman, whose name was Lisa Ramirez, and treated herself to a reading, and that she'd had very good reason to do so, thank you, as she had not heard a word from her boyfriend, Victor, a soldier stationed in Afghanistan, in over a month. "I just couldn't stand the waiting any longer and I didn't know what else to do," she said almost apologetically to Ronnie, whose face reflected total commiseration.

"Oh, Victor, my Victor, my sweet soldier boy!" her kid sister teased, showing the immaturity of her younger years.

"Oh, shush, Nettie!" Ronnie chided. "Tell me, Marsha, how did the meeting go? Did she help you? Were you satisfied? Do you think she's on the level?" Ronnie pumped her friend with these and a slew of other questions, so many and in such rapid profusion that one would think she had more than a passing interest in the subject.

"Oh, Lisa's on the level all right," Marsha said with an unmistakable air of pride in her own keen eye for character. "I'd bet my bottom dollar on it, and, in fact, I almost did. She doesn't come cheap. Bring your credit card with you just in case, if you go."

Ronnie nodded gravely several times, as if she had already decided to do just that.

"But I'll tell you," Marsha continued, "that session was worth every penny to me, and more. Lisa is not your usual cliché of a fortuneteller—there's no cape, no crystal ball, no Tarot cards, no coffee grounds to read—none of those BS props. You see, she's a *bruja*."

This strange word, obviously foreign, and therefore terribly exotic-sounding, made even Annette sit up and listen. "A *bru ... ja*? What on earth is that?" she asked, with a half-mocking grin, but also with obvious genuine curiosity.

"Yeah, what's that?" Ronnie seconded.

"A bruja is, literally, a witch or a sorceress—"

"—*A witch! Oh my God!*" Nettie shrieked in mock hysteria. Ronnie put her hand over her mouth in silent disbelief.

Marsha just sat there waiting for the dust to settle, and when it did, she continued in the same even tone of the sainted instructor laboring to enlighten idiots. "Lisa is from Mexico. A witch isn't the same thing at all down there as she is up here. In Mexico a bruja is part of mainstream society and has a totally different—and higher—social status. People respect her for her skill in prescribing herbal cures. Even doctors go to brujas for their specialized knowledge. A lot of educated people have a family bruja along with their family physician. And for the really private stuff—you know, mental issues, emotional issues, things like that—a bruja is often preferred to a psychiatrist or psychologist. – I've been to Veracruz and Mexico City twice on family vacations; my mom's a Spanish teacher. That's where I learned all about these fascinating women.

"The problem in Lisa's case is that she had the misfortune to fall in love with an American sailor on leave in Veracruz. They got married and she followed him home to New Jersey. He worked itinerant jobs but was never a steady earner. So now she's stuck here selling chestnuts and just getting by on his miniscule navy pension while he's become a semi-invalid who rarely leaves his bed.

"Anyway, as I said, Lisa was worth every penny. She told me that Victor had suffered a minor injury to his right arm and shoulder and was laid up and couldn't write or operate his phone for the time being. But also that he would soon be back in harness and would be calling me any day now, certainly within the next week or so." All seemed happy at this prospect and were impressed with the specificity of the bruja's information.

The three girls hung out chatting, sipping lemonade and listening to music for the rest of the afternoon and well into the evening, but, truth to tell, Ronnie was secretly impatient for the visit to be over—so she could pursue her by-now burning desire to locate and consult with the bruja Lisa Ramirez, to know at last and with certainty, so she ardently hoped, whether Anselm truly had eyes for her. Telling her dad, who had returned from the park, that she wanted to give Marsha and Nettie a lift home, Ronnie took the girls down to the building's underground parking garage where they all climbed into Manheim's Lexus and headed for an address just off Kennedy Boulevard on the north side of Journal Square.

Dropping them off at their house some fifteen minutes later, Ronnie then drove east the few blocks to Central Ave., from which she knew, heading north, that she could easily find the great viaduct that would take her down to Willow Ave at the north end of Hoboken. From there she could, if necessary, hoof it to the bruja's house, which, as Marsha had told her, was a ways off the street grid, set back beyond the northwest edge of town, tucked away somewhere in the untamed weeds and trees that hugged the base of the palisades separating Hoboken from Union and Jersey Cities. Marsha had also mentioned that the bruja saw people only on Wednesdays and Saturdays after sundown, but then was open for business all night long till dawn. So the girl wouldn't have to wait, sitting on pins and needles.

The Hoboken viaduct is an immense ramp, a little over half a mile long, linking Jersey City and Union City Heights, which lie atop the palisades, with Hoboken, which lies at sea-level. The ramp's narrowness at its high end—two lanes of traffic each way, no shoulders—can be intimidating for drivers who struggle with acro-, agora- or claustrophobia. This is the bridge that Ronnie drove down as she descended into Hoboken. Who could blame her if she felt as though she were descending into hell— with no guarantee she would rise again on the third, or any other, day? When she finally came to Willow Ave. at the bottom, she decided to park the car and walk, since the area around and under the viaduct was much too dark to read signs through the windshield. Marsha had told her that the bruja's house was off the beaten path and had no street address, since it was located, literally, on the other side of the tracks, precisely two tracks, that bore freight-train traffic and marked the western border of the "mile square city." She had described the house as a tiny clapboard affair standing semi-hidden among the thick brush and weed trees that clung to the foot of the palisade under the viaduct.

This was all Ronnie had to go on as she locked the Lexus doors with the e-key and turned—with a shudder—to face the vast inky blackness framing either side of the viaduct. She figured she had a walk of about five short blocks, west from Willow Ave. to Madison St., to reach the inkiest, most isolated area. Her heart sank as she started out, one hand clutching a flashlight in one sweater pocket, the other a can of pepper spray in the other. But she was a tough little thing, Ronnie was, made of sturdy stuff, and, as she walked tentatively along, she gave herself a mini-pep-talk ("Come on, let's do this. It's well worth a bit of nerves.") to steady herself. She negotiated the four-block stretch from Willow Ave. to Jefferson St. easily enough, as this section was fairly well lit and dotted with bars, clubs, restaurants and even a dog park, most of it part of an effort in recent years to revitalize this run-down extremity of the city. It was the next, and last, block, from Jefferson to Madison, and beyond that, that gave her pause—and the willies.

This was a dark wasteland, filled with industrial yards and warehouses and high chain-link fences, with no sign of life. Still, she took a deep breath and proceeded, flashlight at the ready. When she got about halfway down the block, she heard a sudden, sharp cracking sound, like gunfire. This shocked her, and she threw herself hard up against the nearby chain-link fence, clutching its zigzag weave, not realizing that this was no good at all as a defensive posture. Then, just as suddenly, she heard a rapid series of cracking sounds, but this time accompanied by the tiny yet keen flashing of fireworks. As the firecrackers went off, she could hear the shrieking laughter of two young boys, probably tweens, inside the fenced-off yard as they ran off to avoid detection by any security guard who might be lurking nearby.

Ronnie breathed a deep sigh of relief and soldiered on. Finally she crossed the tracks and was glad she was wearing sneakers. From there she stepped gingerly into the thick brush of no-man's land, an area so overgrown and grungy from the soot of passing trains that even the rats steered clear of it. She raised the beam of her flashlight to pierce the blackness, hoping to spot the little clapboard house. At first seeing nothing, she moved further under the viaduct stretching high above her and could hear the occasional rumbling of cars and trucks passing overhead in both directions. Finally, as she found herself just about midway under the viaduct, she saw a tiny light, the barest particle of a glimmer, couched behind what seemed to her like an impenetrable density of growth. She moved towards the light slowly, as best she could, and came at last upon a kind of path, defined only by its relative lack of impeding nature. And suddenly there it was, the little clapboard house, the light a single nightlight bulb hanging from the front-porch ceiling.

She took heart and climbed the three wooden steps leading to the porch and the front door. Then she stopped and stepped carefully back down onto the lawn, such as it was, to check something. Looking up, she realized she was directly underneath the top of the massive viaduct, which now struck her as forming an immense cross over her head, the vertical "beam" the viaduct itself, the horizontal beam the crossroad at its high end built against the palisade. Shaking her head skeptically to negate the involuntary associations to Christianity that immediately flooded her already fretful mind, she climbed the three steps again and moved close to the door, searching for a bell to ring. Finding none, she raised her fist to knock and was startled to see the door appear to open itself before her with a loud, whiny creak. She stuck her head inside before stepping in and squinted as she scanned the living room, the lighting being very dim. Seeing no movement, sensing no presence, she finally entered, though just barely, and called out, "Hello! Is anybody home? I'm looking for a Lisa Ramirez. Does Lisa Ramirez live here?"

The only response was a pitch-black cat that strolled past her, stopping just in front of her and looking up at her with searching eyes. Taken aback by the surprise, Ronnie just stood there rooted to the spot, looking down at the animal as she leaned back against the doorframe. The cat walked away from her heading towards the stairs, stopped about halfway there and turned its head back towards her, letting out a very distinct "meow!", unmistakably indicating she should follow. Up the stairs they went, the cat stopping at a door at the end of the corridor. Another "meow" and this door too swung open, revealing a large room full of strange objects, a second black cat and several other small animals—among them hamsters, guinea pigs and two bats, one in flight, the other perched on a curtain rod. The room was astir with what looked on the surface to be hugger-mugger, almost chaotic, activity.

"Ah, so you've finally come, child! I've been waiting." The greeting came from a corner of the room where an old hag sat bent over a table crowded with bottles of all sizes and shapes, some empty, some containing roots, herbs or liquids of various colors, mostly shades of yellow and green. Ronnie was so stunned by the array of objects and creatures that she entirely missed the woman's implication of foreknowledge of her visit. "Are you Lisa Ramirez?" she asked tentatively.

The old woman smiled a semi-toothless smile and answered in her native tongue, "*Si, si, muchacha. Ven aqui*—come here, let me have a look at you. Yes, yes …"

Ronnie was still too much at loose ends to notice the odd note of familiarity in the hag's words. It was all she could do to take in the scene as a whole. The room seemed to be a combination kitchen and old-fashioned sitting room, with modern, tacky plastic furniture. There were all sorts of herbs hanging from ceiling racks in clumps, both fresh and dry. In the corner opposite the table stood a stove, on it a pot with something bubbling in it. On the worktable, among the aforementioned bottles were a number of other items, notably a skull, a little statue of Our Lady of Guadalupe, a plaster pair of Jesus and Mary, and, perhaps to cover all the bases, a bronze bust of the laughing Buddha. Plus an array of Amerindian articles, masks and feathers. In the midst of all this lay something that, by its grotesqueness, brought Ronnie's attention back into focus. It was the crucified head of a rat, the cross rigged from one long and one shorter bone, at the point of intersection a poorly prepared rat's head, decapitated with something blunt.

Ronnie looked from the ghastly cross to its maker, observing in a flash the old woman's straggly graying hair up in a bun, her black non-descript granny dress and shawl, and her flat Indian nose showing two hideous parallel burn marks on its left side. She shuddered and seemed about to fall prey again to anxiety, a prospect abetted by the infernal racket now being made by the motley crowd of bats and birds and guinea pigs and mice, all apparently in a tizzy over the first-time visitor. Suddenly the bruja grabbed a spray can from the table and, holding it up above her head, pressed the button. Out came a tight little cloud of something black, which almost instantly spread out and filled the room, making not only the room's contents but also its noise completely disappear. After a moment, as the light gradually returned, Ronnie blinked her eyes several times in an effort to make sense of what she now saw: an ordinary living room with some cheap drapes, a rug, a sofa and two easy chairs—no creatures, living or dead (the black cat being the sole exception), no work table, no bottles or herbs or roots. Even the bruja herself now seemed somehow less intimidating—her face less dentally challenged, younger; her Indian hair darker; her movements spryer; her granny dress now looking more like a shift.

She gently led Ronnie over to the sofa, raising her hand to rest it on her taller guest's shoulder. Despite the bruja's modest rejuvenation, Ronnie could still feel the bony texture of her arthritic fingers digging slightly into her neck, undermining the woman's attempt to relax her. When they were seated next to one another, the bruja began, "I know very well why you've come to me, my child. You want to know whether Anselm will marry you once he becomes a professor. Isn't that so?"

In her astonishment over this impossible invasion of her most private thoughts, which added to her befuddlement over the room's physical transformation, Ronnie could do no more than nod assent. The bruja knew she had her victim precisely where she wanted her. "Don't be so shocked, my dear," she continued, driving her point home. "Who do you think was behind that violent attack on your tender feelings towards Anselm earlier today. That attack 'out of the blue,' as you dismissed it, to be rid of it. That was me. I was with you there on the sofa doing my best to sober you up from your futile fantasies about a blissful future with that young man … Let go of him, girl! Let go of him! He's not for you. He knocked my chestnut stand over, the one my husband and I tend at the Journal Square strip mall. My poor chestnuts all over the filthy ground! Normally by magic those puppies would come rolling back to me out of the pockets of hoodwinked customers and I'd sell them again. But he ruined it with his damned clumsiness … Listen, child, Anselm is in league with the old man, who is my deadly enemy. He's already been working for him for a few days now. The day before yesterday he sprinkled some arsenic drops on my face … they almost blinded me. Look here," she said, pointing to the spot, "See what I mean? … Let go of that one, Veronika, he doesn't love you. He loves that cursed music of the spheres, the music made by the Archivist's daughter, who is of the realm of the serpents, just as her father is of the realm of the salamanders. He wants to marry his daughter off to Anselm. Anselm will never be a professor, Veronica, because he is now in the service of the salamanders and will fall in love with the green snake. Forget him! Rid yourself of him! He's nothing but trouble."

But the bruja's words missed their mark. Rather than persuading Ronnie, they aroused her ire. She knew what she wanted and was not about to be told to give it up by some old hag, however preternatural her damned powers. In a firm, resolute voice she replied, "Look, old woman, I've come here seeking the same kind of help you generously gave to my girlfriend only recently. I thought you might assuage my anxieties about the future just as you assuaged hers. But all I've gotten from you so far are cynicism and insults. Worse yet, you slander my Anselm, the man I love and wish to marry, with all your stupid allegorical talk of snakes and salamanders. It's obvious I've come to the wrong place. Good night!"

At this the bruja dropped to her knees, impetuously embracing Ronnie around the hips and crying out dolefully, "Ronniekins, Ronniekins, don't you recognize your old au pair Lisa ... who used to bounce you on her knee and play paddy cake with you! I taught you your numbers, one to ten, didn't I? The three of us—you, your father and I—would count with the Count on Sesame Street and I would imitate his Transylvanian accent, remember? ... Which was easy for me since I already had a Spanish accent: vun, too, tree. Your father thought it was hilarious ... It was you, baby girl, who broke me in as an au pair when I first moved up here from Veracruz." Ronnie stared down into the bruja's face, deeply, sympathetically, for she was now moving into the slow shock of recognition. Finally she burst out, "Lisa! Is it really you? Yes, of course, I remember. You're older, of course, but your face is basically the same ... Oh my God! How is this possible? ..." She instinctively looked around the room as if to find someone to confirm her absurdly improbable discovery. Then, turning back, she pressed the woman, "But, Lisa, tell me, how could you have—"

"—Never mind, child, never mind. I've become what I am because I had no choice in the matter. The Archivist is the wise old man but I am the wise old woman. As I said, he is my archenemy and Anselm has fallen into his hands ... I can see you are still the same headstrong girl you were as a toddler when you would burst out of the closet and try to scare your father or me. We would pretend you were a monster—a two-foot-tall monster—and cringe as if terrified. You loved it. – Look, Veronica, if you are serious about winning Anselm, I have the skills to help you do that but you must help me help you. We must break the old man's hold over him and sabotage his devotion to the daughter's music. Are you prepared to do what is necessary?"

Ronnie nodded yes, this time decisively. She was ready. The bruja continued, "All right. So, what we'll do is this: On the night of the autumnal equinox—that's September 23, coming up soon—you will slip out of the house around ten o'clock and come here to my place. Understood?" Again a firm nod. "Good. From here we'll drive up to Weehawken Stadium and perform the necessary rituals on the baseball field there. Nothing you experience there will do you any harm, I guarantee it … That's about it. Now, good night, child. You'd better get home before your father starts wondering where you are. By the way, how did you get here?" Ronnie mimed holding a steering wheel. "Ah, you drove. Very good."

Ronnie left the bruja's house and walked at a fast pace back to her car, parked on Willow Avenue. As she walked, she vowed to herself, "Nothing will keep me from making that equinox date. Lisa's right. Anselm is entangled in something mysterious, something beyond his powers. I'll free him and then he'll be mine … Yummy!"

VIGIL 10

The Not So Jolly Green Dragon

The room was dimly lit and bare, except for a plain tan rug and an old-fashioned console radio placed against the rear wall. Suddenly the doors were thrown open and what entered the room, fat and succulent, its sides voluptuously swelling, footless, pushing itself along on its entire underside, was the green dragon.

"Come right in, my love," the hostess said in her most endearing voice. He smiled, though somewhat annoyed, and said that, as she well knew, he couldn't do that, as he was too long. He couldn't get all the way in. This meant that the doors, as usual, would have to remain open, which, as usual, would make things quite awkward. It was time she learned to accept that. "As you know, I've come quite a distance," he said, "and my underside, as always, is scraped quite sore. But I'm glad to do it; you know you mean everything to me."

"I know, I know, and you to me," she said, a spark of passion spiriting her words. "Well, I suppose we'll just have to continue to make do with things the way they are. After all, we always have."

"Yes, and I don't see that changing anytime soon. And yet …" he said thoughtfully, pulling his hefty green torso as far into the room as space allowed.

"Yes? 'And yet' … what?" she questioned, a barely suppressed note of concern in her voice.

"I don't know," he answered, "It's just that I've been getting these little brain spasms lately, TIAs I think they're called, little interruptions—more like intrusions, really. They come unannounced and totally cut off whatever I'm doing or thinking. They last only a nanosecond and leave behind this curiously pleasant afterglow, a sense that all is well. It's not unlike the moments after one of our liaisons. I shouldn't complain really; I just wish I knew what they mean, if anything."

"Well, if they're pleasant, why don't you just enjoy them and not worry about the rest?" she said teasingly, lightly blowing at a tuft of hair that hung from the underside of his snout.

"You're right, of course," he answered, "but you know me, can't just enjoy anything at face value, always have to know why it's come to me, whether I deserve it—all that justification crap ... In fact, I wouldn't be surprised if that's one of the reasons I can't come all the way in here, why part of me is always stuck outside this room," he said plaintively, trying in vain to pull more of his hinter part into the room.

"That's funny—I mean, *interesting*, very interesting," she said nodding, "but I don't know if I'm getting you quite right. Could you explain a bit?"

"Well, it's just that this half-in half-out arrangement of ours always leaves my back half out in the cold, so to speak. Our meetings are never quite as intimate, as satisfying, as I would like them to be—frankly, as I *need* them to be. It's as if the part of me left outside, the rear part, is just waiting around out there for us to do our business and for me to leave. It's not involved. It's even a little self-conscious, I would say, always nervously on the lookout for passersby who might happen to 'catch us in the act,' *in flagrante delicto*," he concluded melodramatically. (If he'd had arms, he would have raised them.)

"That's so odd, so strange," she said, as much to herself as to him, "Speaking for myself, our *rendesvous* usually leave me quite fulfilled, I'm happy to say, and yet I think I know what you mean. There's almost always this vague, lingering sense that something's not … quite … right. It doesn't pre-dominate—no, it niggles at the edges, like the subtle unwanted aftertaste of an otherwise fine wine."

"I wish it were subtle with me," he went on, "But I'm afraid it's anything *but*. It's as if there were two of me, the one watching the other, and the other, aware it's being watched, can't throw itself into anything completely, not even this! You know what Freud said, don't you? He said the sense of being watched, being observed, is only one step away from the pain-ful feeling of being criticized—and *that* is only one step away from full-blown paranoia!"

"Oh well, we're not going to worry about what old Freud said, are we? He said a lot of things that nobody believes any-more. Like your sore underside, for instance. You know only too well what he would've made of *that*, don't you—bloody organs and such—but we don't believe it for a minute, do we?" she said in a tone perhaps more hopeful than assertive. And just as she looked at him in sympathy, she felt a slight twitch within, almost a click, as if a switch had unexpectedly been thrown in an adjacent room. She had flashed on his "TIAs", as he had metaphorically described his own micro-blackouts, and, noting that she was suddenly feeling refreshed and tin-gly all over, not unlike following an explosive, head-clearing sneeze, wondered if she had had one. "If we're not careful, pretty soon we'll be reading these trysts of ours as enactments of some sort of Oedipal drama," she laughed, now feeling bracingly free of inhibitions, free to speak her mind and to enjoy doing so.

He was somewhat taken aback, though delightfully, by her sudden expansiveness and reminded by it on a subtle, almost latent, level of awareness, of the afterglow of his own TIAs. "Right, right!" he answered, eagerly joining in the mildly euphoric spirit of it, "Aren't we the textbook phallic couple now, me the lumbering, war-weary male organ, all banged up and bloodied by the vicissitudes of life—but nonetheless all the juicier and more succulent for that. Bloodied but unbowed, as the expression has it," and he roared with laughter, tickled by the cleverness of his own phallic pun. "And you," he continued, "well, you're the perfect receptacle, aren't you, the room arranged especially for my needs—even if I can't come all the way in, even if I can't totally go home again ... Do you know, German has a word, or, I should say, *used to* have a word—it's obsolete now, swept into the dustbin of history by the great wave of modern feminism—a word that embodies this fundamental sense of woman as a receptacle? The word is *Frauenzimmer*, literally "women's room," a "room for women," but actually meaning woman herself. Which makes it a contemptuous word, really, since it identifies the female with her genitals, reducing her to her most basic biological functions, sex and reproduction. In fact, Freud comes in here too: He says, somewhere in The *Interpretation of Dreams*, that women are often symbolized in dreams by rooms of various kinds and sizes. This holds true, he claims, for dreams of non-German speakers as well, French or Italians, say, who have no equivalent word for *Frauenzimmer* ... And here we are," he chortled, "a giant green sausage stuffing an inviting receptacle."

They both laughed heartily and were simultaneously struck in mid-laugh by a particularly emphatic TIA, followed on his part by a gong-like ringing in the ears. They immediately recognized the mutual quality of the event—it was obvious, there was no hiding it—and each searched, in vain, for something reassuring to say to the other about it. He was more profoundly rocked by it than she and could not shake off the sense, which he now experienced for the first time, that some alien force or entity was trying to break through to him, trying to enter and occupy his mind, not necessarily in a hostile way but perhaps more in the welcoming spirit of his own occupation of her. In support of this theory, there were, of course, those post-TIA periods of euphoria he had mentioned to her, one of which he was enjoying just then in especially full measure and assumed her to be doing the same.

"Something very strange, something utterly mysterious, is going on here and apparently it involves both of us," he said finally, breaking the impasse.

"No question," she replied tersely, afraid to move her line of sight from his eyes.

"I can't say I'm terrified by the uncertainty of it," he went on, "it's more like a mix of intense curiosity, expectation and maybe just a dash of anxiety coming from an intuitive sense I get of its monumentality. Whatever these so-called TIAs are, I feel they're finally coming to some sort of fruition, for better or worse, for both of us."

And indeed they were. For no sooner had the dragon spoken the word "fruition" than he was rocked by another TIA, this one even deeper than the first, and accompanied this time by an effulgence of radiant light that would have brightened the room beyond endurance for ordinary eyes but was perfectly comfortable for the two of them. And with this light, what one might tentatively call the dream's meaning or significance came clearly to awareness in the dreamer, who of course was none other than our hero Anselm himself; and its significance was that Anselm's personal identity in the dream was not the one he would have assumed, or expected, or preferred, but the other one, that is, the room itself—or rather *her*self. He felt, beyond question, with an intuitive certainty, that *he* was the receptacle, *he* the container, *he* the wrap-around protector and nourisher of this bloodied male member seeking to wrest comfort and bliss inside her/him. It was the strangest sensation, utterly novel, this sudden seismic shift in gender identity, an impossible opportunity to experience what sexual union was for the woman, something he'd often wondered about in the course of his life but from the experience of which he knew—or thought he knew—he was forever barred. But lo and behold, he *wasn't*. This was it! *He* was now doing the holding, the caressing, the nurturing, no longer the plunging, the prying, the piercing. And as he gently allowed himself to surrender to the moment and relax into it, as into a warm bath, he felt he would be more than content to remain in this empathic, almost maternally feminine, condition indefinitely.

But the moment was not yet done with him. For just as he was relishing the sense and feel of his own new-found womanly nature, his "eternal-feminine" essence, the question occurred to him as to who was being the green dragon here, who the *male* member, especially since *he* was busy being the woman? And just as this question, with its niggling uncertainty and demand for an immediate answer, an "accounting," threatened to annoy the dreamer and exile him from paradise, a flow effect was initiated somewhere in (un)consciousness, shifting his sense of identity back to the dragon, back to where it normally was. But, astonishingly, the flow back to masculinity was not exhaustive, not total, as some of the energy tied up in her/his being the embracing room remained shimmering where it was, this in turn leading to the dreamer's even deeper insight, with a correspondingly deeper attendant delight, that she/he was ... she/he! Or s(he)! Or ...? The oppressive sense of the impossibility of a word naming the transcendence of gender, naming the end of the battle of the sexes and a return to the primordial paradise of androgyny, before the Fall into a divisive History by whose storms we feel ourselves tossed and turned and battered about in this life; the sense of despair over the profound gulf left by what amounts to the futile stammerings of language even at its noblest and loftiest—all this fell away from the dreamer entirely as he lost all need to put this experience of the ineffable, this moment of the identity of opposites, into something as paltry, as trifling, as utterly ineffectual as words.

The flipside to this falling-away of linguistic shackles was the dreamer's felt buoyancy of being somehow emancipated into an enjoyment of words, phrases, sentences, in a way he had never known before, not as tensely held arrows aimed at targets of "meaning" forever to be missed, but as valid objects of play in and of themselves. The surrender of the need for a significance never quite here, always off in the distance, or not so far off, even close by, in the next breath, but never fully exhaled, never fully expressed and assimilated—was this so different from "coitus lite?" No, it wasn't, he could now see, reeling with a new wave of delight that beggared description; in fact, it was precisely the same thing, and therefore, having healed *that* split, he realized he had healed this one too. Word and thing, signifier and signified, were one. And she/he *was* that One. The very idea of a split, or division, or gap, or crevice, or fissure, in anything anywhere, was seen to be a delusion, a practical joke played by the universe on itself. And if this delusion hadn't been the cause of all human misery down through the ages, it would, he thought, be a laughing matter.

Of course, it must be remembered that what is here necessarily represented as a succession of events, in effect a narrative, actually takes place in a dream, on the stage of the unconscious, where a three-act play can unfold in a few seconds. This accounts for the relative paucity of language in the recall of "dialog" in dreams. But it is the recall that is laconic, not the dream world itself. Therein, language is moved to full, rich, abundant expression, and, freed of its constraints to mean this or that or the other, can mean anything it damn well pleases, and our attempts to pin it down, whether over a breakfast cup of coffee or in the claustrum of a psychoanalytic session, are like grasping at so many fluff strands of a pussy willow blowing in the breeze.

And so the reader will not be surprised to learn that, upon awakening the next morning, Anselm would recall from this dream only the vague confines of a room and an unspecific sense of deep significance connected with it. For Anselm was a "work in progress," the project of a cosmic alchemist, still in the womb of the retort, and was therefore not yet ready, not yet sufficiently ripe, to appreciate on a conscious level the manifold specifics of self-knowledge revealed to him in the dream. "Fruition" here was a way station, not an endpoint.

One of the curious "specific" elements in the dream, fully appreciated by the green dragon but forgotten by the dreamer upon awakening, is the console radio facing the dragon from the room's rear wall, aside from the rug the only object in the room besides the dragon himself. Why does the dream feel it necessary to put that radio there? The answer is simple: The room, a synecdochic or genital-part-for-whole symbol, needs a vocal apparatus of some kind in order to carry on her conversation with the dragon. The radio thus becomes her mouth, her mechanical-electrical means of vocal self-expression. It seems that, at times, even dreams make a perfunctory attempt to go by the rules.

VIGIL 11

The Work Begins

"It's just possible that double shot of Jack messed me up last time," Anselm speculated. He was stuffing his laptop into his backpack before heading out for a second attempt at gaining entry to Lindhurst's house. "All those crazy, creepy phantasms that plagued me at the door could've been a consequence of drinking alcohol on an empty stomach … Well, this time I've got a heavy PB and J in me and I'll skip the booze, thank you. That, plus whatever substance is in that little bottle the old man gave me, should cover the bases."

"Covering the bases" was Anselm's homey way of expressing the rift that had recently burrowed its way into his maturing view of the world. One base, the culturally prevailing empirical-scientific one, was the one he had grown up with, and refined and formalized in his schooling, the one that told him all valid knowledge was wrested from careful observation and precise measurement. Here it took the form of medical materialism: hallucination brought on by physiological complication, the proverbial "undigested bit of beef" producing Ebenezer Scrooge's own "three-ghost hallucination." The other base, inchoate, quiveringly nascent, hardly more than a nervous suspicion, might be captioned as "the reality of the unseen," or "the seldom seen," or "that seen only by those with eyes to see." Anselm, it seems, had one eye firmly trained on first base and the other tentatively searching for second, obviously a non-position he could hold for only a while. At some point he must advance or fall back.

Not that he typically thought of himself in such grandiose terms. The various "-isms" of an intellectualized *Weltanschauung* (theism, atheism, agnosticism, materialism, monism, etc.), while academic *lingua franca* to him from reading and study, were still relatively alien to his self-image, which at age twenty-four was still very much bound up with experience and events of an intimately personal, primarily religious, nature. Like the time he tripped over a seam in the chancel carpet and fell into the priest who was distributing communion wafers, knocking the chalice and the hundred-fifty or so hosts nestled therein to the floor. Or the time in first grade when he asked Sister Generosa, who had been teaching the class about fasting from midnight before receiving a.m. holy communion, whether it was okay to spit into a glass and then drink it since you were only taking in liquid that was already inside you, already "yours," anyway, and, instead of appreciating the intellectual subtlety of such a question coming from a seven-year-old, she—and the class—reacted with total disgust: "Ewww!" Or the time, during a closed retreat in his senior year of high school at a rural Jesuit compound, when a gray-haired priest with a far-away look in his eye told him that the moment he died he would go straight to hell if he didn't give up the sin of self-abuse. "Self-abuse" he called it, an act that felt like anything but, more like self-pleasuring, self-coddling even. Where was the abuse? In any case, by age twenty-four Anselm had jettisoned the Catholic Church, at least intellectually (vomiting it up from his gut, wrenching it apart from his deepest values in his struggle to form a reasonable conscience, was another matter entirely), and was just beginning, very gingerly and tentatively, to draw a distinction in his mind between religion, of which he'd had a snootful, and spirituality, which he hardly dared hope might be a way to avoid the mistake of throwing out the baby with the bathwater. And, over time, more and more he sensed there *was* a baby, even if one not easily kept or nurtured.

As he opened the door to leave, he realized that the little bottle of witch repellent was still standing on his desk. He ran over and grabbed it, shaking his head over his own incurable absentmindedness. *For chrissake, it's all I can do to manage* this *world. What am I gonna do with another one!* Then, as he headed out on foot for the PATH train to Hoboken, all the marvels and visions and fantasies that had been toying with him of late sort of jelled at once within him, producing an emotional frisson that made him swoon with delight, and he realized anew that everything he had done during this period was in service—in *devotion*—to the mesmerizing music he had first heard on the 4th of July in the Journal Square subway station and after that here and there at the most unexpected times. "It's all for you, my muse!" became his mantra, as if the enchanting stream of sound were a nubile goddess.

An hour later he stood once again before Archivist Lindhurst's door, this time ready to do battle with whatever chimaeras might present themselves. But as hellacious as his first encounter at the door had been, this one was, thankfully, a bit of a fizzle, since, as soon as Anselm pressed the bell with his left index finger and the old bruja's face ballooned out of it, all hideously swollen, and opened its jaws wide as if to bite that finger, if at all possible, off, he whipped out the little bottle with his right hand and shook a few drops of the yellow liquid onto the crone's nose and she immediately withdrew amidst a slew of curses and imprecations, leaving the doorbell plate and button looking exactly as they should. Then, without further ado, Anselm opened the door and stepped inside, cautiously, tentatively. But his wariness seemed unwarranted as he was greeted by an array of sensory delights—the delicate pinging, dinging and tinkling sounds of bells and mobiles moved by the sudden inrush of air and, once he moved inside, the strange but uplifting fragrance of an incense that pleased his nostrils like none he had ever breathed in during the innumerable Benediction services he had attended in boyhood as an acolyte.

Encouraged by this pleasant, if impersonal, reception, Anselm made his way past the rows of ancestral portraits decorating the anteroom straight ahead to a grand wooden staircase, outfitted with finely carved posts and spindles and wide, curving bannisters that led up to a landing on which he paused for a moment to take in all the splendor. Only once in his life could he remember being surrounded by such aristocratic refinement, and that was when, as an altar boy, he had accompanied his parish priest, Father Declan Fitzhugh, to the bishop's residence to provide moral support for a request for desperately needed funds. Anselm then bounced up the second half of the stairway to the top, finding himself at the very midpoint of the building and not knowing whether to turn left or right down one of the halves of an extremely lengthy corridor. He was rescued from this dilemma by the Archivist himself, who stepped outside one of the rooms along the corridor wearing a brown tunic with a white sash, looking for all the world like a Franciscan—or even a Buddhist—monk. (He was neither.)

"Ah, welcome, Anselm," he said extending both hands in greeting, "I'm so glad you were able to make it this time. I trust that little solution I gave you—pardon the pun—did the trick … But come, come with me, I want to take you right to the laboratory," and with that he turned back in the direction from whence he had come, striding all the way to the corridor's end and making a smart left turn down a shorter, narrower corridor. Anselm had all he could do to keep up, hardly noticing the exquisite burgundy décor of the walls, dappled with strange yellow symbols—suns and moons and planets and odd shapes and letters. After another turn or two, Lindhurst finally led Anselm through another door into a dome-shaped greenhouse, a massive space that made Anselm's jaw drop. Covering the rotunda was an immense umbrella of glass that appeared to capture the shifting patterns of light that existed outside it and hold them steady on the inside. This is to say, the interior light seemed somehow to be equally distributed throughout the sphere, all unaffected by time, the relative position of the sun having no bearing on its intensity or quality. This brilliance of light, shimmering all in between and around a jungle of exotic grasses and flowers and plants and shrubs and trees, caused Anselm to swoon momentarily and loose his bearings. The layout of the circular space did not help either, with its intricate network of crisscrossing paths that seemed to stretch indefinitely into the distance and then simply disappear. Obviously looking up did not help as there was nothing material on which to focus, nothing by which to orient oneself. Add to this the plethora of exotic plant shapes and colors along with the babbling fountains with their marble basins and a palette of intoxicating fragrances, and poor Anselm, overwhelmed by it all, was beginning to experience a touch of agoraphobia. Where were the protecting walls! Where the boundaries? Where was the Archivist? Certainly nowhere in sight.

This anxiety that now began to grip Anselm—partly a fear of dissolving boundaries, partly a paradoxical fear of anxiety itself—was spiked considerably by a cacophony of sounds, vocal and otherwise, that now began to affect him in a paranoid way. An infernal chorus of tittering, sniggering and cackling, even the gurgling "laughter" of the fountains, seemed to affront him on all sides. To be sure, these were not human sounds, they were the sounds of garden creatures, predominantly birds, yet they somehow seemed to form words, and eventually phrases and sentences, a mounting patois of mockery that threatened to throw him into panic: "Hey there, Anselm, looking good! Where'd you get those Mickey Mouse cufflinks? … Why don't you leave a quarter in your shoe and let the shoe fairy put it on Silky Sullivan in the fourth at Belmont? … Come on, don't be shy! Join us! We're just rapping here about the banana skin you slipped on in second grade. Remember? What an ap-peel-ing memory, no? …" And so it went, on and on, from near and far, throughout what was becoming a vast circular booby hatch, and it wasn't long before Anselm began to fear losing his mind. All creatures—birds, frogs, insects—seemed to be converging around him, pressing in, closer and closer, tighter and tighter, a hellish phantasmagoria growing ever more sinister, ever more threatening. The yawping birds were, of course, the worst of it. Just as he was about to scream, what he took to be a fire-lily bush standing nearby walked right up to him. Anselm flinched in terror but it turned out to be Archivist Lindhurst wearing his floral afternoon dressing gown with its brilliant orangey-red blossoms that covered its satin sheen from head to toe.

"Forgive me, lad, for leaving you momentarily in the lurch here," he said while picking a few needles from his robe, "but I had to attend to my favorite cactus which is scheduled to blossom sometime tonight. But tell me, what do you think of my little house garden?"

"'Little house garden,' he says, right!" Anselm answered with a smirk, but then, noticing the old man's knitted brow and the eyes beneath that were boring into him, he backtracked to, "My God, Professor, it's beautiful beyond measure! Staggering, really. But I don't think the, ... er, residents here are so happy about me invading their space. I think they think I'm crowding them, so now they're crowding me back a little. The screeching birds are especially hard to take," he added, sticking his index fingers into his ears and shrugging, as if to say, "Whaddya gonna do, right?" Then, remembering again who he was talking to, he gathered himself and put on an overly stern and serious expression. But this time the old man agreed with him. Looking around the grand circular space and realizing how closely gathered and, in consequence, how raucous the birds were, he raised both arms high like a prophet of old and shouted, "Silence, you buzzards! Cease and desist!" And so it happened. Command given and obeyed to a T. Not a creature was stirring, not even a mouse. The very air itself, with its precision-controlled humidity, seemed momentarily to cease to circulate. Then, "Now go back to whatever piddling pursuits you were engaged in earlier and leave my guest in peace," he brayed.

Just then, a large gray-feathered parrot emerged from the green labyrinth and fluttered its way onto a myrtle branch next to the Archivist at about eye-level. He was very serious of mien, the bird was, with a pair of thick-framed eyeglasses perched on his sharply curved beak. Anselm thought he must enjoy some superior status in this society of creatures, a thought confirmed by the fact that he now proceeded to speak for them: "Please, sir," he rasped to Lindhurst, "don't take offense at the excessive exuberance of my young charges, but, really, the young man has only himself to blame—"

"—Quiet! I won't hear it!" the old man snapped. "And you—I expect more from you, my old friend," he said, actually touching the bird's beak with the tip of his index finger. "I expect you to keep the troops in check, especially the younger birds. Where are we without discipline, hmm?" he asked, rhetorically. Then, turning to his guest, he said, "Please excuse this little contretemps. They have much to learn. In any case, let's proceed," and he led Anselm along one of the paths out of the dome and through a series of rooms of breathtaking beauty, rooms filled with rich furnishings and gold-framed mirrors and impressive mythic-historical oil paintings and all manner of strange objects he couldn't identify. It was all the bedazzled Anselm could do to keep up with Lindhurst who moved at an annoyingly quick pace for anyone who had to follow behind him. Finally he arrived at and opened one of the double doors to a huge room, almost a hall, politely standing aside as he waved his guest in. As Anselm stepped inside, his jaw dropped for the second time that day, for the dazzling and complex beauty that distinguished the rooms he had just passed through was here offset by a simplicity equally impressive in its relative featurelessness. The walls were of a subtle azure-blue color giving them the illusory texture of infinity. They were walls depicting the wall-lessness of the heavens. Out of this azure infinity came golden palm trunks that swooped upward towards a ceiling that was totally hidden by the emerald brilliance of the fronds. Anselm stood there transfixed, while the Archivist stood absolutely still next to him with bowed head, apparently lost in some meditation.

After a moment Anselm lowered his gaze and beheld, in the precise center of the room, a large tabletop made of porphyry, a red-purplish stone dotted with tiny diamond-like crystals. The stone rested on three dark-bronze Egyptian dragons, or ouroboroi, and at its center sat a simple golden flowerpot, from which, the instant he laid eyes on it, Anselm could not turn his gaze away. It wasn't the pot's shape or luster that held him fast, as pleasing as these were, but rather the shifting forms and colors that seemed to be reflected on its surface, shapes and shades and loops and lines and circles in continuous muta-tion, somewhat like the patternless pattern of a kaleidoscope but less fractured. At first it was the ceaseless movement of these forms in a room in which nothing was moving that hypnotized him, as though the forms were being generated by the pot itself entirely from within—in other words, an impossibility. But as Anselm continued to gaze, the question of possibility quickly became the least of his concerns as the forms began to morph into what he could swear were recog-nizable people, places and things. Was he suddenly caught up in some sort of absurd surreal review of his life? He thought he caught a glimpse of his father hitting fungoes to him down at the Lemoyne College ballfield. Then one of himself alone at age eight, all glum-faced, being kept in third-grade detention after school ... And on it went, the pot's surface now become a golden screen for rapid-fire "clips" from old home memory movies, and from other, more mysterious, sources: friends, some still, some gone ... a coveted Action Comics book accidently found covered with dust balls under his bed after weeks of futile searching ... yet another scolding in the confessional from Father Fitzhugh who was sick to death of delivering the same inane message to every hormone-driven boy to whom he opened his screen ... three tiny maidens warming themselves on a bed of sun-bleached bones, their long, lustrous hair not quite preserving their modesty ... a dinger blasted over the centerfield scoreboard to beat Bishop Keane High ... a Mello Roll ice cream cylinder sliding neatly from its wrapper into the cone custom-fitted to it ... a bridge not far enough across the Mohawk River in Amsterdam, New York ... lying together with a biology grad student he barely knew on her ratty rented couch and loving it ... And so it went, one forgotten—and now hungrily remembered—scene or object or person after another, each emerging from the thing preceding it and melting into the thing following it, each evoking its own uncanny feeling-memory, a party favor of emotion utterly unique to it.

Until, at some point, the flow of images on the pot's surface seemed to slow down, and finally coalesce, around a row of subway turnstiles, the ones whose syncopated clicking he had heard in perfect harmony with the hum of florescent lights and the gabbling of commuters on that fateful July 4th afternoon. And as he listened once again to the, at first, banal noise, totally absorbed, it soon enough began to shape itself into a panoply of enchanting sound, once more slowly and subtly transmuting itself until finally burgeoning into breathtaking symphonic beauty. Only this time the music seemed in a strange way to move backward in time, moment by moment, iteration by iteration, until arriving finally at that solo violin that had produced the original seed-phrase of the subway symphony. "My God! There it is again! What is that music? Who is playing it? Is it really your daughter?" he practically shouted at Lindhurst. "I must find out. This not-knowing is killing me!"

"Whoa, my boy, not so impetuous," the Archivist, who was still standing nearby, said calmingly, patting Anselm on the shoulder. "*Of course* it's my daughter. Who else? The fact is, just now she is in the middle of a practice hour. But if you can hear her from here, you must have x-ray ears, as her rehearsal room is way over in the other wing of the house. Then again …" he made as if to speculate, stroking his chin thoughtfully, obviously enjoying the contemplation of a possible telepathic connection between the two. When he teasingly suggested this to Anselm, the young man shrugged sheepishly. "Oh well, as we used to say at the university in the old country, *Wie dem auch sein mag*," Lindhurst quipped. "Let's move on, shall we?" and he now took Anselm by the arm, not quite trusting the lad's physical stability following this onrush of exotic new sensations.

Anselm's next conscious experience was feeling the old man let go of his arm and announce, "Ah, finally! Here we are." He looked up and around as if awakening from a trance to see that he was standing in the middle of a conventional library room, though, it must be said, a most impressive one, with shelves filled with books literally from floor to ceiling, most of them with gold-embossed spines. In the middle of the room stood a handsome, though otherwise ordinary, executive desk with cut-off corners. "You'll be working here, for the time being at least," said Lindhurst. "Only time will tell whether at some future point you'll advance to the blue room we just visited ... First up, I would like to assure myself of your basic computer literacy," which Anselm took as a cue to unzip his backpack and pull out his laptop, which he then made bold to place neatly down on the middle of the desktop, smiling proudly as he did so and nodding approval of his own adroitness. The old man, however, looked askance at this, sneering sourly, cynically, then lowering his head and shaking it slowly from side to side in mock despair. This incensed Anselm, who wanted only to lash out and whose face flushed deeply as he took a few deep breaths to regain control. "It seems the master is less than impressed with my equipment," he said finally, in the steadiest voice he could summon but unable fully to suppress an implied sneer of his own. "I assure you that my laptop, the Turnover 6.0, is the best one available on the market today. It gets highest marks in *Consumer Reports* and *Engadget*. And I assure you, my typing skills are off the charts. I've been told I could easily find work as an executive secretary." But, despite himself, he wound up saying the words more as a hopeful plea than a confident assertion, which only caused the hard-assed old goat to shake his head a second time.

"My boy," he said, taking a more conciliatory tone, "I'm afraid that for now I'm going to have to rely more on your sincerity, on your good will, than on your accomplishment. And as for *this*," he said contemptuously, pushing the young man's computer towards him at the edge of the desk with an offended left index finger, "please dispose of it, will you, as it has no purpose here." Anselm was dumbfounded and felt a sudden shiver run up his spine. *What next?* he wondered. Never had he asked the question more sincerely.

And, as it turned out, more appropriately, for, raising his arms in a sweeping arc like a sorcerer, the Archivist lit up the air between his hands like a tiny rectangular movie marquee, or so it appeared to Anselm. He then lowered the little patch of twinkling and blinking lights to the desktop, angling it like a computer monitor, which indeed it was, and inviting Anselm to inspect it as though it were a physical object, which it wasn't. Anselm extended a finger to and through the thing, haltingly to be sure, then withdrew it and tried scrambling the boilerplate text formed by the lights by running his hand through it willy-nilly—in vain. He scratched his head and looked sheepishly at the old man for enlightenment.

"This, my boy, is the computer you'll be working with," said the latter with an air of deep self-satisfaction. "A little invention of my own that eliminates messy hardware entirely." And with that he gestured again, this time with a finger, and a photoelectric keyboard appeared just beneath the screen, the two hovering there on the desktop, one flickering above the other, together forming a perfect photoelectric replica of a computer workstation.

"Professor, I'm afraid I'm way out of my depth here. I don't know anything about—"

"—Tut-tut, my lad. There's nothing to fret about. My 'air computer' works just like the ordinary one. It just takes a little getting-used-to, that's all. In fact, once you *are* used to it, you should find that the elimination of all physical encumbrance increases your work-speed a good threefold ... So, let's have at it, shall we," and with that, plus a little pat of encouragement on the young man's shoulder, which he also used to push his ambivalent new employee gently down onto the upholstered wheeled armchair, he walked across the room to a locked file cabinet. Taking a pair of plastic gloves from one robe pocket and pulling them over his hands, he then withdrew a key from the other pocket and unlocked the cabinet, pulling the draw all the way out and carefully withdrawing a manuscript, itself wrapped in plastic. He carried the manuscript over to the desk and unwrapped it, again slowly and gently, then untied its two cloth bindings, opened it and laid it down on a lectern beside the light computer.

"And there you have it," the old man smiled, crossing his arms in satisfaction. Anselm looked down and found himself facing a sheet of classical Arabic inscription. But he did not panic; on the contrary, he felt the keen abdominal tingle of recognition, arising from the odd fact that, though having no formal instruction in spoken or written Arabic, he did have some superficial acquaintance with its strange, squiggly, right-to-left written characters, acquired from an Islamic friend in high school with whom he shared a curiosity about foreign tongues and who enjoyed conversing with him in "pidgin" Latin.

And so it was with a commingling of trepidation and confidence that our hero proceeded to study the dual-language keyboard, English and Arabic letters sitting next to each other on the various keys, all lit up and twinkling and seemingly itching to be tapped. After a moment, though, he thought he'd better move from study to practice as he could feel his employer standing behind him, arms crossed and feet planted firmly on the floor in growing impatience. Slowly, tentatively, he tapped a key and watched the letter appear on the lit screen. Bravo! Then another. And another. So far, so good. No blown fuses or blackouts! For a while thereafter he was just hunting and pecking and making more than the occasional mistake, knocked off center by the sheer novelty of the job and the old man's annoying presence behind him. The latter, for his part, just stood there watching silently, his only visible response a slightly curled upper lip that expressed his typical cynical reaction to yet another "lemon" of a job candidate. After a while, he turned and left the room shaking his head.

But, predictably enough, the old man's exit was like a tonic for Anselm. Though it took him a while to get the hang of the right-to-left movement of the text, it wasn't long before he was typing along at a smart pace and beginning to feel that the work was within his power. Indeed, within a half hour he could hardly believe how comfortable and efficient the whole operation was becoming; his acquaintance with the Arabic alphabet from adolescence, precarious and half-forgotten though it was, stood him in good stead. Moreover, the old man had been right: Typing "air keys" was so much easier than regular keyboard keys, which had, in turn, been so much easier than typewriter keys. What was next, he wondered. Wi-Fi thought keys? Keys in the mind directing an external response?

The work moved along swimmingly until, on the stroke of three, the Archivist called Anselm into an adjacent room for a coffee-and-snack break. At table Lindhurst was in high spirits and inquired about Anselm's friends, Manheim and Branden, then telling him in turn a slew of not always sanitized anecdotes about the latter, whom he knew well, such as the time he, Branden, accidently in a drunken haze, deleted the grades of the entire senior class about to graduate. (Of course, there were backup files, but the question was whether these could be found and entered into the system in time.) Anselm gobbled these telltales up faster than his liverwurst and relish sandwich and was thinking about how he might tease his friend with them, when the clock struck four and he immediately stood up, almost like a robot on a timer. This, however, seemed to please his native-German employer, who valued nothing more than punctuality, and this more than ever since emigrating to the New World of Whenever, Man.

If the work had gone smoothly before the break, it went spectacularly after it. Anselm couldn't believe the ease, the grace, with which his fingers danced around the little rectangular ballroom of lights, rarely making a misstep, feeling as if they had been typing Arabic all their life. So it's understandable that at first he hardly noticed the far-off rising strains of the violin that accompanied the movement of his hands across the lit-up letters, so focused was he on the task in front of him. But soon the instrument was crooning fortissimo, as if released from silent bondage by the seemingly flawless dexterity of a master performer. At some point the aural beauty could no longer be ignored as it wove itself gently into the fabric of Anselm's consciousness. *What? The music? Again? How exquisite! Where is it coming from? Who is this mystery fiddler? This is one mystery I need to solve, and solve now.*

He rose from his chair and at first just stood there, all ears, as if spellbound by the flow of rapturous notes and chords and dazzling runs. Though a devotee of classical music, he did not recognize the piece. It seemed to him to fuse German form with Russian feeling, yet it wasn't anything by Brahms or Tchaikovsky or Khachaturian he was familiar with. And as for the brilliance of sound, the exquisite playing, it put him in mind of some of the great modern-day violinists he was familiar with—Heifetz, Menuhin, Oistrakh. But how could that be, unless the Archivist, Svengali that he was, was keeping a potential musical superstar all to himself, under wraps, draped in the chains of the master's hypnotic will? Such was the spell cast on Anselm's youthful imagination by the Archivist's darkly charismatic persona. He was soon to learn that he was way off in his impetuous thinking but also that the truth of the matter was even more fantastic than that.

He stepped outside the library into the corridor, making sure to close the door noiselessly, and listened; and, although he focused his ears as acutely as he could, he found himself beset by a question of ontology: Was the music he was listening to actually coming to him physically from down the corridor or did it exist only in his mind? Assuming the former, and aware the daughter's practice room was in that area, down the corridor he padded, on tiptoe, probably an unnecessary precaution since the carpet was quite plush. Passing beneath the grand chandelier marking the hall's midpoint, he decided there was no good reason why the music couldn't be both physical and telepathic, carnal and ethereal, and again sharpened his hearing, determined to identify the right door and avoid opening the wrong one. Drawn to a door on the left wall maybe three from the end, he pressed his ear against it, closed his eyes and just let the sound, which by now he knew to be minimally physical, caress him. Then, without even deliberately deciding to, he turned the handle and opened the door. And there, inside the room, standing near an open window, a gentle breeze fluttering through an artfully braided plait of her golden-brown hair, stood a lovely young girl of around twenty or twenty-one. She was dressed in a green gingham smock made for ease of upper-body movement, and, her playing having been interrupted, her slender arms hung down at her sides, violin in one hand, bow in the other. She had the face of an angel, with a sweet, sensitive, caramel beauty by which Anselm was instantly enchanted. One or two stray strands of hair that had escaped her plait framed the gentle curve of her unblemished cheeks.

"Hi, I'm Tina. You must be Anselm. Wonderful to finally meet you," she smiled—radiantly—putting the bow down and extending her hand. Anselm hardly knew where he was.

"You ... You know me?" he finally managed to stammer, taking her hand and holding it cupped in both of his, then realizing the impropriety of the gesture and blushing like a schoolboy.

She laughed, a soft, gentle ripple of delight, without attempting to withdraw her hand so as not to embarrass him. But leaving it there also caused him embarrassment, which caused *her* embarrassment, which in turn caused them both to laugh together.

"Well, I know a little about you from my father. He told me you'd be coming here to work with us," she said, taking a seat at the high-arched open window and inviting him to sit next to her.

To work with us. Us! He liked the sound of that, even without knowing what it implied. But he thought it must be something wonderful, wonderful and mysterious. Anything that put him together with her had to be wonderful, didn't it? After all, she was obviously the source of the music that had bewitched him of late. He couldn't believe it. He was actually meeting the heart of his obsession, and that heart beat *outside* him, in the flesh, totally independently of him. *How was that possible?* He hadn't a clue, but in any case, now in the full presence of the *fons et origo* of a months-long infatuation, in an encounter whose inevitability he now realized he had sensed from the beginning, he was already having trouble telling the music from the music-maker. Come on, she didn't just *execute* the music, did she? She wasn't merely a performer. He already knew he would never again think of the music apart from her, nor of her apart from the music. She was the music, its instrument and herself all at once. Any attempt to disentangle these was a fool's game. This he knew implicitly yet hadn't a clue as to how he knew it.

These strange, magical thoughts held him in thrall even as the two of them sat there chatting and enjoying the autumn breeze. At some point she picked up the violin and began playing again, this time a sad, sweet melody that seemed to convey the tenor of these very thoughts of his on the inevitability of events and the futility of human effort to avoid or change them. But entwined with the tune was a whispery voice. Whether real or ideal, it was unmistakably *her* voice, which, in strange counterpoint to the music, seemed to promise glad tidings to him who remained faithful to this destiny. *I'm close to you, Anselm—close—close! I will help you—have courage—don't be afraid, dear Anselm! — I will struggle with you so that you'll be mine.* Here, enveloped in music, she could express sentiments implicitly that she would never have allowed herself to utter on early acquaintance. Music was the language of the unconscious, the language of woman, of the Eternal Feminine, but, miraculously at the same time, also the language of *a* woman, in this instance *this* particular creature of flesh and blood sitting at the window next to Anselm, the scent of whose fragrant, freshly shampooed hair he could breathe in to his heart's content.

When she finished, she put the instrument down and looked out over the Hudson, letting the river's breeze play with the few loose strands of her hair. "I do hope it all works out, Anselm," she said smiling, "and that you'll be able to stay on here. As you can see, the view is breathtaking—look, you can see from bridge to bridge, George Washington to Verrazano—and the working conditions are certainly ideal." Anselm couldn't help but think of *her* as the most ideal working condition he could imagine, but limited himself to saying, "I hope it works out too, Tina, and if it does, I also hope I might expect to be entertained now and then by your beautiful playing? That would really seal the deal for me." This last he spoke a bit shyly, out of a reticence to say too much too soon, but also out of an even stronger need to signal to her his desire to be in her presence. He felt he was walking a fine line and needed all his wits to get it right.

"Oh, not to worry," she said warmly, looking straight at him, "there'll be plenty of opportunity for that. I practice almost every day, but usually all alone. It'll be ..." she hesitated, searching for the right word, " ... pleasant to have an audience, especially such an ... appreciative one." As she complemented him, putting an ever so slight emphasis on the word "appreciative," she seemed to nod her head just a tad, smiling up at him so to speak from under her eyelids, a gesture that thrilled him with its blend of modesty and seductive allure.

Then suddenly it occurred to him he'd better get back to work if he expected there to be any future of private concerts, any future on these premises at all. "Well, Tina, listen, it was delightful to meet you," he stood up with a clap, as if waking himself from a mild trance, "but I'd better be getting back. I'm guessing your father is a pretty tough taskmaster."

"He certainly can be, Anselm, but I have my ways with him. I wouldn't worry," she smiled, with the faintest note of allure in her voice, which both tantalized the young man and made him wary. It was all happening so fast. So many events, particularly inner events, bulging with significance. What was he getting himself into? He made his way back to the library room with the dragonesque desk and set immediately to work, determined not to lose a moment to the pull of wishful fantasies. Oddly, however, even though he succeeded in not giving in to the tug of libido, that voice of earlier, *her* voice, insinuated itself into the rhythm of his typing, empowering it, paradoxically, to move along at lightning speed. *I'm with you, Anselm. I'm always with you. Keep faith with me, in me, and you'll know what it is to be free, free to enjoy the vison of the golden pot.*

Before he knew it, the clock struck six and in came Archivist Lindhurst, walking without greeting or ceremony straight over to his desk and, without excusing himself, nudging Anselm in his wheeled armchair aside so that he could scroll up and down the luminous screen unhampered. Anselm could only watch in anxious silence, but after a moment, he suddenly turned inwardly atingle to see the old man's face morph slowly but profoundly from its default snarling smile into something akin to stunned wonder. Lindhurst's gaze softened, his lips unpursed and his ashen cheeks blushed as he raised his hand in bewilderment to his brow. Then he looked down warmly at Anselm as upon a long-lost son, a prodigal son returned, and spoke: "Young man, I know all the hidden ties that bind you to my daughter. Tina—Serpentina—loves you. Remain faithful to your apprenticeship here with me and she will eventually be yours and together you will behold the wonders of her dowry, which is the golden pot." Then, shifting his tone deftly from enchantment to business as usual, he patted Anselm on the shoulder and dismissed him saying, "Well, your first day's work is in the books. Well done. Well done, indeed. Be back here tomorrow at noon sharp and we'll see if your skills hold up."

As he exited the building and walked down the front steps, Anselm stopped and stared at the mighty Hudson, sitting there in all its watery corpulence, unfazed as always. Then he heard a window being raised behind and above him. He turned to see the Archivist leaning out on the ledge, apparently eager to deliver some further parting words: "Please convey my best greetings to your friends, Manheim and Branden, when you see them. And check out your PayPal account when you get home. Today's wages have already been deposited in it."

But this financial boon did not especially gladden Anselm. His thoughts were far too consumed with the mysterious sea-change in outlook going on both inside and outside him. *I don't know what's happening to me, and it scares the hell out of me. I need a guidepost, something to hold fast to in this storm, and what better one than Tina? If I go down in this struggle, let me at least go down* in devotion to her.

VIGIL 12

Return to Sender

Anselm, the beach bum! There you sit at your Venice Beach window, of an evening, dreaming all sorts of dreams to yourself—of golden sands lit by the setting sun, of serpentine blacktops twisting through fields and over mountains and around cities and running on forever, of coast-to-coast superhighways called Interstates or "I's," as in I 70, I 80, I 90, that take you from one bottleneck, the George Washington Bridge, to another, the San Diego Freeway. You dream of the superspeed with which people and things move from one end of the great continental tabletop to the other. And so it is with supreme confidence that you send your message to the Grand Poobah sitting on his throne in his lavish palace at the other end of the table. You seal the envelope and stick it in your mailbox gritty with sand, push up the pickup signal and return to your window and your dreaming. You dream that the mail carrier picks it up and takes it, along with hundreds of others, to the processing plant. There it gets scanned, barcoded and sorted. Finally, it's placed in a large tray along with thousands of others that fall within the same east-coast ZIP Code range. The tray is then taken to the airport to fly across the country. After the plane lands at its Dulles Airport destination, postal workers take the tray containing your letter to the mail processing plant that serves the Post Office branch that will deliver it. At the plant, the letters in the tray are fed through a barcode sorter, which separates letters to a specific ZIP Code from other letters in that ZIP Code range.

After this, your letter receives its final sortation. A delivery barcode sorter sorts it to the particular carrier who will deliver it. The delivery barcode sorter also arranges that carrier's letters in the order of delivery. Next, all the mail for this carrier is taken by truck to the Post Office branch for which the carrier works. The carrier loads trays of mail, including your letter, into a motor vehicle. The carrier drives to the street where the letter is to be delivered, safely parks, then loads his or her satchel with the mail to be carried to each house or business. Within minutes of leaving the truck, the carrier delivers your letter to the addressee. That's how it normally works. Your dream is correct. And not only that: It is also rich in detail, informing you of the several particular steps in the mail delivery process of which you consciously have no clue. But alas, you walk out of your shanty bungalow of a sunny morning in your nightshirt and slippers to get the mail, and, when you open the box, you pull out your letter all inked up with cancellation stamps that say:

Return to sender.
Address unknown.
No such number.
No such zone.

But then, since it is merely me sitting here at my keyboard telling you all this, it doesn't really matter, does it?

VIGIL 13

The Smartest Phone of All

"Well, that's it for me," concluded Paul Manheim drowsily from his favorite armchair, as he laid his hardbound copy of Sumerset Maugham's novel, *The Razor's Edge*, aside and proceeded to knock the contents of his pipe into a nearby ashtray. "Time to drift into the arms of Morpheus," he said with a smile, rather pleased with himself for topping off the evening with a smart classical reference.

"Sounds good to me, Popsy," quipped Ronnie deflatingly; she was seated at the dining room table, poring over a textbook as thick as the telephone directory. "I'll be following right along. I've got a history test tomorrow ... Oh, don't bother, I'll do it," she added, meaning the CD player on the mantle, which was playing a Bach *Brandenberg Concerto* at a low volume, the "Second," which was one of her father's favorites. She switched off the player and they both headed for their respective rooms.

"Oh, can I give you a lift to the Square in the morning?" he asked.

"No thanks," she answered, "my test is in the afternoon and I'll be here all morning studying for it."

And thus the great subterfuge was set in motion. There was no history test tomorrow and she had no plans to turn in anytime soon on this dark, windy, rainy September evening, if, indeed, she got to bed at all. For it was approaching September 23, the autumnal equinox, and there was great, important work to be done, and, weather notwithstanding, she had to venture out to get it done.

She had been positively obsessed with Anselm since her tryst with the Hoboken bruja Lisa weeks earlier. She sensed an inner voice, possibly under the witch's influence, telling her that her young man was being "svengalied" by a powerful negative force, that he must be ripped from its clutches, and that it was she who must do the ripping. She shrank inwardly from the strangeness of it all, from its terrifying, ghastly, gothic aura, and at times thought she must be going mad. But Veronica was no pansy, she was a girl with backbone, and spunk—who doesn't admire spunk?—and wasn't going to allow a few chills up and down that backbone to scare her into a pusillanimous retreat.

So, after a while, opening her bedroom door and sticking her ear out, she listened for her father's apneic wheeze and her sister's gentler slumber sounds to assure herself that the way was clear. Finding it so, she tiptoed to the vestibule closet, sneakers in hand, threw on her lightweight waterproof rain jacket and slipped out the door, noting that if she hurried, she could reach the bruja's place by 11 pm, the appointed time for … whatever it was, God help her.

She drove the same route to Hoboken she had taken weeks earlier on her first visit to the bruja, but this time the culminating sprint down the long viaduct into that city aroused a dread in her that almost made her turn around and speed home. The winds blowing in off the Hudson were fierce and seemed to grip the car and shake it as it rolled down into them, as though demanding she cease and desist from this mad foray into the black arts. When she got to the bottom, she made a sharp U-turn heading back toward the base of the bluff, knowing this time precisely where she had to go. Yet nothing looked familiar because the darkness was as black as pitch. Even though there were lights here and there, they seemed to illuminate only themselves, like stars in the night sky, leaving the surrounding space as dark as it would be without them.

Parking in the bruja's gravel driveway, she got out and headed for the barely visible porchlight. Intermittently she could hear the thick, heavy raindrops as they noisily pelted her plastic jacket, presaging the oncoming downpour and arousing in her scarified mind thoughts of a hail of bullets. "Ah, there you are, my dear, right on time as promised!" the old woman suddenly shouted down, raising an upstairs window. "Stay right there, stay where you are. I'll be down in two shakes." Not exaggerating, she almost instantly appeared before Ronnie, a dark rebozo shawl draped over her head and shoulders, her black cat dancing infinity signs between her legs. (Apparently this was to be a magical mystery venture for three.) She handed Ronnie a covered basket to carry to her rusty old pickup truck parked behind the house. When they got there, Ronnie could make out some sort of a basin, a tripod and a spade lying in the truck's cargo bin, each of which delivered to her its own special jolt of anxiety. What she had heard about witches' paraphernalia blended with her general confusion and anxiety to make her feel as if on the brink of madness.

Nevertheless, she had enough presence of mind to note that the bruja turned left on Willow Avenue and headed north over the city-boundary bridge into Weehawken. This unexpected turn in a direction even farther away from home only fed her near-riotous apprehension. She soon felt gripped by panic and actually began checking the truck's doors and door handles in anticipation of a swift exit and getaway. But each time her panic spiked, she would mentally beat it down and drag herself back from the brink, forcefully reminding herself of the nobility—and self-interest—of her cause: *Anselm must be saved! Anselm is worth saving! He will be mine!*

Lisa Ramiriz drove over the Willow Ave. bridge and sped into Weehawken, picking up Park Ave. but going only a couple of blocks before turning right into a small parking area behind the dugout to a baseball/football field named, appropriately, Weehawken Stadium. It was a patch of green in the unlikeliest of places, located precisely in the middle of a massive concrete monolith that served as the Jersey-side entrance to the Lincoln Tunnel. This was one of the most mind-boggling architectural-engineering anomalies of the northeastern United States, overlooked or ignored by those who lived around it yet mesmerizing to all tourists who chanced to behold it. Not to mention a unique spot perfectly suited to the bruja's nefarious purposes, as Ronnie was soon to learn. Picture, dear reader, a colossal traffic circle arcing gradually downward in a clockwise direction from the Union City heights, feeding traffic into the gargantuan three-mawed tunnel entrance. Think of it as a circular viaduct, as indeed it was, located no more than half a mile north of the straight one Ronnie had just driven. Picture now that great arc turning sharply inward at about the three-quarter mark, like a radius, feeding all Jersey traffic towards the circle's center where the three tunnel maws stood. Now imagine a baseball/football field resting squarely on top of these three gigantic tunnel entrances, which would only be possible because of the considerable depth at which those entrances had been excavated way back in 1934. But that's the way it was, in fact, and that spot, at precisely the fifty-yard line of the Weehawken Stadium football field, resting atop the tunnel portals, was where Lisa and Ronnie stopped and began their preparations to invoke the aid of the dark powers in securing Anselm's allegiance.

Lisa Ramirez was a clever and knowledgeable bruja, who, despite her straitened circumstances, felt blessed to be living so close to a location of incredibly rare preternatural possibilities. So many of nature's warring pairs of opposites came together here on this improbable fifty yard-line, providing a cosmic gap or "sweet spot" for changing the course of events that would otherwise seem preordained by rock-hard cause and effect: Vertically, they were between the above and the below, between the open sky and the rumbling tunnel traffic, the latter just barely audible if one paid close attention; horizontally, they were at the midpoint of the football field, at the seam between offensive and defensive antagonists, and, more broadly, at a nexus between land and water, Weehawken and the Hudson, the former engaging, even penetrating, the latter. Then there was the surrounding circular viaduct itself, dubbed "the helix" by some locals, the "corkscrew" by others. Physically it was not a complete circle, it's true, only three quarters. This deficit, however, was not an impediment to exploiting its magical properties for a bruja of Lisa Ramirez' long experience. She knew she could, so to speak, "supply" the fourth quarter-arc to complete the circle through the powers of her highly developed imagination, as long as, according to the bruja's unwritten manual, the circle had a physical existence of at least fifty percent to begin with.

Ronnie helped the bruja as best she could in digging out the earth for a Veracruz-style fire hole and filling it with driftwood pre-soaked in kerosene. Then, as she held the flashlight beam steady while the old woman set up the tripod and basin over it, Ronnie noticed that the rain had stopped, but that the storm itself had become much more menacing, a thousand shrieks and howls seeming to rip through a punishing wind. She also noticed that the profound rumbling of thunder from the black clouds overhead now blotted out that of the tunnel traffic below them, making it seem as if the above and the below had suddenly switched places, deepening her already consuming dread.

At length, and with the aid of the wind, the old woman was able to coax a flame out of the pit, which grew stronger by the minute and soon enough was producing a reddish glow at the bottom of the cauldron. At this point she began dropping various indistinct objects into the vessel—flowers, metals, herbs, small creatures—all the while stirring the mix with an industrial-sized metal cooking spoon and shouting over the wind to the cat, who was walking circles around the action as sparkler-like sparks shot up out of the tip of her raised tail. These spark-circles were much more than window dressing added to the ritual; on the contrary, they were an essential part of it as they gave concentricity to the massive traffic circle above and around them, thus increasing the potential for magical transformation.

Every so often when there was a lull in the wind, the howls of the cat could be clearly—and chillingly—heard. Ronnie crouched there next to the old woman, numb with terror, as the latter continued to stir her brew and murmur strange maledictions in a foreign tongue or tongues. Sensing her old-time ward's mounting panic, Lisa took Ronnie's trembling hand in her own free one and gently squeezed while trying to calm her with soothing words: "There, there now, little one, you're doing wonderfully. It'll soon be over. Just keep your thoughts focused on Anselm. Remain steadfast now and soon I will give you something fine and pretty out of this boiling pot, and Anselm himself to boot. Just wait and see!" To herself Ronnie whispered, more as a hope than as a confident pronouncement, "I'm staying till the bitter end, come what may." "That's the spirit, that's my feisty girl," the old au pair encouraged. Then she asked Ronnie for the two agreed-upon, meaningful personal possessions, her high school graduation ring and a lock of preserved baby hair, throwing these too into the infernal concoction. With each addition to the mix the cat let out a wind-piercing howl, as if sensing the formidable, burgeoning potency of the ritual she was circumambulating. Even though totally complicit in his mistress's invidious designs, like a loyal black cat, he still felt compelled by his animal instincts to widen the sparkly circles and give that boiling bomb the widest possible berth.

Would that you, dear reader, had been there on the 23rd of September—no, no, I don't mean right there on the ground with the two conjurors, but above the ground, far above it, riding in a Port of New York Authority helicopter, being taxied from Manhattan to Newark Airport to catch a late flight on important business. You'd been warned because of weather conditions to delay your departure till the next day, especially to stay off the chopper, which, though a heavy "executive model" machine, was no match for the ferocious gales blowing that night. No, you insisted, time was of the essence, departure could not be put off. So, there you are, high up in the turbulent night sky flying west across the Hudson, passing over the spot where, just a few years ago, "Sully" Sullenberger, cool as a cucumber, landed his US Airways Flight 1549 in the river after both engines had been disabled by a bird strike. You look nervously out the fiberglass bubble but see no signs of flapping wings. What you do see, however, is just as hair-raising: a strange flickering light on the ground, off in the distance. As you approach, you distinguish a ring of fire surrounding the light, which itself turns out to be a fire, one placed directly under a cauldron causing it to boil. Out of the cauldron pours a thick vapor with quivering red flashes and brilliant sparks. Unaccountably fascinated, you tell the pilot to approach and descend a bit, with extreme caution. This enables you to see two contrasting figures crouched down beside the cauldron, only partially illuminated by its light. One an old hag in a dark, heavy shawl, out of which a withered arm extends holding a large stirring spoon which she patiently rotates through the ungodly brew. The other, right next to her, a pretty young girl in a jacket much too light for this weather, all color drained from her face as she stares, petrified, into the pot. The wind has blown the hood of her jacket down, freeing her lovely blonde locks, the only part of her body in visible motion. Her angelic face hovers in the angry red light cast by the flickering flame under the trivet, but in the icy terror which has frozen it, it is as stiff and white as death; and you realize her fear, her complete horror, from the raised eyebrows and from the mouth, vainly opened to emit the shriek of anguish that cannot find its way from a heart oppressed with indescribable torment.

I can imagine, intrepid reader, that, although there were little in the world that could evoke a bone-chilling fear in you, your hair would nevertheless have stood on end at the sight of this hellish scene from Breughel or Mussorgsky or Stephen King, here brought to pulsating life. Still, your eyes could not help but remain rivetted on the sweet young child seemingly entrapped in the ghastly ritual, and soon enough your parental instinct would kick in, sending a bolt of angry electricity up your spine to douse your fear and move you to an act of rescue, damn the potential consequences to yourself. You would defy the circle of fire and bring the full fury of your wrath to bear on its hideous harpy, releasing the innocent girl into your custodial embrace. Slowly and precisely, you guide the pilot to a spot overhead and slightly aslant, giving you the best view of the ghastly goings-on. Ready for anything, you grip the bone-carved handle of your fold-up pocket umbrella on the unimaginable chance that the situation should come to blows. You alert the pilot to hold steady because you're about to open the sliding door on your right, which you proceed to do. You then tell the pilot to turn on the copter's powerful searchlight with its thermal imaging camera and train it on the ground fire and its two suspicious attendants below. Which he promptly does. You lean slightly out the doorway, making sure of your firm grip on the overhead leather strap, and shout into the wind and rumbling thunder in the most menacing voice you can conjure, "Hey, you down there! Old woman! What's going on? What are you up to?" There, in the very heart of chaos, between the claps of thunder and the clapping of the copter blades, amidst the screaming wind, the repetitive squeal of the switched-on copter alarm and, most disruptive of the black arts being practiced below, the harsh exposure of the searchlight, you watch as the witch topples over into her own fetid brew, causing a great panoply of black smoke to billow up out of the cauldron and blot out the fiendish scene entirely. I cannot tell you whether you would have found the precious girl for whom you then desperately searched, but you certainly would have destroyed the spell of the witch and would have broken the magic circle that Veronica had thoughtlessly entered.

Alas, beneficent reader, neither you nor anyone else flew overhead on the 23rd of September during that stormy night so favorable to witches. Poor Veronica had no choice but to remain crouched there beside the cauldron next to the bruja and simply endure it all until the nefarious work was done. She did keep her eyes tightly closed and so could at least defend herself visually against the pandemonium, but her ears were a different matter as she was wracked again and again by all that howled and shrieked and raged about her. She felt with a doomed certainty that, were she actually to lay eyes on the miscreant spirits that were producing this bedlam, she would fall into irreversible madness. Just to endure was a mighty feat of heroism.

Presently the bruja stopped stirring her brew and, within minutes, the black smoke thinned out to almost nothing. Soon there remained only a small spirit flame shooting up from beneath the cauldron. At that point the old hag cried out, "Veronica, look! Look, child! Down into the bottom of the pot! What do you see?" But Veronica wasn't seeing anything; it was as if her eyes had been grouted shut. She actually had to use her fingers to pry them gently open. After a few terrified blinks, she tried to focus her still cloudy vision on the contents of the cauldron but could only make out a hodgepodge of indistinct shapes and colors drifting up out of it. Then suddenly there rose up, almost like a man-sized balloon being inflated all at once, an effigy of none other than Anselm himself. Or *was* it an effigy? A simulacrum? Or the man himself? Who could tell? In any case he stepped out of the cauldron, brushed himself off, smiled at Veronica and walked off into the folds of darkness. "Oh, it *is* him! It *is* Anselm. I was *right* to come here and do this!" she proclaimed, deliriously happy.

Eagerly the old woman placed a three-by-six-inch rectangular iron mold near the bottom of the cauldron beneath the petcock and opened the latter. Out gushed a bubbling stream of molten metal, filling the mold and overflowing it. She closed the valve, stood up and announced triumphantly, "The work is done, my child! Our goal is accomplished … And *you*, my faithful soldier," she cried out turning her gaze on the cat, "you kept watch! You let nothing interfere with our crucial purpose. You—" And before she could add another catty compliment, she was interrupted by the whoosh of what looked like the immense wings of a bird—possibly an eagle—but an eagle as large as a Cessna 150. This gargantuan creature just hovered there above them, the flapping of its gigantic wings extinguishing the flaming circle and just beating all hell out of everything within it. A voice as deep and fearsome as hell itself then commanded, "Leave off, scoundrels! Cease and desist! Get on home or you'll cease to exist!" The hag raised her fist and cursed the creature in an unholy wail, then fell to the turf in a swoon. Fell next to Veronica, who was already unconscious.

When the girl came to, she found herself lying in her own bed, covers up. At the foot of the bed stood little sister Sally who had just brought in a cup of hot coffee for her. "Hey, what's up with you, sis?" Sally asked, "You've been tossing and turning and moaning in bed all morning. Daddy was worried enough to take off work. He just went out to the pharmacy to pick you up a cold and fever remedy … Boy, you put on some show!" she laughed, in childish obliviousness to the potential gravity of her sister's condition, setting the coffee down on the nightstand. "You were calling out and crying and moaning something about 'Big Bird.' Whoever heard of anybody having a nightmare about Big Bird?" she mocked in an exaggerated tone. "And every so often you'd mention Anselm's name and that would set you off on another crying jag. Now *that* is something I can understand."

Ronnie answered nothing. She sat up in bed leaning back against the upholstered headboard, covers drawn over her knees, sipping her coffee and keeping her own counsel. Her mind was abuzz with questions, doubts, astonishment, dread. *Was it all a dream? An anxiety dream? But how could that be? It was September 23, so I must have gone to the old woman, no? It's true I wasn't feeling great all day yesterday and I suppose it's possible some bug got into me and I just fell asleep and dreamt it all. All this obsessing I've been doing lately about Anselm and that old woman who claims to be Lisa … It'd make anybody sick.*

On and on she ruminated, unwilling to face the fact that her fear was making her rationalize the events of last night. But then Sally came back in and unwittingly settled the matter: She was holding up her sister's rain jacket, then shaking it to show some raindrops flying out of it and dropping to the floor. "You must've left this on the chair by the window. The wind must've blown the window open and the rain rushed in and soaked it," she laughed, lobbing it onto the bed in front of

Ronnie's covered feet. Ronnie brushed the jacket off the bed onto the floor in annoyance. But she was much more annoyed by the dread of virtual certainty the wet jacket raised in her mind than by her sister's childishness. *So it was real! It did all happen! Oh my God! What now?*

As soon as she managed to shoo her sister out of the room, she pulled the covers up over her head and listened to her own teeth chatter as her mind searched frantically for some recourse, some offramp from this nightmare of a highway. Then, just at the point where she felt she was about to dissolve in despair, some impulse made her turn over in bed, lean over the bedside and pick her jacket up from the rug. She stuck her hand in the pocket and felt a familiar shape, that of her cellphone. But when she pulled the phone out, she was stunned to see that it wasn't hers, or at least not her usual one. It was the same size but that's where the similarity ended. It was silver instead of black, and not just in color but in substance. It was *made* of silver. "The old woman's gift!" she cried out. As she gazed at it transfixed, a kind of radiance began shooting out of it, shafts of brilliant light that, oddly, did not hurt her eyes. On the contrary, her eyes felt refreshed by the warm, healing light flowing out of the phone up into her face. And not only her eyes, but her whole body soon felt that it was thawing out from icy fear and being cradled in a warmth, a euphoria and a buoyancy that made her earlier misery seem like a fast-fading bad dream. Another moment passed and she was well! No, she was better than well, she was robustness incarnate.

Yet this swift transformation of Ronnie's condition was only *one* of the phone's beneficent properties. As she continued to gaze into its rectangular silver surface, a foggy aura gradually gave way to an image of the one who was always on her mind. Behold Anselm! Oh joy! She could conjure him on the screen by simply concentrating her thoughts on him as she focused her eyes thereon. But was it *him*, or just an image of him, an effigy, a reproduction? Or could it somehow be both? This was the first time in her life Veronica found herself troubled by a question of ontology, a question of the very nature of human identity, and even identity itself in the deepest sense. What was real? Was anything real? Really real? It was really all too much for her, and she resolved the issue by deciding that the real was whatever made her life more fun. And who can argue with this simple pragmatism, ontology be damned!

As she continued to lounge in bed sipping coffee and watching her beloved on phone TV, she noticed that she was increasingly feeling as if the barrier of location separating them were disappearing and that she was right there with him in whatever place he was. And where was he? He was in a room, a strange, albeit magnificent, room she had never seen before. Around them was a sort of aureole of yellow and gold, which, as she trained her gaze on it, turned out to be the gilded spines of an enormous collection of books lining all four walls. Anselm seemed oblivious to her presence; he was sitting at a desk in the middle of the room occupied with some sort of writing or note-taking, she couldn't tell. She wanted to walk across the room to him, tap him on the shoulder and say, "Look, Anselm, I'm here!" or some such banal surprise greeting. But after taking two or three steps towards him, she found herself hitting and rebounding off some sort of invisible and pliable, but also impregnable, barrier, something like an industrial-sized rubber band. This suggested to her that she wasn't really *there*, that is, *there there*, in the same physical location as Anselm, but since such a conclusion wasn't much fun, she immediately dismissed it. The effect, however, was to reestablish the duplicity of locations, he at work in Lindhurst's library and she sitting in bed viewing him on the screen of her very, very smart phone. This would have to do, and why shouldn't it? It was a boon all by itself.

But she wanted more, so she once again concentrated hard on Anselm while viewing the phone screen, giving free rein to her, by now, routine fantasies of life as the admired wife of an important member of the local academic intelligentsia, herself an elegant and successful fashion mogul on a first-name basis with Ralph Lauren and Givenchy. And soon enough, after a moment or two, she found she could rouse the young man's attention. Anselm, for his part, experienced this as nothing more than a passing thought of Ronnie, one of several thousand he had mentally fondled since the ferry ride across the Hudson on July 4th last. He did wonder for a fleeting moment why he should be thinking of Ronnie just now of all times, only days after meeting the great love of his life, his muse, his heart, his soulmate, the enchanting Tina. But Ronnie it was, and the thought of her was anything but unpleasant. Oh, you are so sweet, he thought to himself. Is it possible that I'm just confused and it's you I really want?

Just then her father walked into the room with two echinacea tablets and a glass of orange juice. "Here, drink this," he said to her, dropping the pills into the juice. "The pharmacy has nothing to offer. I don't know why I even bother going there anymore. The supplement store is where the action is."

VIGIL 14

Training Day

It was the first Friday of the month, which meant another training day had arrived. Each first Friday was earmarked for assessing new animals for their trainability. It was, more specifically, the first Friday of the second quarter of the year, which was reserved for tigers. Anselm took off his pith helmet, which he found to be a nuisance, annoyedly tossing it aside so that it almost landed at the base of the bars of the surrounding cage. The cage itself was enormous, almost the size of a public hall. Its long vertical bars, however, were not made of the usual iron but of a sort of radiant gold that stretched high up into the rafters of the barracks that housed the operation. A gilded cage, indeed.

Anselm cracked his whip a few times and kicked the sawdusted floor as they wheeled in the beast in his smaller cage and let him out onto the sawdust; he wanted to show the animal who was boss right from the get-go. But the tiger didn't seem interested in any contest of wills; having recently been plentifully fed, it just lay there on the ground drowsily resting its enormous orange, white and black-striped head on its thick paw. This amped up Anselm's annoyance considerably. How was he supposed to judge the animal on a spectrum ranging from refractory to docile if it did not cooperate, that is, did not behave somewhere between those poles like a normal tiger? A sleeping tiger was about as useful to him as a dead one. Anselm tried cracking his whip a few times in the vicinity of the tiger's head, but it didn't even bother to raise it, merely blinking once with each crack and resuming its own recumbent after-lunch reveries.

In frustration, Anselm called a halt to the session and summoned the members of his team to a little impromptu meeting to discuss plan B. Since the training cage was circular, they could not retreat to a corner but had to huddle near a point on the cage's circumference that was farthest away from the beast that now lay in peaceful slumber.

"Can you believe this bullshit?" Anselm said to them with a caustic snort. "It's midday and the animal falls asleep on me. I'm a big-cat trainer with nothing to train. I don't have time to wait for His Highness to finish his nap. Any suggestions?"

One of the crew speculated, "I think he was given his shots yesterday. Heavy doses. Maybe it's knocked him off center a bit, you know, dulled his instincts. He'll come around. Though maybe not till tomorrow."

"Well, I'm afraid that's just not good enough," Anselm replied churlishly. "I've got an impossibly tight schedule this week, and the weeks just ahead don't look much better. It'd be a shame to lose him. He's a beautiful animal—"

"—I was thinking," another assistant inserted himself, "it might not be the shots at all. I've never known these meds to cause this sort of reaction—which is not to say that this tiger might not be a rare exception. He may well be ..." and with this the poor man seemed to lose his train of thought and just stood there nervously rubbing his left wrist. Anselm shifted his stance from one foot to the other, a clear signal for the man to get on with it, and suddenly the poor fellow found the missing thread and continued, "... Anyway, it could be his feeding schedule, you know? He ate a lunch of heavy red meat only thirty minutes before being brought in. He probably needs a little more time to digest it and get his second wind, so to speak."

Anselm's face assumed a stern and serious look as he considered this. "That could be," he said finally. "I've never been in favor of feeding animals during the three hours preceding a training session. Most trainers agree with this. How is it the zoo's dietician is not aware of such elementary strictures … I'll have to have a little chat with him … Anyway, for the time being let's give the cat another hour and a half or so to sleep it off, okay?" Everyone nodded in unison. "Maybe we can still salvage at least part of the afternoon." And the group of them sat down at a little card table and commenced to play poker, a quarter ante, while the tiger slept.

Anselm, it seemed, couldn't win a hand. Whenever he folded, he would realize at the end he should have stayed; and vice-versa. No strategy he tried improved his luck. He had lost about fifteen bucks when he finally got up in disgust and turned his back on the table, muttering "Deal me out this hand." He walked towards the tiger, who hadn't moved, and stopped about midway, standing there in the sawdust with arms folded, just studying the dozing animal.

"All right, men—and lady—let's give it another shot," he snapped, some ninety minutes having now passed. "Hand me the whip there, will you?" he curtly ordered the junior assistant, who fell all over himself grabbing the whip from under the poker table—an eight-foot kangaroo-hide bullwhip—and, in his eagerness to please, practically shoving it into his boss's chest. Anselm grimaced and turned to face the slumbering beast, which had yet to move its head. He snapped the whip once, twice, three times, causing the tiger's eyelids merely to flutter briefly and close again.

"There's something wrong with this animal," Anselm said with a mixture of disappointment and sympathy. "Nothing else makes sense. I'm afraid we'll have to call in the vet—I think we're justified in calling this an emergency—and see if he can figure it out." Which they did. The vet, an old man with white hair and a bushy white moustache, who knew Anselm by reputation, came immediately and, after injecting the beast with a syringe of fast-acting tranquillizer, had Anselm's team hoist the animal onto a make-shift examining table in order to run a series of checks on it. The old man took the animal's vitals, then poked and prodded and pressed, now here, now there, even prying the beast's massive jaws open with a strength that belied his years and could only have come from decades of repetitive practice. After a half hour of exhaustive examination, he removed his stethoscope from his ears, pulled off his plastic gloves, tossing the latter carelessly onto the card table (in disregard of possible bacterial contagion, which, in the case of a feral animal, could be very serious) and said tersely, matter-of-factly, "Mr. MacGregor, I can find nothing wrong with this animal. I could take him in and run some further specialized tests, but, at this point, I think it would be a waste of your money—"

"—The *company's* money," Anselm rushed to interrupt.

"Excuse me?"

"A waste of the *company's* money," he repeated with almost surly emphasis. "Please note the distinction and forward all bills for services rendered to my superiors."

"Yes, yes, of course," the old sawbones muttered, packing his things and heading out. Just before stepping out of the cage, he turned to Anselm and said, "You know, it may well be nothing, nothing at all. These animals do have bad days, just like us. They're not machines. Maybe you caught him on a day of depression when all he wants to do is sleep. We all know how that feels, don't we?" he laughed as he exited the hall. "Yeah, we all know how that feels!" Anselm called after him in his snidest tone, steamed over the wasted afternoon, for which he would still have to pay his employees.

The upside of it all was that, after having the tiger taken away and dismissing his employees, he had some free time on his hands, with nowhere he needed to be. Not knowing what to do with himself, he just shambled aimlessly around the cage absently checking things out—the whip, which he was still holding and which, upon close observation, looked quite frayed; the sawdust, which struck him as of uneven quality and probably in need of changing; the card table, which had a slightly short leg making it wobbly and an unsightly brownish-red streak across the top which looked quite suspicious. He made mental notes on various items of the cage inventory, intending to pass them along to the appropriate staff members.

Finally, having nothing else to do and turning towards the exit, it struck him that he had left out of account, having totally forgotten it, the cage itself, this massive enclosure of vertical yellow-gold bars that stretched from the floor high up into the darkness of the rafters. He mildly slapped his own forehead in self-reproof. How could he forget the single most important requirement of effective lion taming—a good, solid, spacious cage? Perhaps its very omnipresence, its absolute reliability and close-to-zero maintenance requirements, caused one to take the cage for granted, like a fish forgetting it's in life-sustaining water or Chopin so lost in his playing that he didn't notice his breathing was being compromised by his creeping tuberculosis until he began coughing up blood of an arresting crimson shade onto his ivory-white piano keys. The irony of these and other striking examples of blissful ignorance, of failing to become "woke," did indeed flit through Anselm's consciousness, making him feel stupid and vulnerable at once. He knew he had better have a look, a close look, at those bars before leaving for the day or he would get no sleep that night.

Still holding his whip, now in hands folded behind his black, he stepped up close to the bars just beside the poker table. He studied them just as he had earlier studied the sleeping tiger, with a fierce determination and a prodigious analytical power. But as with the animal, he got little return on his investment of energy. He tried again, giving it everything he had, but again, after several minutes, had to give up in frustration. He was at a loss. His very intellectual impotence signaled to him, not only that it was the cage that held the answer to the mystery of the sleeping tiger, but that he needed to try another approach. But what other approach? Brain power was the only one he knew. Sheer brute application and analytical penetration.

Then, continuing to stand there in front of the yellow-gold bars, his mind exhausted and empty of any strategy, feeling almost a sense of respect for these bars that would not yield their secret, even to a formidable intellect, he looked. For the first time, he really looked at the yellow-gold bars, looked without an intention and without an agenda, looked without demanding to know. And that was when he saw. And the instant he saw, he knew. And the instant he knew, he raised a hand and gently, ever so gently, stroked, not a bar, but the yellow-gold spine of a book. It seems there were no bars, never had been any, only books—old, gilt-spined, hardcover editions of books. Books forming a circular library all around the training hall, forming an enclosure that had never once been breached.

Anselm, of course, was thunderstruck. Then, acting purely on instinct, an instinct of ravenous curiosity, he pulled out the book he had just touched and opened to the title page, which read: *The Lonely Crowd*, by David Riesman. He knew the book from college days and was delighted. Gripped by a sudden burst of manic energy, he felt he needed to know every title comprising the cage, and so he ran about, this way and that, not knowing which book to pull out next, like a kid paralyzed by choice in a candy store. Finally, he stopped on the other side of the cage, reached in without looking and pulled out another volume. It read *The Mass Psychology of Fascism*, by Wilhelm Reich. Ah, another classic he had studied years ago. What else is there? And he ran around the arc of the "cage of books," stopping somewhere on impulse and once again reaching in: *Repression, the Price of Civilization*, by Sigmund Freud, a neglected work of the master's middle period.

Anselm, to be sure, was delighted by all this; yet just beneath his delight was frustration. Yes, he felt he had penetrated the mystery of the sleeping tiger; his "discovery" of the golden cage of books made him feel certain of this. But what exactly was the animal's problem? What did classic studies of social psychology have to do with a somnolent tiger that couldn't read them? Wondering, considering, weighing a plethora of competing theories as they sprang to mind, he walked aimlessly around the cage for quite some time before eventually finding himself at exactly the spot where the tiger had lain. Still lost in thought, he looked down and noticed the slight thickness of the straw that had made up the animal's bed. It looked warm. Inviting. He lowered himself carefully onto the bed, assuming roughly the same position as the tiger, and laid his head on his forearm. Unable to resist a sudden, profound wave of exhaustion, he fell fast asleep.

VIGIL 15

Prehistory

The days and weeks Anselm spent working in Lindhurst's library were the happiest of his young life. Unlike most of us, he woke up every morning both relaxed and full of energy, eager to go to work and lose himself in a language he didn't understand, but which spoke to him in a way his own never had. For the mere physical reproduction of its strange markings on the monitor evoked sights and sounds and smells that put him in the orbit of a bliss available to most others through artificial stimulants alone—and even then only in its grossest strain.

Anselm's relation to Arabic was, of course, intuitive, not intellectual, connotative rather than denotative; what the letters and sounds suggested to him was more important than what they meant, or, put round the other way, what they suggested *was* what they meant. This intuitive affinity somehow allowed him to copy the marks quickly and correctly, without the strain of scrupulous attention. Unfailingly, whenever he finished copying a manuscript, the Archivist would enter the room with another one, taking the one just copied with him without saying a word. (Conversation took place only during snack breaks.) Every now and then the old man would briefly check Anselm's "air computer" and Wi-Fi setting, using some sort of e-monitor he wore on his wrist like a watch, but, aside from such perfunctory maintenance, he came and went silently.

To be sure, the cause of Anselm's happiness was Tina. His rich sense of her—who could deny it was love?—blended into everything he thought, said and did. In this way she was transformative for him in the subtlest yet also the most revolutionary sense, for he was beginning to regard his work as a mission, an almost sacred charge, a quest of some kind involving not only himself, but, through her, in a way he could not yet fathom, the world itself. Somehow the world needed him as an instrument through which to renew itself, and he had no idea how or why this should be, only that it was so, that Tina was an essential agent in the process and that he must not fail. He did not see Tina often, no more than once or twice a week for an hour in her practice room; he would sneak away from his desk the instant he heard the strains of her violin. But he didn't mind the limited time together, he didn't mind it at all, for some deep instinct told him that even a smidge of impetuosity could be dangerous. He must keep his balance, bide his time and have faith in the work; then all would be well.

On those biweekly occasions when he would sneak off to her practice room, she would always welcome him with a warm hug, a smile and, after a few weeks, a tender kiss. She would play something lively for him, a "Hungarian Dance" by Brahms or the opening of Erich Wolfgang Corngold's Violin Concerto with its hypnotic half-harmonies, falling always just short of tonal fulfillment. She would play brilliantly and he would be totally enchanted. During many of their trysts, he would think back to summer and that first soaring wisp of a melody rising up from the bowels of the subway, a strain holding him spellbound, promising him an intensity of life he now realized he was already beginning to enjoy. He looked around him, looked at Tina, and the expression "erotic sanctuary" popped into his mind, a strange amalgam of the sacred and the sensual, qualities he was used to keeping separate in his mind and heart. Totally without effort, Tina was teaching him new ways of seeing the world. She was helping him eroticize the world or, better put, rediscover the world's underlying sensuousness that is always already there.

Not that everything was always so serious and profound between them. As they got to know each other better, they naturally made time for the frivolity and teasing and horseplay that give body and sinuousness to love, the delightful strokes of quasi one-upmanship each would play on the other for a laugh. They hid things from each other. He would hide her violin bow, she would hide his notepad or his phone; then the concealer would finally display the purloined item, laugh and immediately hide it again on his or her person, requiring the other to perform an "outraged" and very handsy search of the offending body. Ah, the delightful games reserved for young love! On one early afternoon, she summoned Anselm to her rehearsal room by playing an agreed-upon signal melody. As he opened her door and rushed in to greet her, he found an empty room. Puzzled, he headed back to his desk, but halfway there he heard the melody again. Again he rushed back and opened the door—again to an empty room. He looked around and realized she must be hiding in the small storage closet in the corner. So, pretending to leave, he closed the door to the room and waited quietly beside the closet so that he would be hidden by the opening door. Sure enough, she opened the door, looked around and, seeing no one, quietly stepped one foot out of the closet. Which is when he jumped out from behind the door with the humongous roar of King Kong swatting airplanes from atop the Empire State Building. Then, gently shoving her back into the closet and closing the door behind him, he "had his way with her" (within reason, that is), stealing a few passionate kisses that she didn't mind losing at all. Keeping the door closed and turning on the little 10-watt bulb hanging from the closet ceiling, he could see, even in these dim, tight quarters, that she was wearing his favorite outfit: jeans with the requisite torn-up knees, tennis sneakers and an anti-Trump T-shirt. Her politics only further inflamed his lust, for they showed she was as earthy as she was ethereal, and her ready response to his ardor only confirmed this. She was as ready to fight Trump as she was to love *him*.

He kissed her one last time—those full, supple lips, achingly sweet—and felt as he did so a thin strand of her caramel hair that had caught the corner of her mouth and nestled itself there. He brushed it gently aside with his lips and inhaled deeply, taking in the full fragrance of her hair and, in the stifling airlessness of the closet, the subtle pungency of her sex. This was enough for him, enough for now—more than enough—and he opened the closet door and helped her out.

It never occurred to him, by the way, that this love play was time stolen from work and that Lindhurst might be furious with him if he found out. On the contrary, he felt sure in his bones that the old man knew very well what was going on and was not opposed. And, indeed, Anselm always found his copying skills honed to a fine point following a private encounter with Tina, so that Lindhurst never had cause to complain about the quality or timeliness of his work.

One day, shortly after the stroke of twelve, Anselm arrived at the door to his library workroom and found it locked. But before he even had time to wonder about this, the Archivist appeared at the other end of the corridor wearing his floral robe and called to him, "Anselm, come this way please. Today is the day we meet the masters of the *Bhagavad Gita*. We don't want to be late." Anselm hadn't a clue as to the old man's reference, but it reeked of importance, enough for him to skip-walk down the corridor and then follow the master through a series of rooms that might or might not have been the same ones he had traversed his first time in the house—he couldn't be sure. (After the first few days, he usually used a shortcut route to get from the house entrance to his workplace and back.) When they entered the greenhouse, Anselm was, as profoundly as on that first day, stunned by the vast array of plant and avian life—the shrubs and bushes and trees, each with its distinctive fragrance, the birds of countless stripes and colors, many exotically red and yellow, with the strangest shapes of heads and beaks; even the insects charmed as they buzzed around fluttering their multicolored wings and nuzzling each other in their little round dances. As a dazed Anselm tried to take it all in, he was, for good or ill, again accosted by that pack of delinquent birds that had mocked him the first time he had dared run the gauntlet through their territory: "Hey, college boy, where ya goin'? There's no class today—the professor fell into the Hudson and died of lead poisoning. Flinty old geezer. Ha ha ha! ... Hey A., can ya spare me a ten-spot? I need it to fill the hole in my sole, shoe sole, that is. Wait! I don't wear shoes... Be careful, Master Shuhu, never wake a sleeping tiger or you'll know what fer!" And so on ad nauseam.

They left the rotunda and before long entered the room with the azure-blue walls, the "walls of infinity" projecting palm-tree trunks up to the canopy of fronds. Gone was the porphyry table and its golden pot; in their place, in the middle of the room, was a table decked with blue velvet, behind it a matching upholstered armchair. On the table, all atwinkle, was a new "air computer" that looked much like the one Anselm had been using, except that its keyboard was larger and displayed an entirely new set of symbols that looked to him to be daunting. The old man cleared his throat and began, in a tone that had a touch of solemnity to it, "My dear Anselm, to my satisfaction you have now copied several manuscripts with great accuracy and have earned a promotion. As you might expect, with that promotion comes greater responsibility, for the most important work remains to be done. From now on you will be copying, or perhaps I should say 'reproducing,' certain texts that are written in markings you will find very strange; these are works that I keep in this room and that are never to leave this room. So this will be your new work station," he said, gesturing towards the blue-velvet tabletop. Then he continued, now in a tone that marked a sudden shift from solemnity to gravity, "But I must warn you: One false move on your part, one slip or lapse in concentration, leading, God forbid, to any damage to the original manuscript, and you are lost! Beyond redemption! Plunged into agony!"

As Anselm listened while seating himself, his eyes perused the glistening emerald fronds that shot out from the trunks of the surrounding palm trees. Lindhurst turned and pulled one of these loose from its trunk and laid it on the table. As he spread it out, Anselm realized that it was not so much a frond as a parchment, a strong piece of vellum covered with an array of signs—dots, dashes, curves, squiggles, curlicues—that seemed to represent all manner of plants, grasses, mosses and animal shapes. His heart suddenly sank as he felt overwhelmed by the sheer complexity of it all. He looked at the light keyboard and, observing that each key had three or four symbols "imprinted" on it, knew that he was nowhere near being up to this job. Lindhurst, of course, was expecting precisely this reaction from his apprentice, and had this to offer: "Take heart, young man. Just keep the faith and remain steadfast in your love, and Serpentina will guide you." As he said these words, the old man's voice had an imposing stentorian quality to it, which caused Anselm to look up and take notice. What he saw, standing over him, was a prince, clothed in regal robes, smiling at him with an unmistakable aura of beneficence. Anslem's reflex reaction was to bow down in reverence, but the princely hand stopped him and then, grabbing onto the palm tree trunk, lifted its owner nimbly aboard, from whence he climbed high up into the canopy of foliage on top, disappearing therein. "Probably going up to his study," thought Anselm, "to consult with the planets on what's to be done with Tina and me … Or maybe he's off to his black-hole shortcut on a visit to his brother in the Tunisian mountains. It's really none of my business. My best bet is to get to work."

Anselm sat up straight in his chair and leaned forward slightly in an attempt to make whatever sense he could of the cryptic markings on the parchment, and, as soon as he began to concentrate, his surroundings seemed to come to his aid. The music of the bird and insect life from outside came in through the half-open window and swirled gently around him. It was accompanied by the seductive plant fragrances of the Fall and Winter seasons, the pink viburnum and the red abelia and the gorgeous Tasmanian tiger. The mockingbirds joined in too, flying by the window as they chirped their nasty little epithets in Anselm's direction, though today for some reason he didn't understand them, which suited him just fine.

It was a symphony of the senses of which Anselm was aware only vaguely in the hinterlands of consciousness as his sole intent at that moment was to penetrate in some way the arcane gibberish he was studying. What he would later come to understand was that the "symphony of nature" in the background and the palm-frond markings in front of him were identical; signifier and signified were one and the same. To know one was to know both, since they were, in fact, not-two. But this subtle understanding was for later.

The harder he looked at the uppermost marks on the leaf, the clearer it became that their meaning must be "On the Marriage of the Salamander and the Green Snake." The instant this breakthrough in his understanding occurred, Anselm heard a tremendous triad of bells ring out, whether in his mind or outside it, he could not tell. This was followed by a phrase repeated over and over on the violin redolent of those hypnotic tones heard in the subway on the day it all began. And these were followed in turn by words that, though clearly audible, almost seemed whispered, so richly breathy were they. Like the music, they seemed to come from the palm-tree canopy on high: "Anselm, dearest Anselm." The words ached with longing and Anselm sat up ramrod straight: "Serpentina, is it you? Are you there?" He stood up and craned his neck to see up into the leaves and, lo and behold, a small green snake came out of them and proceeded to slither its way down the trunk. But, strange to say, it slithered, not straight down, but in spirals, most elegant spirals, and, at some point, after receding from his view in mid-spiral and coming round the other side into view again, mirabile dictum, it appeared as the lovely young girl Anselm knew and desired. "Oh, Serpentina, I can't believe this! It *is* you!" She was dressed in the sheerest gossamer material, almost see-through, a blend of both brilliant and muted earth tones like the autumn season itself, and it was marvelous to see how she was able to avoid every knot, needle and branch on the palm trunk as she nimbly pulled her delicate gown after her on her way down.

She sat down next to Anselm in his armchair and put her arm tenderly around his shoulder as she gave him encouragement: "Dearest Anselm, soon you will be mine. By your faith and love you will win me, and I will bring you the golden pot, which will seal our happiness forever."

"Tina, as long as I have you, nothing else matters. Once you become mine, I don't care what visions and wonders and phantasms descend upon me. Let all the powers of hell itself have their way with me. They've been doing that anyway since the moment I first laid eyes on you."

She kissed him softly under the ear and said, "I know how trying my father's pranks and jokes have been for you. Some of them are downright sadistic. All of it comes out of his foul mood, a disposition caused by the witch who is his arch-enemy. But that, dearest, will soon be a thing of the past, for I am here to tell you, right now, all you need to know about my father and me, our relations with the world—this world and the other—and our particular project of which you have become an integral part. I know you are ready to hear this and assimilate it to the deepest reaches of your being."

Anselm was moved to awe by Tina's seriousness of tone and by the philosophical gravity of her words, a style of discourse he was not used to hearing from her and that now opened up to him the vast chasm of her spiritual depth. What reassured him, however, what took the edge off all the profundity, was what he *was* used to and could not get enough of: her warm embrace, the sweet breath, the caramel hair grazing his cheek, her very pulsebeat, which he could no longer distinguish from his own and made him feel as if he could only stir, only move, only have his being, in and through her. She pulled him to her bosom with deep affection, more motherly than erotic in this moment of profound sympathy for the trial she knew he was soon to undergo. He felt an almost electrical surge of energy pass from her body into his and cried out to her spontaneously, "Oh Serpentina, don't ever leave me! You are my life!" "Certainly not today, dearest," she replied, "at least until I have told you everything about my family that your love for me allows you to comprehend." She rustled her gown softly as she snuggled up close to him and began: "Know then, my love, that my father descends from the wondrous race of the salamanders and that I owe my existence to his love for the green snake. Since olden days it has been Phosphorus who has ruled over the wonderland of Atlantis and whom the elemental spirits have served. One day the salamander—my father, that is—whom Phosphorus loved above all others, was walking through the sumptuous gardens when he suddenly heard a lily high on a hill singing a lullaby. He approached her and, aroused by his fiery breath, she opened her petals to reveal a little green snake sleeping in her calyx. This was her daughter. Immediately and overwhelmingly smitten, the salamander scooped up the snake and made off with her, the mother calling after her with a variety of scents that pervaded the garden.

"The salamander took her straight to the palace of Phosphorus and requested that the prince marry them and 'make her mine for evermore.' 'Fool!', the Prince of Spirits rebuked him. 'You know not what you ask for. Do you not know that the lily was once my beloved and ruled with me, but the spark I injected her with threatened to destroy her and it was only our victory over the black dragon, now held in chains by the earth spirits, that saved the lily and kept her petals strong enough to hold and preserve the spark. But if you run off now and embrace the green snake, your glow will destroy her body and a completely new being will rise from her ashes and fly away.'

"But the salamander was having none of it, and, burning with desire, off he rushed with his beloved, taking her in his embrace, the volcanic intensity of which immediately burned her to a crisp. And, as foretold, a winged creature emerged from her ashes and flew up and away. Seized by the madness of despair, the salamander ran here, there and everywhere throughout the garden, spreading fire and flames of rage and wreaking devastation on all fronts, such that the most exquisite flowers and blossoms sank down scorched and filled the air with their lamentation.

"Upon hearing of this, the Prince of Spirits was livid and had the salamander prince brought to him: 'Now you've gone and done it—destroyed my beautiful gardens! You're finished here! I'm extinguishing your fire—gone are your flames, doused your jets. Down to the earth spirits you'll go. Let them tease and taunt you and drive you mad until, one day, your flint reignites your inner glow and you beam forth on the earth as a new being.' And with that the salamander was—literally—sent down. But then the prince's gardener, himself a spirit, stepped forward and interceded on his behalf: 'Majesty, please do not be too hard on him; his only crime is to have fallen victim to love, which has happened to you yourself, and more than once. Besides, no one has more reason to complain of him than I do: He has ruined most of my most brilliant colors in the flower garden, the reds, blues and yellows I labored to create for longer than I care to remember.'

"These words sobered the prince, who then lightened the salamander's sentence, saying, 'For now his fire is out. In that unhappy time to come, when only the vaguest memory of our harmonious existence here is left to man, when a boundless longing is his only link to … he knows not what, having only the most unformed sense of a life lived in nature's bosom, then and only then will the salamander's fire reignite and burn again. But he will not rejoin us here—no, not yet; rather he will remain in that valley of tears, condemned to earn his bread by the sweat of his brow. To make his suffering more acute, he *will* remember his pre-existence here with the pain of nostalgia, and he will retain only partial use of his power over fire and dominion over his fellow earth spirits. And one day, he will find the green snake again, in a lily bush, and the fruit of their union will be three daughters, who will announce their presence among men through their music, through the sweet strains of the violin. But only those who have ears to hear will hear their music, only those with a deep sense of the possibility of a higher life will hear that life announced in their music, and, marrying its embodiment, will enter that higher life and join us here for an endless banquet, an endless celebration of the wonder of it all. But this must happen no fewer than three times: Three young men must be found and each must marry one of the salamander's daughters before he can throw off his earthly burden and return to us.'

"'As you wish, sire,' the gardener bowed, 'but please allow me to provide each daughter with a gift, a sort of dowry; each shall receive from me a pot made of my finest gold, a pot polished with rays taken from my richest diamond deposits. Anyone gazing at its surface with eyes to see will witness moments of our sublime life here in the embrace of nature. In the moment of the daughter's marriage there will sprout up from its inside a fire lily, a flower symbolizing spiritual awakening, whose sweet scent will follow the youth who has been found worthy and will teach him our natural language, the language that communicates directly, without the tedium of words.'

"Now, dear Anselm, you can understand that my father is the salamander in human form, and you can appreciate the sad fact that he is forced to live in a world that is alien to him, forced to bear the slings and arrows of shortsighted, need-driven human beings. It's no wonder that he is subject to sudden shifts of mood and outbursts of anger and, at times, even to ill-treatment of others bordering on cruelty. He has often complained bitterly about the rarity of just those qualities of temperament required of a proper suitor for his daughter's hand—a simplicity, an innocence, or even naivete, about the ways of the world often inciting others to mock him. A proper suitor has the unshakable inkling that there is something fundamentally wrong with human beings that cannot be fixed with 'more' of anything—not love, not money, not learning, not acquiring ... not *anything*! My father calls this naïve worldview 'a childlike poetic temperament' and says it is a disposition only too readily misunderstood by the world.

"But you, Anselm, you heard my music! You sat there in that dark, grungy subway cavern and listened, entranced, and heard what the world truly sounds like, even down there in that hell of steel and grease. You love me, whether in human or serpentine form. You believe in me and are committed to me, without reserve or condition. Soon the beautiful lily will blossom forth from the golden pot and we will live happily in Atlantis as man and wife!

"But I must also tell you that our archfoe, the black dragon, managed to escape a horrific battle with the salamanders and the earth spirits and fly off ... Not to worry, Phosphorus has recaptured him, but the thing is that in the struggle he lost several feathers—black feathers—and these gave rise to all kinds of dark spirits whose entire reason for being is to thwart the noble purposes of our kind. That old woman, for instance, who's been so hostile to you, and who, as my father knows only too well, will do anything to get her hands on the golden pot—that woman is a product of the union between one of those black feathers, ripped from the dragon's wing, and a particular beet root that today is native to Mexican soil, particularly in and around Veracruz.

"She's a witch in every nasty sense of the word, Anselm, and she knows her own origins and is well aware of her own powers. For in the groans and convulsions of the captive dragon are revealed to her the secrets of many an astral constellation, and she uses all such esoteric knowledge to try to worm her way into our inner circles. My father is always ready to fight her with his jets of fire that come from the salamander's innermost being. She extracts all the harmful essences from the various toxic plants and animals under her dominion and concocts from them—as you well know—many an evil spook to befuddle her victims' minds, filling them with terrifying illusions, and deliver them up to the demons spawned by the dragon in his losing battle.

"Please be especially on your guard, Anselm, when it comes to her. She is your mortal enemy because your childlike sincerity has already sabotaged several of her wicked conjurings ... Stay true, true, true to me! Soon you'll reach your goal!"

Anselm, who had kept his eyes shut during most of Serpentina's recounting of her family's history, then felt a soft, gentle kiss on his lips. The kiss lingered there, their lips lightly pressing against each other like tiny warm pillows, until he could no longer contain himself and cried out in a spasm of ardor, "Oh Serpentina, how could I do anything *but* stay true to you? You've taken possession of me fully; my mind is wall-to-wall you. You've become my life! I don't pretend to understand how or why it is that the world has turned upside-down, nor how I could possibly feel more at home here in this preposterous palace than in my efficiency apartment or even in my parents' house in Syracuse, but, strangely, it is so. Coming here isn't coming to work; it's entering the Gates of Paradise. Even on days when I don't see you, your essence pervades everything within these walls as well as the space in between. Even if I never saw you again—God forbid—I almost think I could rest content as long as I were allowed to remain here and continue to copy these arcane documents, for somehow they conjure your presence most strongly ... I don't know ..."

And just then, as he again closed his eyes in this moment of sincere admission of his own ignorance, he felt another kiss—warm, tender, supple. Then, in his ear he felt the breathy words, "Just stay true and all will be well." But when he opened his eyes to reciprocate his joy, she was gone. He looked around the library—no sign of her. He was happy but confused, his steady state these days. He shook his head in wonderment and then suddenly slapped it, realizing he'd been neglecting his work all this time. He hadn't typed a word—that is, a mark—since noon, and it was almost snack time. The old man would be furious with him. But then he looked down at the air monitor and—lo and behold!—there it was on the screen, big and beautiful, the typed copy of the entire palm-leaf manuscript that Lindhurst had left on his desk; and, as Anselm leaned in and studied the text on the screen, he couldn't help but feel it presented Serpentina's narration of the prehistory of her father, of the span of his life in (and presently out) of Atlantis.

Now the archivist came into the room wearing his gray and white blazer and carrying his (decorative) walking stick. Popping a Tic Tac into his mouth, he bent over and peered carefully at the monitor, but only long enough to assure himself of his own assumption. "Excellent, my boy! Excellent! Just as I thought. Now, put it all away and come with me. We're off to Mitzi's for happy hour," he said, already halfway out the door with Anselm scrambling to catch up. "Drinks are on you!" the old man barked, laughing. "Just a small jest," he added, mercifully. As they passed through the rotunda, the birds were at their late-afternoon wackiest, and Anselm was glad their screeches were Greek to him.

When they got to Mitzi's, they ran into Harold Branden just outside the door. There were effusive greetings all around and a moment of chitchat. Branden was smoking a pipe that had gone out and was searching his pockets for his lighter.

"Can't find the damned thing … Where *is* that cursed lighter?" he muttered.

"What is it, Branden? Fire? Do you need *fire*?" the Archivist asked, brimming with a spirit of largesse to be of service. "I've got plenty of fire, and then some!" he quipped as he snapped his fingers and produced a flame on the upraised tip of his index finger. The registrar cupped his hands around the flame, a superfluous gesture as no wind could ever threaten the integrity of a salamander's fire. Lindhurst lowered his finger down to the top of the pipe's bowl and lit its contents without further ado.

"Another one of your little chemical tricks. Eh, my friend?" Branden snorted as he opened the door and they all three went right to the Archivist's round table and commenced to embrace the spirit of happy hour. As the evening progressed, they were joined by a few colleagues from Stoneham, including a professor of chemistry with hair as vertical as Kramer's, whom the registrar, after three mugs of Guinness ale, began pestering with questions as to how on earth the Archivist did that finger-fire thing. After another two mugs, his questioning had devolved to his usual charmingly maudlin, "Are you my friend?" Everyone at the table had to profess undying friendship to him, and when the old man had finally had enough, he got up, slipped two twenty-dollar bills into Anselm's hand and told him to call a cab for their friendship-challenged friend.

VIGIL 16

Anselm's Aporia

Limpid blue sky. If he kept his head at a certain angle, his eyes took in nothing but sky. What was it? What was the blue? What was it made of? How deep was it? He felt a deep tingle in his abdomen, as if some stupendous unknown delight were beckoning to him. He lay in the tall grass of his backyard in Syracuse, in the grass near the back fence where he couldn't be seen, on his back, looking straight up into the beguiling abyss of blue. He was ten and hiding from Mom who wanted him for chores and was pleased with himself for finding the neatest hiding place. It was a perfect afternoon in early June: The sun was shining but not oppressively, the bees were flower-hopping, a light breeze rustled the trees, the birds were twittering. He felt no need to move, to go anywhere or do anything; he was content to stay there, sheltered by the weeds, looking up into the dizzying blue, dizzying because there was no contrasting object that might limit it. Every now and then he would suddenly feel connected to that blue, physically, umbilically, connected, as if his stomach were being gently tugged at by it, inviting him to come out of himself and be absorbed up into that great azure mystery. What would he find there? How would it be? Did it even make sense to speak of being "inside" it? Who's to say it wasn't just a façade? A David Hockney sky? But he had an almost mischievous sense that it was more, much more, than a façade.

These and other fanciful ideas he lay there entertaining, and being entertained by, before finally drifting off to sleep, there in his bed of tall grass, at one with it all. He couldn't know this, of course, but this was the first moment in his life given up solely to philosophical, quasi mystical reflection, and the first time he had experienced being alone to be more fulfilling than being with others.

But his slumber was brief, for just as he slipped into unconsciousness, he felt a slight but unmistakable tug on his neck which brought him rudely to. He slapped the nape of his neck with his hand, thinking there must be something back there pulling on him, but he felt nothing. Then it got serious. He felt violently yanked by the neck in a head-first direction. He could see nothing, feel nothing, do nothing. His anxiety was off the charts, feeling as he did completely at the mercy of whatever force was pulling him backwards through the grass. Before he knew it, his head was at the precipice of a hole, a hole he *knew* wasn't there when he came into the yard. He was terrified. Utterly powerless. Then, as the force pulled him about halfway across the hole, he felt an involuntary let-go totally engulf body and mind, such that he was now an indifferent, though perhaps also oddly curious, witness to what was taking place. Downward yanked the force and down the rabbit hole he went, down, down, endlessly down the dank, pungent blackness. After what seemed like an eternity of falling, the sensation of descent lessened, and then finally faded out entirely. Conversely, there was an awareness of light coming up from below. Where was it coming from? Had he stopped falling? He didn't know. He was absurdly, impossibly, suspended in light, but at least he could now see his own body and, more to the point, what it was that held him in bondage.

It was not one, but two chains of wrought iron with twisted links so as to cause great pain to a struggling neck. And, indeed, both chains were secured around his neck, one going up, presumably toward the top of the hole, the other down to … who knew where? He could look up and down and see both, as they stretched away from him in reverse directions. Since, as far as he could tell, his neck, though badly chafed, was neither broken nor critically injured, and since he wasn't being pulled by the lower chain, he concluded that the upper chain was, for the moment at least, running slack and that, wherever he was, the principle of gravity was operative. Neither chain was causing serious damage, at least not yet.

Then, ever so gradually, the light began to dim and he thought he could again detect, just barely, the pull of gravity. All of this was confirmed over the next few seconds. He fell freely for a moment or two; then at some point he blinked and found himself standing in the assembly yard of his old grammar school, Holy Cross Elementary, in DeWitt Township, an eastern suburb of Syracuse—chains forgotten, hence gone. It was around 8:20 on a crisp, sunny Spring morning and the children were waiting for the bell to ring that would call them to assemble in their class lines. But he was oblivious to all that, standing there half-crouched as he was with his fists raised, ready to start pounding them into the tall but woefully thin body of one Richard "Macky" McNamara, in happier times his best friend in third grade, but now, suddenly, for reasons buried in the great cosmic memory book, turned deadly enemy. Several of the kids in the class, mainly boys and a girl or two, had formed a "ring" around the two combatants and were urging them to get on with it, since there were precious few minutes left until "the final bell."

He lashed out with his left and caught Macky flush in the face. The stringbean crumpled up and went down like a discarded Kleenex. What happened next was strange and, possibly, accidental: As Macky rose to his haunches and lingered there for a moment to gather himself, his head happened to be located perhaps a foot or so above Anselm's left knee, and, before Anselm knew it, the knee had jerked upward in an apparent reflex movement that caught Macky under the chin, sending him back down to the ground, his face by now a mask of blood. The ooh's and aah's of the bystanders rang out all around and he couldn't help but feel them as injections of heroin (or at least, what he *thought of* as heroin) into his ego. How odd, this strange mix of pride and guilt, for he still had a deep affection for his longtime friend and only recent foe. But soon the pride took over, squeezing out the guilt and allowing him to know the matchless thrill of social adulation, the intoxication of being, in some important respect, regarded by the others in one's circle as superior. The only lingering shadow was the question, significant to him alone, as to whether the upward jerk of the knee had been deliberate or, as he secretly believed and hoped, accidental, a mere reflex action and therefore beyond his control. This way, he could enjoy the adulation without taking responsibility for the harm. The perfect moral scam.

But he had almost no time to savor his victory, for he suddenly woke up and found himself lying hidden in the tall grass of his yard as before. Or at least he *thought* he was awake: This time, with a minute shift in geographical location, the result of a slight cosmic recalibration, the hole appeared directly under him and down again he went. It struck him immediately that the principle of gravity applied between worlds as well as within them. Again, as he fell, he gradually felt the two chain-link nooses form around his neck and, as the light again came up, he sensed a slowing-down as he approached what he would later come to understand as the bardo realm, the realm between worlds (objective) or between lives (subjective). He wasn't nearly cocky enough to believe that he understood any of this; he just knew he was headed *somewhere*, possibly for the purpose of a revisit, for reasons he couldn't fathom.

That "somewhere" this time turned out to be his father's study, decorated during Anselm's late adolescent years with dramatic posters of Italian opera, from the witches stirring their toxic brew with frenzied glee in Verdi's *Mabeth* to Rodolfo at the bed of the expired Mimi in Puccini's *La bohème*, crying out her name in anguish. Archie MacGregor, though Scotch-Irish to the bone, was a fanatical devotee of Italian music, everything from those passionate Neapolitan love songs like "O sole mio" and "Core 'ngrato" to the more "serious" symphonic music of Respighi and Busoni. But his deepest love was for opera, particularly those lush, eminently hummable melodies of Giacomo Puccini. Of these he could not get enough. Every Saturday and Sunday, the stentorian tenor of Pavarotti or Domingo or Corelli would ring out from the Bose CD-player through his study walls and render all conversation and other radio or TV communication going on anywhere else in the house virtually mute.

This is where Anselm's dream journey now took him, to a comfortable seat in the leather armchair in his father's study. His father was sitting at his old-fashioned oak roll-top desk and had just removed a bottle of Asbach Uralt, a fine German cognac, from its bottom draw and was pouring about an inch into each of two glasses. Anselm had just arrived home from college on Christmas break and Archie had decided he was old enough to enjoy a father-son shot or two of whiskey.

On recent visits home, Anselm had taken to teasing his dad, at times rather cruelly, about his obsession with Puccini—"How can you listen to that olive oil drivel? … 'Che gelida manina' makes me comatose—I actually think I'm pre-diabetic from it!"—and then he would press the stop button on the Bose and slip in a CD playing some extravagant piece by Wagner, the grave and towering Teutonic answer to the lemony Southern sunshine of Verdi and Puccini. Back and forth they would argue, North vs. South, the glowering baritone of Bryn Terfel's Wotan versus the silvery tenor of Pavarotti's "Nessun dorma." Archie, who rarely rose above his phlegmatic disposition, would jump up and rant about Wagner's many musical (and personal) deficiencies ("heavy … slow … mawkish … no arias … reprobate …anti-Semite … heavy … bombastic … over the top … heavy").

But on this occasion, a little miracle happened. Leaning back in his chair and sipping his Asbach, Anselm said, "Well, Dad, what do you say? Bring on the Puccini. Bring on the Pooch. It's time for another round in the opera heavyweight championship, don't you think? Go ahead. 'Che gelida' the hell out of me. I can take it." Archie, who was considerably shorter and of smaller stature than his son, got up, walked over to the Bose sitting on an end table and, with a faint smile on his face, slipped a CD he apparently had already selected into the player. Expecting South, Anselm got North. He could scarcely believe his ears, but there it was: Out of the Bose streamed the restless, brooding opening of the orchestral "Prelude and Liebestod" from Wagner's *Tristan and Isolde*, perhaps the most erotically passionate piece of music ever written. Anselm, who knew the piece from first chord to last from countless hearings since childhood, was transfixed, less by Wagner's genius in this instance than by the fact that the father, voluntarily and without coaxing, had put on *the son's* music, giving it, at least on that day, precedence over his beloved Puccini. What volumes that simple little gesture spoke to his son. He knew his father wasn't being polite or kind; such a motive in that context would have been foreign to the texture of their monkeyshine relationship. No, it was because his father had had an awakening, an epiphany; he had actually *heard*, as opposed to tolerated, Wagner's music for the first time in his life. During an errant, possibly even accidental, playing of the "Liebestod," some phrase or patch of musical text must have slipped past Archie's inner censor, almost unconsciously beguiling him—a seed that, once planted, would, with repeated, increasingly compulsive hearings, froth up into a love potion. And this narcotic draught would, in turn and over time, cause the whole mystical fabric of the "Liebestod" to unravel and lay itself at his feet, a boon to his soul forever.

Anselm now sat there sipping the last of his Asbach, totally in awe of this presumed event in his father's recent interior life, an event at which he hadn't even been present, but to the effects of which he was now witness. There smiling before him, his head resting on his elbow on the rolltop desk, was his father, swept away by the irresistible flow of the music—obviously a happy man, enjoying the heady freedom that follows from seeing through one's own petty biases. Anselm was happy for his father, even grateful, for giving expression to something that happens only too rarely in life. Truth be told, he was even a little jealous.

They both listened in total silence. Finally, as the violins swelled and died away at the music's end, Anselm waited a respectful moment and then spoke to his father amiably, though with a note of astonishment in his voice: "Dad, I don't get it. Wagner? Wagner, the German beast? What gives? Are we changing sides here in our little North-South competition. I mean, come on! *Wagner*? 'Too heavy ... bombastic ... self-important ... Germanic.' Remember? Remember, Dad?"

Archie just sat there looking at his son, beaming with pride and gratitude, and spoke not a word. Finally, he slowly lifted his head from his hand, sat up straight and, closing his eyes, moved his head from side to side with the utmost solemnity, unmistakably communicating, "No. That's all rubbish. I see it differently now."

He was about to pour a second shot of Asbach when the bottom fell out once again. This time Anselm descended still sitting in his chair, even if the latter did mysteriously disappear by the time he approached the bardo realm. Before he knew it, he was past that and standing in a vast, dark, indoor space surrounded by young people, couples, dancing to music that amounted to little more than a steady pulsebeat—boom-chick, boom-chick, boom-chick, ad infinitum. As if they were all hooked up to somebody on life support. The only lighting was provided by multicolor strobes that panned up, down and all around the crowd, lighting up sweat-glistening faces in ghostly flashes, everyone in a frenzy of hypnotic rhythm, gyrating, shaking, spinning, twerking, sweating through their shirts, blouses and summer shorts, and blissfully freed, for the moment at least, from the boredom of college or work. It might have been spring break in Virginia Beach or Fort Lauderdale or La Jolla. He couldn't tell.

All seemed well until a strange kind of staccato interference—static, perhaps— began to throw the monotonous beat off by nanoseconds. People danced through it in the expectation that it would smooth itself out, but it didn't; on the contrary, the noise increased in volume and frequency until all were forced to revise their interpretations of its source in line with more sinister possibilities. A moment later, when the shouts and shrieks began coming from that part of the room where the entrance was located, all interpretations instantly coalesced into one: gunfire. Pandemonium was immediate, Anselm alone remaining unaffected; he simply stood there in the middle of it all watching the dancers as they rushed to the corner opposite the sound of the shots. He was present, he was *in* it, but not *of* it; he had enough awareness to recognize that his primary function in this moment, and throughout this whole experience, was to witness.

And witness he did: a writhing mass of bodies, some two hundred young people, pushing, crushing those up against the steel-armored, emergency-exit double doors, which were, as fate would have it, locked from both inside and outside, leaving those up against the doors in the throes of suffocation and those crushing them in a panic oblivious to all concern for anyone but self. Men punched women or flung them aside in an effort to get a step closer to the doors that must surely swing open any second now. Women were no less barbaric: One who wore a dress and heels took off her shoe and began hammering the pointy heel into the skull of a young girl in shorts and tank top in a fever to get past her. Both of them were soon sodden with blood. The more agile in the mob climbed up the backs of others, thinking to take the only express route to the doors physically available, but only ended up crawling up the backs of other, equally agile types, who had had the same idea a moment earlier. Pity the poor souls suffocating underneath all this surface drama, the ones nearest the damnably unforgiving doors, having now to contend with both vertical and horizontal crushes. Many had already given up, simply allowing the mob to move them about willy-nilly without resistance. And some had, by now, succumbed to the ultimate non-resistance.

Meanwhile, during this bedlam at one end of the room, shots were ringing out from the other end, in no particular direction and in all directions at once, not individual shots but the rapid-fire clusters of an automatic weapon, which made the event maximally terrifying. A bevy of shots took out a large strobe-light fixture from a sort of carousel attached to the ceiling above the rioters, red, yellow and blue shards of glass showering down upon them, heaping yet another "fresh hell" onto the one already tormenting them. One shard landed on the head of a girl wearing a garland of flowers who stood dithering on the periphery of the mob, seemingly more terrified by *it* than by the shots coming at her from behind. The hot glass lodged momentarily between her blond hair and the floral netting, just long enough to cause the plastic roses in the rear arc of the garland to catch fire. Anselm, forgetting his role as a non-participating witness, instinctively rushed towards the girl, who was screaming for help and frantically swinging her flaming head every which way. He got to her and, in one deft wave of his arm, swept the fiery garland off her head and onto a nearby tabletop. Then he darted over to another table, ripped off its cloth covering and turned back towards the girl to put out her flaming hair. But instantly he knew this move would be futile as just then the floor gave way beneath him and he knew his time there was over. As he began to drop, he did, however, barely manage to toss the cloth underhanded to the girl in need and catch a glimpse of the scorched garland flowers lying on the nearby table. There was something about those flowers, but now was not the time …

This time, as his fall again slows upon his passage through the bardo realm and his chains again materialize, he can discern in the bardo light the vague figure of a man in bushy black hat and uniform, standing at attention, his rifle perched on his shoulder, guarding God knows what, perhaps thirty paces off his axis of descent. He wants desperately to ask the man about his chains and just generally engage him in a Q and A exchange, but his mind is suddenly possessed by a very old joke, the one in which a window washer high up on a skyscraper falls from his scaffold. As he passes an open window on the seventy-fifth floor on his way down, an office worker inside happens to turn his way and asks, "How's it going?", and the falling worker answers, "So far, so gooooood." By the time Anselm clears his mind of the sadly yet hilariously appropriate joke, alas, it is too late for a Q and A of any kind, as he is now on the radius beneath the bardo and again falling rapidly.

Then a funny thing happens. (Yes, I'm aware of the absurdity of that statement in a book like this.) His fall slows and stops and then begins a slow rise back up to the bardo realm. When he gets to eye level with the uniformed guard, he stops, suspended in air and feeling quite woozy. (For some reason, it occurs to him that the axis between the guard's eyes and his own is a perfectly horizontal line bisecting the vertical plumbline of the shaft.) Within a moment he falls asleep and commences to dream. He is in the arms of his beloved Tina, she of the caramel hair and sweet ruby lips. They're lying, bodies entwined, on a patch of green in the middle of her father's arborium. Between full, flush, open-mouthed kisses that intensify the mounting pressure, from head to toe, of Eros, she whispers in his ear the "sweet nothings" that are the intoxicating currency of Atlantis: "Stay close to me, Anselm … Stay true … Do not waver now that the goal is almost in sight … Remember, though, the closer you come, the more subtle and dangerous the delusions that block your path. These are the frantic phantasms of our enemy who fears your escaping her clutches. Soon you will have me and we'll retire to a sumptuous villa on the sunny shores of the Aegean, or some equally lovely spot (wherever Atlantis is building these days) … Think of the pleasure, the delight, the pure joy of life!" And just as Anselm bends over her, hungry for her lips, he suddenly sees he is holding, not Tina, but Ronnie, his other paramour. But his senses are by now so inflamed that he just can't be bothered fretting over the exchange of identities. He'll deal with the issue later. Right now he wants Woman! He breathes in her lustrous blond hair with its subtle but distinct scent of patchouli, a fragrance that has always acted on him like an aphrodisiac of steroidal power. This is Ronnie, the girl who wants him, along with the niveau of social life his career promises, and is prepared to do whatever it takes to get him, not excluding opening her lean and lissom legs here and now. But as he looks down upon her supine body, he is amazed to see the commencing of a rapid but exquisitely subtle series of transformations of female face and hair, back and forth between blond and caramel, between mythic and mundane girls—faces, lips, eyes, hair, breath. Who is who? Whom does he love? Are they both real, or is one an idealized, or earthbound, version of the other? What should he think? How should he act?

As he frets frantically over these imponderable questions, he loses touch with the body, both hers and his own, and falls into a swoon, which puts him back to sleep. (Wasn't he already sleeping?) When he opens his eyes, he finds them focused squarely on the guard, still some thirty paces away. Immediately he knows what he wants to ask: "Tell me, you work here, so you must know something about the place. Why am I in these two chains? They don't seem to serve any function so ... what's the point?"

The guard switches smartly to an order-arms stance and answers, "The chains are intended as a backup system in case the principle of gravity should fail."

VIGIL 17

The Prophesy Is Fulfilled

As the season moved into the flaming foliage of Fall, Anselm was feeling less and less like a solid citizen of the earth (and even less than that of greater metropolitan New Jersey-New York), so bewitched and beguiled was he by all the fantastic occurrences of late. He had lost touch with his friends and looked forward every morning only to the witching hour, which for him was high noon, when the Gates of Paradise on the Hudson would once again be thrown open. And yet, most strange, every now and then he would find himself thinking about the nubile Ronnie. Several times a day, in fact, she would wend her way into his thoughts, linger there for a while in various attires—dresses, gowns, shorts, jeans, nothing—lying under him or bending over him, planting a tender kiss or unleashing a French one—and finally recede from his inner theater of the body-mind with promises of many encores to come. The faintest essence of imagined patchouli would linger after her, delivering him up to paroxysms of unalloyed bliss.

Sometimes her mental presence would be more insistent, intrusive even, than charming or alluring: She might, for example, invade his thoughts as he was drifting off to sleep, during that moment called by the psychologists "hypnagogic," when, in the mysterious zone between waking and sleeping, one's characteristic defenses have been lowered and one becomes emotionally vulnerable. More than once she seemed almost to appear standing at the foot of his bed, abject and tearful, declaring her undying love for him and her profound concern over his involvement with the dark, mysterious forces haunting the Archivist's house. On these occasions he would feel nothing less than chained to her, so powerful could her beseeching presence be. For example, in the night following Tina's unveiling of herself to him in serpentine form and her subsequent revelation, in her familiar human form, of her family's history, Ronnie appeared to him with such incandescent sensual vividness—eyes moist with tears, blond hair wickedly swept over her left eye, firm yet supple breasts yearning to be fondled—that he fell asleep believing she had actually been there physically.

It wasn't until he awoke the next morning and drank his coffee that he arrived at the view that Ronnie's presence had merely been a dream, an especially pellucid one to be sure, but a dream nonetheless. But why was he dreaming so often, so intensely, of Ronnie? The question bedeviled him, confusing and upsetting him. Certainly he was attracted to her, and very much so sexually, but, on the other hand, there was no question that Tina was the light of his life, his true love in every sense, his raison d'etre, all the woman he needed and then some. Even logically, he thought, he should feel no strong pull towards Ronnie: As alluring as she was, she was not unlike a dozen other girls he had known and found beautiful but never seriously considered as a possible mate, a lifelong partner. He felt like a cluster of metal shavings being pulled towards a magnet, away from his heart's desire. What to do?

To shake off these ruminations and clear his head, he grabbed his jacket and went out for a walk, south along Kennedy Boulevard. As he was passing by the entrance to Paul

Manheim's high-rise, he ran into the man himself, on his way home with a bag of goodies from the bakery.

"Well, well, look who it is! My dear friend! ... Anselm, where have you been keeping yourself these days? Veronica is positively bereft over the loss of her musical duet partner," Manheim said, propping up his large white bag of rolls and pastries. This was his casual, oblique way of signaling to Anselm that his daughter really was pining for him. She hadn't been out of the apartment in days, he complained; indeed, she had hardly left her room. The few times he had stuck his head in her room to inquire after her, he found her sitting up in bed in her robe and pajamas, knees drawn, staring intently into the face of her cell phone.

"Ah, well, young girls on the cusp of adulthood," he concluded. "Who understands them? As Freud put it, *Girls! What the hell do they want?*"

"Women," Anselm corrected.

"Women? What about them?"

"What do *women* want?"

"How the hell should I know? I'm just a poor widower trying to raise two daughters. Why do you ask?"

"No, no, I mean ... er, never mind ... Anyway, it's been good seeing you, Paul," Anselm said, trying to ease his way out of the encounter. But Manheim was having none of it.

"Oh, no you don't!" he chortled, wrapping his free arm around his friend's shoulder with the ferocity of a tentacle and practically dragging him to the double-glass-door entrance. "You're coming with me! Branden is stopping by this afternoon, so it'll be a fine occasion for us all to catch up and hoist a few. I've got a fresh bottle of Hennessy that's itching to be cracked ... Come on now, and don't even think of refusing."

For the most part, Anselm wasn't interested, but he let his friend cajole him into agreeing, for a part of him, a part on the dark side, was interested, in an egotistical, schadenfreude sense, in seeing how Ronnie would react to his appearance. Would she be sad? Would her sadness betray itself with longing glances towards him? Would she attempt to sit near him, or possibly even abscond with him to her room?

As they entered the lobby, they saw a small group of people, staff and residents, clustered around the elevator, whose door was open, exposing its forbidding dark maw. Inquiring of an acquaintance who lived on the same floor, an elderly woman pressing a tiny toy poodle to her flapcake bosom, an absurd looking animal with a football-sized tuft of white fur sitting on top of its head, Manheim was told that there had been an accident: Another resident, a young graduate student at St. Peter's U. down the boulevard, had inadvertently stepped into the open shaft and fallen one floor to its bottom. He had been chatting with the concierge when the elevator door opened and not noticed that there was no conveyance there. An electrical fluke, but one with potentially deadly consequences. The astonishing thing, however, was that, when they had finally gotten him up and out of there, the young man was found to be totally uninjured, not a scratch on him, just a smear of grease on his left cheek and across the front of his beige cashmere sweater. All were in awe of the "miracle," but the fellow himself just took it in stride, even quipping that, "I could swear the laws of gravity were suspended just as I was about to hit bottom. I seemed to slow down about a foot above ground zero and was, somehow, gently lowered the rest of the way, just as if I were in an elevator … Hell of a thing!"

Manheim and Anselm looked at each other in wonderment, the latter especially so since the incident struck a mysterious chord of familiarity in him, an eerie intimacy, though without any rhyme or reason he could fathom. A shudder passed through him. They climbed the stairs to Manheim's apartment on the third floor, Anselm unable to shake off entirely the weirdness of the incident, nor the feeling that there was, in Jung's sense, some element of synchronicity embedded in it. But what, exactly? *The longer I live, the less sense the world makes. But at least it's not boring. Actually, I could stand a little boredom right about now!*

When they got to the apartment door, Manheim opened it with his key, shouting, "Oh, Veronica! Come see who I found! We may just be enjoying a duet today, a bit of *West Side Story* perhaps—'There's a Place for Us' or possibly even 'Tonight.' That's my personal favorite." As Manheim said this, he was occupied with putting away his hat, coat and gloves in the hall closet; at the same time, Anselm, who stood just in front of him facing the living room, was astonished, and delighted, to lay eyes on Veronica as she came out of her room, a vision of elegance, dressed splendidly in a snug gray pencil skirt, tucked-in white blouse and low-heel black pumps. Her blonde bangs swept seductively past her left eye, and as she came right up to Anselm without hesitation and looked him straight in the eye, lips ever so slightly mock-pouting as if to scold him for his extended absence, the young man was so overcome that, momentarily regressing to his juvenile clumsiness, he backed up hard into the coffee table, knocking Ronnie's handbag from the table onto the rug. Out of the bag spilled some of its contents, including her cell phone.

"My goodness, girl, why such sartorial splendor? One would think you were *expect*ing our friend's visit!" quipped her father, who for once was saying far more than he knew. Meanwhile, while Manheim excused himself, retiring briefly to his study to write an email, Anselm was crouched down on the rug retrieving Ronnie's things. Having tucked all of them back into the bag except the phone, he hesitated as he held the device in front of him, perhaps enchanted with its peculiar sheen. As he stood up staring into its screen, Ronnie came up quietly behind him and rested her chin on his left shoulder, the shoulder of the arm holding the phone, and just stared into it with him. He could feel her sweet breath as it grazed his cheek.

Then suddenly all manner of chaotic images, snapshots of recent history, began to appear on the phone's screen, and Anselm soon felt himself being wrenched into an internal civil war—Archivist Lindhurst holding court at Mitzi's, Tina playing her violin, the little green snake spiraling down the tree trunk, the Edenic garden and its destruction by fire, and on and on. Anselm felt himself caught in the middle of it all, between the devil and the deep blue sea, as it were. Who should he turn to? What, or who, was his heart's desire? Lowering the phone as if in self-protection, he just stood there, his other hand covering his brow, trying not to think at all, sensing that his own mental efforts to escape his plight would only get him into deeper trouble. Finally, all the inner chaos coalesced into the solid conclusion that it was Ronnie he loved, always had been, Ronnie and only Ronnie, and that even yesterday the figure who appeared to him in the blue room had been Ronnie and that the fantastic saga of the marriage of the salamander to the green snake was something that he himself had dreamed up and written and had in no way been told to him. He was aghast at his own mental aberrations of late, fearing that they bordered on the pathological, the hallucinatory. Was he going mad without knowing it? Did a madman ever know he was one? How could he know, living like a recluse as he had been since the summer? There was no one around to tell him if he was spinning off course.

At length, needing some convenient way of living with his own profound doubts about what was real, he forced himself to rationalize it all, attributing his recent "eccentricities" to the exalted state his love for Ronnie had produced in him, and, no less, to his work in Lindhurst's blue room whose atmosphere was constantly suffused with one exotic, and possibly narcotic, fragrance or another. He had to laugh at his own gullibility, a lethal weakness that had led him to fall in love with a green snake and to regard a distinguished archivist as a salamander. What nonsense!

"Yes! Yes!" he rejoiced inwardly. "It's Ronnie and no one else but!" As he turned around to affirm this new hard-won clarity of mind with a victorious fist-pump into the air, he almost clipped the poor girl on the chin; she had been standing close behind him waiting patiently for him to come around and shower her with tender attentions and loving gestures. He looked into her blue eyes, alight with love and longing. She sighed as their lips came spontaneously together, and Anselm felt as if his victory over his own immature nature had been indelibly sealed with a kiss. What I merely fantasized yesterday has become reality for me today, he thought with the confidence of a man who has finally found himself and could now stand on his own two feet.

"I want to send you into paroxysms of unalloyed ecstasy," he whispered in her ear with more than a hint of lechery in his tone.

"Ouu, I love it when you talk dirty, Professor MacGregor" she whispered back. "And will you marry me when you become a professor?" she asked, pressing her white blouse with its voluptuous contents softly but firmly to his chest.

"The black dragon take me if I don't!" he blurted out, and immediately felt like a fool. The black dragon? Where on God's earth did that come from?

Just then, Manheim came back in carrying a handsome amber bottle. "Voilà!" he chirped. "Feast your eyes, my friend," he said, holding the bottle of expensive cognac out to Anselm, who was surprised to see an Irish name on a bottle of French cognac. "Hennessy!" he read aloud, smiling, as Ronnie furtively cupped his left rear cheek with her dainty hand. *Who needs booze?* he thought happily.

"But first, lunch," said Mannheim. "I'm afraid you're stuck with potluck, Anselm. Soup and sandwich, with pastries and coffee for dessert." *If he only knew what I usually have for lunch—that is, when I have lunch—he wouldn't speak so modestly of his own menu* thought Anselm. They all three repaired to the dining area and took their seats, as Sally, off school for Columbus Day, brought in a large tureen of lentil soup and a platter of cold cuts, assorted cheeses and sliced bread. (It was a dining "area," not a walled room as such, in accord with the current vogue of interior living spaces with "flow." Walls divide, space brings together, bathrooms excepted—usually.)

"Harold Branden will be joining us later for coffee," added Manheim. At this Anselm's spirits sank a bit. Hoping to steal some choice one-on-one time with Ronnie, "the more the merrier" wasn't what he was looking for. Still, he was fond of Branden, and if he had to be a monk that afternoon, Branden was the man to be it with.

Just then, it struck him like a bolt of lightning that it was a weekday and he had completely forgotten about work. How could he have? How on earth was that possible? "Paul, forgive me, please, but it seems work completely slipped my mind! This is a workday! I just can't believe I ..." he stammered as he fumbled and stumbled around looking for his jacket. "I'm so sorry to have to reneg on your splendid lunch, and the wonderful company and all ..."

"Uh, *excusez-moi, mon ami,*" Manheim retorted, holding out his wrist before Anselm's eyes, the wrist displaying a cheap Rolex replica that said 12:30 pm. "I'm afraid that ship has sailed. I doubt the old man will even let you in at this point. You might as well write off today and enjoy yourself?"

Anselm thought for a moment and quickly came to see the wisdom of his friend's point of view. What am I so worried about, he asked himself. It's just another day of tedium copying a damned foreign language, assuming it even *is* a language. I've been working hard lately and I think I'm entitled to a day off. A mental health day. Comfortable with his decision, he turned his attention to the lovely Ronnie, who was seated on his right and already resting her open left hand on his right thigh. The hand, *sub mensa,* was heading north by northeast. The further up his leg it travelled, the surer he was that he had made the right call. By the time it reached what is known in football as "the red zone," he was overflowing with silent gratitude not only for the sexual diversion itself but, even more, for the freedom from torturous delusion it seemed to promise. It was time to "partay!"

Almost as if in response to this, as it were on cue, Harold Branden arrived for coffee carrying a bottle in a discrete brown paper bag. He doffed the bag and proudly held up a fifth of Drambuie, a liqueur made up of scotch and honey, which, so he'd been told by friends who were discerning drinkers, was the perfect complement to any good cognac. One poured two parts Hennessy and one part Drambuie into a snifter glass and "*Ecco!*" (Branden preferred Italian to French), one had oneself a serious cocktail called a Rusty Nail, "serious" in the sense that one Rusty Nail was about equivalent to two Manhattans in potency. Sip, don't gulp!

Needless to say, the company didn't linger long over coffee and dessert. The table was swiftly cleared, the two handsome bottles were placed side by side in its center, encircled by snifters, and the four of them, Sally being dismissed, resumed their seats with great expectations. Branden, as the one in the know about Rusty Nails, did the honors, filling about a quarter of each glass with the concoction and handing it out. Notwithstanding her tender age, Ronnie was included among the recipients, this in keeping with her father's "enlightened" European attitude towards the consumption of spirits, which regarded them, within reasonable limits, as a normal part of a child's upbringing. "But absolutely no more than one. Understood, sweetheart? … This is a potent cocktail," he cautioned, as Branden handed her a glass containing the golden nectar. She eyed, first the glass in front of her, and then Anselm, as if that gesture were the unspoken language of eros. Anselm smiled at her and gave a conspiratorial wink.

"So, tell us, Harold. What have you been up to lately?" Mannheim asked his friend. "Oh, right now it's the annual Fall post-midterm fiasco," he replied, "with the usual five percent of failing students begging, bullying or bribing us not to send warning letters home to their parents."

"Oh, that must be annoying," Mannheim sympathized.

"I'm for doing away with grades entirely!" Veronica interrupted. "After all, who do they really help? Only students' future employers, I think. They're of no benefit to the kids themselves so far as I can see; all they do is turn the A-students into intellectual narcissists and the flunkies into self-hating drones," she asserted, with an edge in her voice aided in no small measure by the two sips of her drink she had already taken.

"Now, now, dear daughter. We don't want to put our friend in the position of having to defend a system of evaluation that's as old as formal education itself, do we?" the father intervened.

"Oh, please, Paul, I don't mind it at all," Branden hastened to offer. "In fact, to an extent I even share Veronica's point of view. I like very much the concept of the alternative university, where students get to devise their own curriculum and receive detailed written evaluations at the end of a course instead of grades. Bard College does it that way, if I'm not mistaken. And do you know who else holds such a radical liberal view? None other than our mutual acquaintance, John Lindhurst. I was sitting with him at Mitzi's the other day, and he was telling me how he has argued with the Stoneham administration and trustees for years over the issue of grades. He insists that ubiquitous grade inflation has made them worthless, that a "B" is really a "C" these days, if not indeed a "D," and that "F's" on student transcripts are as scarce as honest politicians."

Anselm was charmed, and more than that, by the sudden appearance of Ronnie's opinionated tongue, powerfully barbed and winged as it happily turned out to be; this was a side of her he had rarely seen, emancipated no doubt by the gift of temporary fluency provided by Hennessy and Co. For him it added yet another facet to her already high desirability.

Charmed as he was, however, Anselm did not actively participate in the conversation himself; he merely sat there, sipping his Rusty Nail. This was not because he wasn't interested in the subject, but because he was finding, as he began to feel tipsy, that the mental Pandora's box he thought he had shut tightly earlier that evening was beginning to rattle, and he didn't like that at all. The matter was settled, he told himself. God, let it *stay* settled!

But the dreary prospect of yet another battle in an internal civil war in which he had just declared victory nettled him profoundly, and, so it seemed, the others as well, as if by osmosis, for, with the second round of the golden elixir, everyone's dander would have seemed to a fly on the wall to have risen noticeably. And none more than Ronnie's, for, when her father excused himself for a bathroom break, she immediately fell upon Branden, wheedling him and, finally, trying to strong-arm him into pouring her another drink. Poor Branden, torn between his self-assigned role as the girl's de facto guardian during her father's brief absence and his own libido, which was decidedly more permissive, finally gave in, resentful towards her for putting him in such a bind. But then, when Ronnie practically chugged the drink, he could not hold back any longer: "Ronnie, what's the matter with you? Are you in your right mind? You'll find yourself on the floor in less than ten minutes. And who do you think will get the blame for it? Huh? Who? Certainly not Anselm!"

"Hey, easy there, Harold! Easy!" the wronged young man chided. "Who made you *almus pater* all of a sudden? Ronnie's her own person. She's eighteen and has a level head on her shoulders. I'm okay with letting her take the lead in—"

"—Yeah! You see? There you go! The voice of reason! Cool it, will you, Harold!" Ronnie practically shouted, bulldozing her way into the exchange and already making Anselm a tad regretful of his noble defense of her maturity. "Anyway," she went on, "I *had* to chug the drink, Howard. Don't you see? I couldn't let my father come back and see me with a full glass. He saw me finish the *first one*." Then, bursting into hysterical laughter for getting Branden's first name wrong, she made a mock apology, unable to keep a straight face during it: "Please forgive me, *Ha-rold!* Ha ha. I don't know whatever could've made me think of you as a 'Howard'; all the Howards I've ever known were, *ha ha*, complete—OW!" She was abruptly cut short by the pain of a severe pinching of her right underthigh, compliments of the Voice of Reason. She shrieked, alternating between squeals of pain and hysterical laughter, which profoundly confused her father who was just returning from the privy.

"Apparently I've missed something of considerable amusement, and mirth," he said in his overblown style, which would always escalate to nothing less than baroque whenever something made him feel uneasy. For it was too late in the discussion for mediation by a neutral party. The triangular exchange was already gathering an alcohol-fueled momentum of its own, one that excluded Paul Manheim and would, in fact, leave him in the end as its (metaphorically) most bloodied victim.

"Welcome back, Paul!" Branden bleated, in a tone that was friendly enough but at a volume that was at least twice his normal one, which prickled the hair on the nape of Manheim's neck. "We were just comparing 'Great Professors I Have Known and Loved,'" Branden dissembled, adroitly changing the subject, "and I was offering our friend the Archivist for consideration, who is certainly one of the oddest, most mystifying academic birds I have ever come across, wouldn't you—"

"—That, my friend," Anselm interrupted in a tone of competing volume, "is because the Archivist is, in actuality, not a bird at all but a salamander who unfortunately let his anger get the better of him and laid waste the garden of Phosphorus, the Prince of Spirits, all because the green snake got away from him."

"What are you ... I don't ..." Manheim stammered, the picture of befuddlement.

"That's right, that's right!" Anselm hissed at him, as if the latter had just fired a cannonball at him. "That's why he is now forced to be an archivist here on earth, specifically a householder in Hoboken—for his three daughters, you see, who themselves are wee little gold-green snakes who play the violin most enchantingly and, like the mythical sirens themselves, seduce young men like me."

"Anselm! Anselm!" the Assistant Principle cried out, "Did a synapse just go dead in your head? What in the name of heaven are you babbling on about?"

"Oh, he's right, Paul, he's right!" the registrar interjected, all fear of ridicule gone now, carried off by the last sip of the second Rusty Nail. "That man—our esteemed Archivist—*is*, in fact, a goddamned salamander," he announced, pointing his thumb in the general direction of Hoboken, "and he's got this creepy way of giving you a light by snapping his fingers. The son of a bitch could set you on fire if he wanted to! Burn you to a crisp! ... I'm telling you, everything Anselm just said is true, and anybody who denies it is my enemy!" And with that the registrar hammered the table so hard with his fist that the glasses jangled, the registrar's own falling over, thankfully empty.

"Harold, for Christ's sake! What on earth is the matter with you? Have you gone non compos mentis, too?" Manheim shouted at him. "This is all your doing, Anselm! You've infected everyone around here with your insidious delusions!" he yawped, turning viciously on the young man.

"Oh, foo, Manheim!" Anselm answered. "You're nothing but a big gasbag, a stuffed shirt, who never met a four-syllable word he didn't prefer to a two." The remark was so on point, so apt, that Ronnie and Branden only managed to half-suppress a guffaw.

Manheim was mortified.

"How dare you!" he hissed. "Calling me, of all people, pompous ... grandiloquent ... linguistically profligate! Deeply insulting words from a ... a perfidious popinjay like yourself!" he railed, the last phrase ejecting an unsightly bit of spittle onto his stuffed shirt. "Why, you're daft! That's all there is to it. You're totally mad!" he concluded.

"That's because he's got the old woman on his back!" Branden brayed.

"Yeah, I'm afraid the old girl is powerful," Anselm agreed, "even though she comes from humble origins—her old man nothing more than a shabby feather duster, her mom a mangy beetroot … She gets most of her power from all those hostile creatures around her, toxic lowlifes that they are."

"That," Ronnie suddenly cried out with fire in her eyes, "is a despicable slander! Old Lisa is a wise woman, and her black cat, far from being a 'toxic lowlife,' as you call him, is really a highly cultured young man with elegant manners—her first cousin, in fact."

"Hey! Tell me, Ans!?" Branden practically bawled, having momentarily fallen into a stupor of drunken reflection. "How can that salamander eat anything without singeing his beard and going up in flames? Will you tell me that, please?"

"Now that's a stupid question, even for you, How-, uh … Harold," Anselm replied all smug and besotted. "Obviously, whenever he eats, he assumes his human form. The same goes for his daughter Tina, or 'Serpentina,' as she's called when she's in serpentine form. But either way, snake or sylph, she loves me because I have a genuine poetic disposition and have gazed deeply into her serpentine eyes."

"Yes! Eyes that the cat will scratch right out of her head," shouted Ronnie, red-faced with anger.

"Oh my God! The verkakte salamander has bewitched them all—all three of them!" the Assistant Principal roared in a fit of rage. Then, in the shock of self-reflection, "Wait a minute! What am I saying? Am I in a madhouse? Have I too gone mad? I can't believe I'm beginning to spout this insane drivel myself! Yep, that's it! I'm crazy too! … Me too!" And with that the Assistant Principal chugged the rest of his second Rusty Nail—Branden and Anselm were already working on their third—and, winding up like a baseball pitcher, flung the empty glass full speed against the stone hearth clear across the room, shattering it over a three-foot radius. Folding his arms, he stood there beaming with pride, as if that was the most liberating act he had performed since college days.

Not to be outdone, Branden emptied the last inch of cognac from the bottle into his glass and heaved the former in the general direction of the stone hearth. But, alas, he was not the control pitcher his friend was and overshot his mark, the bottle crashing into an unassuming turquoise ceramic cremation urn sitting on the mantle shelf above the hearth—an urn containing the ashes of Paul Manheim's deceased wife—smashing, first the urn, and then itself, to pieces, the entire mess of glass, ceramic and dust now littering the stone floor in front of the hearth. "Long live the salamander! ... Down with the old woman! ... Down with her! ... Smash the spy phone! ... Hack that fucking cat's eyes out! ... Attack, birds, attack! ... Banzai!!!" Such cacophony, and worse, shrieked and howled by the three men in their drunken debauch, scared the bejesus out of little Sally, who had been eavesdropping nearby; she ran off to her room whimpering. Ronnie, herself dazed by the hostile barrage, retreated to the sofa where she lay down to stop the room from spinning. Manheim would not notice that his wife was all over the place until the following morning.

Just then, at the height of this bedlam, the doorbell rang and, without waiting to be admitted, in walked a little man in a gray, double-breasted trench coat. He wore thick, horn-rimmed glasses on his huge curved beak of a nose and on his head sat a little Sam Spade fedora. He carried himself with an unmistakable gravitas.

"Good evening," the little man said in a slightly gravelly voice, "I was told I might find the student Anselm MacGregor here."

Anselm raised his hand very tentatively.

"Ah, yes," the man nodded, "I extend to you friendly greetings from Archivist Lindhurst. I'm to tell you he waited in vain today for you to show up at work. He requests that you make every effort to be there tomorrow, at the appointed hour."

And with that the little man turned, walked to the door and let himself out. As he left, they could all clearly see that this serious fellow wasn't a man at all, but a gray parrot. Manheim and Branden stood there looking at each other, stupefied. Then they exploded into fits of hysterical laughter that rattled the chandelier. Between waves of guffaws, one could hear, just barely, Ronnie, moaning and weeping on the sofa. As for Anselm, he had been struck by terror on first sight of the "little man," whom he instantly recognized as the Archivist's assistant. In a fit of panic he ran out the door and down the two flights of stairs into the street, and just kept running, not *to* any destination, just *away from there.*

After a while, he slowed his pace down to a jog, and, finally, a brisk walk. He walked for hours, well into the night, all around the city's central area, from McGinley Square to Journal Square, then west along the boulevard to Sip Avenue, then further west to West Side Avenue, and, finally, south to Manheim's street. He walked that circle twice before caving in, physically and emotionally, and heading straight to his little flat on West Side, where he ended up sober as a judge. It was all intended to dispel (read: run away from) the chimaeras unleashed by the bespectacled parrot, in essence, his entire fantastic experience with Tina and her wizardly father. By the time he reached his flat, he did feel some measure of control over it all, but it was like the tentative sort of control one feels when trying to hold a gas-filled beach ball under ocean water, a fragile control aided by emotional exhaustion and sure to dissipate after a good, long sleep.

He crawled into bed, pulling the covers up over his head and, minutes later, when he peeked out from under them, he saw Ronnie sitting at the foot of his bed, smiling.

"Sweetie, in your inebriated state at my place, you gave me such a scare," she purred. "You all did, even Daddy, who normally couldn't scare a crow. Please, I beg you, be on guard at work against all the bogies and bugbears the Archivist has in his conjuror's arsenal … And now, good night, my dearest," she whispered, planting a tender kiss on his lips.

Anselm reached up to embrace her but grasped only air. He immediately fell asleep and woke up cheerful and invigorated. Eating his breakfast PB and J sandwich, he had a good laugh over all the drunken high jinks of the previous evening, and when his mind turned to Ronnie, he felt the spread of a warm, tingly current of well-being. She alone is the reason I haven't gone completely bonkers, he thought, sipping his coffee. God, for a while there I was like the sorcerer's apprentice—Mickey Mouse trying to bail out the house with a bucket … Well, one thing's for sure: As soon as I get a tenure-track position as a professor, I'll marry Ronnie and be done with it. Snakes and salamanders be damned!

As he entered the Archivist's house at noon and proceeded up the central stairway, he was whistling a tune and feeling no pain. Deciding on such a fine morning to stroll through the greenhouse, he casually scanned the surrounding plant life; it struck him as a quite ordinary penumbra of green, and he wondered how it all could have seemed so exotic, so enchanting, on previous visits. He saw only potted plants, geraniums, myrtle and the like. Instead of the multihued bird life, the magnificent birds of paradise that loved to tease him, there were only a handful of bland brown sparrows fluttering around, making unpleasant, meaningless squawks and shrieks as he passed under them. Even the blue room struck him as a hideous eyesore: He couldn't understand how the garish blue walls and the grotesque trunks of the palm trees jutting out of them with their outsized, misshapen fronds could ever have captivated his fancy for even a moment.

The Archivist came in and looked at Anselm for a moment, an ironic smirk playing about his lips. "Well, my lad, I hope you enjoyed the Hennessy yesterday."

"Oh, yes, that," Anselm replied, a little embarrassed. "The parrot must've—" he began to say, then interrupted himself, for it occurred to him that even the parrot's visit was probably just one of the more hallucinatory features of the general mayhem of the moment.

"No, no, not at all. I was there myself," the Archivist contradicted. "Didn't you see me? The fact is, I could've been seriously injured during all the lunacy you people had got up to. I was sitting in the empty cognac bottle, enjoying the fumes, when the registrar grabbed it for pitching purposes; I got out in the nick of time and hid in the bowl of his pipe, which was in his pants pocket. Otherwise I would've had poor Mrs. Manheim all over me, and I have no magic for that. – Well, carry on, my boy. By the way, I'm paying you for the missed day, since you've been doing such fine work lately."

What a load of malarkey! The old man must be entering his dotage, Anselm thought, as he sat down at his desk to begin his copying assignment for that day. As usual, the Archivist had laid the manuscript out on the right side of the desk next to the air computer. But when Anselm bent over the parchment to study its markings, he was dumbfounded by a sea of strange jottings, lines and squiggles, an utter gobbledygook that gave his eyes no rest no matter where he focused them. My God, it's pure gibberish—how do you transcribe gibberish, he asked himself in mounting anxiety. As he sat back, breathed deeply and took in the manuscript as a whole, it no longer even looked like parchment but more like a richly veined slab of marble or a stone mottled with patches of moss.

Still, he was determined to do his best, and so he sat up erect, intending to move his chair in close for a serious look at the manuscript—which is when his old bugaboo, the clumsiness gremlin, showed up to turn a perfunctory adjustment into a catastrophe. As he raised his haunches, lifting his chair with him, his front thighs inadvertently rammed hard into the lip of the desktop, knocking the priceless "stone parchment" from the desk onto the onyx tile floor surrounding the immediate desk area. There it lay, broken in two! He stood there, gawking at it, aware of having made the very mistake the Archivist had most gravely forbidden. Suddenly blue flashes shot up simultaneously from each of the two pieces, entwining into an indigo braid that made its way ominously up to the ceiling. The higher it rose, the more it also fanned out like the branches of a blue tree, the branches then raining a thick, black vapor down into the room, filling it and totally blotting everything out. Winds of hurricane force came from nowhere, blowing fronds loose from the surrounding palm trees and turning their jutting trunks into enraged, fire-breathing basilisks that clanged their hideous scaly heads together to produce a metallic din intolerable to the human ear. At that point, Anselm was on the floor on his back, pressing his hands to his ears in a futile attempt to protect his hearing. At the same time, cataracts of fire were falling from the maws of the giant serpents towering over him, wrapping him in a kind of flaming cocoon. Then, all at once, a brilliant aureole shone above the field of fire, a radiant light in which the salamander appeared in princely form, wearing his crown and royal raiment. Like a clap of thunder, his voice rang out in fearsome judgment: "Madman! Now you will suffer the punishment for what you have done in your insolent arrogance!"

Such were the withering words of despair Anselm was forced to hear before losing consciousness. The streams of fire from above continued to encircle him, forming something around his body that felt, oddly, not like fire at all, but its opposite, a hard, ice-cold mass. And as he became more aware of this hard surface congealing around him and confining him ever more narrowly, his thought process finally stalled and he passed out. When he woke up, he found that he could barely move. He felt as if enveloped by a diamond-hard gloss, against which he kept knocking whenever he tried to move a hand or a foot. – Alas! He was sitting in a hermetically sealed crystal bottle on a shelf in the library of Archivist Lindhurst.

VIGIL 18

Sancho and the Don Have a Few Beers

A hot afternoon at a tavern somewhere in early modern central Spain. Don Q., a knight-errant, and his squire, Sancho P., sit at a round wooden table chewing the fat over a mug of beer.

DON Q.: Anyway, enlighten me, will you, Sancho? Why did you come along on this particular sortie? I didn't ask you to. Besides, I thought you wanted to stay home and get used to milking the new goats.

SANCHO P.: Well, yeah, that was the original idea, but I changed my mind. I just couldn't see you going off and having all this fun all by yourself.

DON Q.: Oh, really! Is that what you think we're doing on these expeditions—having fun?

SANCHO P.: Well, that's what *I'm* doing. With you, of course, it's a very different matter.

DON Q.: How so?

SANCHO P.: Well, you see, you take these crusades very seriously. For you they're missions or quests to battle evil giants, save damsels in distress and, just generally, to right wrongs and fight for social justice and freedom. After all, you're the Man of La Mancha.

DON Q.: I see. And for you, I take it, these things are not serious? Not important?

SANCHO P.: On the contrary. Like you, I see suffering everywhere. Let's just say that I've learned to take a more sanguine, a more optimistic, view of it.

DON Q.: I don't get it. How can you be "cheerful" or "optimistic" about human misery? Wouldn't that make you some kind of mass sadist?

SANCHO P.: It would if I believed the suffering to be real.

DON Q.: So it's not real?

SANCHO P.: Oh, it's real enough all right, but only to those, like yourself, who believe it is. You see, suffering is caused by beliefs, which by definition are not real. They're only sentences in your head which cause you to see the world in a certain way. Drop the sentences, the characteristic way of seeing the world, and you can't help but drop the suffering. Pain may still be there, but suffering, which is a cluster of beliefs about the meaning of the pain, is gone.

DON Q.: Hm. That's an interesting distinction you make between pain and suffering … Tell me, though, how did you come by this more sanguine view of suffering?

The barmaid stops by the table, leaving two full mugs of beer and removing the empties. Sancho waits for her to leave, then continues.

SANCHO P.: Believe me, it wasn't easy. It took years. I did it by reading books about myself, or rather, about the sort of man I wished I were—you know, a knight errant like yourself, a 17th-century superhero, who goes around fighting crime and injustice, all to honor the special lady to whom he's pledged his love—and troth, whatever that is.

DON Q.: Wait a minute. That sounds very much like what I did myself to prepare for my chosen way of life. I read every romance I could get my hands on—El Cid, King Arthur, Perceval, Roland, Tristan ... Are you pulling my leg here, Sancho?

SANCHO P.: Not at all, my lord. It shouldn't surprise you that our lives are so parallel. After all, I've practically been your shadow for years, once you plucked me from my little plot of land to be your squire. – God, was I happy to get away from that harpy of a wife and those screaming little brats! – Anyway, when I joined you, I felt like the Buddha going off into the forest for seclusion. Except that you and I did the reverse—we went out into the wide world to see what we could see and do what we could do. – But, about those romantic adventures ... I have to tell you that they had a quite different effect on me than they had on you.

DON Q.: How's that?

SANCHO P.: Well, over time, they made me a free man, while in your case they constricted and confined you ever more tightly until they became more asphyxiating than that suit of armor of yours, standing over there in the corner.

Warily the Don eyes the armor standing like a mummy in the corner behind Sancho.

DON Q.: I beg your pardon, my friend. That's most presumptuous of you. There's no way you could know how I feel about the armor. I've made it a point never to complain about it. As for the romances, they mean everything to me. They've given my life direction, a goal, an ideal to strive for.

SANCHO P.: Yeah, I know, the impossible dream and all that. Striving to reach the unreachable star.

DON Q.: How dare you stick your tongue in your cheek to make light of it! What's better, what finer, than spending your life in the service of a noble idea? Truth, goodness, beauty? The eternal verities.

SANCHO P.: Only one thing is better, and that's spending it to learn how to drop those ideals, which are only a complex of images and sentences in your head—in other words, beliefs. Desirable, consoling beliefs, to be sure, but beliefs nonetheless, with all the oppressive mental entanglements all beliefs entail. You see, it's not just bad or harmful beliefs we must learn to give up, but the consoling ones as well—beliefs of any stripe. Put it this way: the mechanical function of the mind to make maps of the terrain, in other words, belief formation, must go. The only exception is "beliefs" concerning physical reality, otherwise known as "facts": For example, it takes ten minutes on horseback to reach the blacksmith's shop from here. Whenever anything is added to that bare physical fact, say, "That's too far for me," is when the trouble starts.

DON P.: But how do I get from Madrid to Barcelona without some kind of map?

SANCHO P.: Use a map, of course. Just don't add any kind of judgment about the information the map yields—too long, too far, I'm too tired today, that blacksmith's no good, or: he's terrific, I'll go right over. As harmless as those judgments seem, they are beliefs, opinions, that contribute to creating the ego, the master illusion of individual selfhood, which teaches: *Someone* there is for whom the distance is too long, too far, etc. That makes it not just a distance, but a distance *for me.* Voila, the self!

DON Q.: Assuming, for the sake of argument, that I am persuaded by your view—which I decidedly am not!—how then does one get rid of all the beliefs and opinions that collect so automatically around the so-called simple facts of life, which, I suppose, is just a synonym for "reality?" How does one get to reality directly, without mediation?

SANCHO P.: Remember now, you can't get rid of facts—say, it's raining today—nor, obviously, would you want to. After all, maps—in this case, weather maps—are facts too, and facts are always helpful. But, to answer your question, the way to contact reality directly, to see how things really are, is to see through the fundamental illusion generating all opinions and judgments about how they are, which is the illusion of separate selfhood. Drop the self, the sense of (or belief in) separateness, and beliefs fall away with no effort on your part. Drop the self and see the world! See its interconnectedness.

That interconnectedness, which is, strangely, both empty and full, is what you really are. It's your True Self. So, drop the self and *be* the world!

DON Q.: Okay, drop the self. But you're evading my question, which is *how*?

SANCHO P.: I'm afraid there is no *how*. Any direct attempt to drop the self merely binds one more tightly to it. It's like being told not to think of a pink elephant. Bingo, there it is! A pink elephant. To be ruthlessly honest with you, there is no way, no method, which, even perfectly applied—whatever that means—can guarantee an experience of no-self, or, put positively, World-Self. Many use meditation in one form or another, which may teach you to be calmer and endure the slings and arrows of life with greater equanimity, but no technique can automatically bestow that delicious taste of freedom I call World-Self, which happens when you see, without any doubt, that you are what you are aware of.

DON Q.: Well, that's a hell of a thing! Nothing at all you can do?

SANCHO P.: That's right, but that's only the negative side of it. The positive side is there's nothing you *have to* do. No requirements, strictly speaking. It can happen to anybody at any time, and probably has to most at one time or another, but they were too busy to stop and recognize it. – But there are things that can be helpful, that increase the chances, the odds, to put it crassly, of its happening. Meditation is one of them. It clears the mind and makes room for the spontaneous. My particular form of meditation was to read all those books about heroic knights of old. All the ones you mentioned earlier plus so many more. When I began the reading, the epic hero was an ideal for me, a paragon to be imitated—you know, fake it until you make it. But the more I read, the more I began to see through the image, to see its made-up nature, its artificiality; and the more clearly I saw through it, the less bound I felt by it. Simply put, I saw its emptiness and was free of it. So all those books about my ego-ideal became for me, over time, a mirror in which to inquire honestly about this so-called heroic self of mine, in order, eventually, to drop it.

DON Q.: But, as I said, I read those same books and they had no such effect on me. On the contrary, I found them inspiring. They reinforced my love of knightly nobility and kept me going when my spirit was low. Actually, between you and me, I could never have found the courage to tolerate my own stupidity, had I not read about Perceval's stupidity in failing to ask the king about his mortal wound. If Perceval could be an idiot and still become a great knight, well then, there must be hope for me, right?

SANCHO P.: Ah, but you see, hope is a set of future-oriented *beliefs* that blind you to the emptiness of the ego, and, as such, are the fuel that keeps the illusion of ego going. Similarly, it was your own beliefs about your intelligence: "I'm stupid"— which have nothing to do with your intelligence itself—that chained you to those books, and to the empty ideal they portray ... Your beliefs about yourself are like those windmills you were always tilting at in the low countries. Red herrings all of them. All images of self are red herrings since there is no entity, no substance, that the image represents. That's why we call it empty. Search as long and as hard as you will, there is no self, no individual identity, no ego to be found anywhere. In this respect, the Buddha had it right.

DON Q.: That's all well and good, but it doesn't do much for me, does it? I seem to have completely missed all you claim to have learned from your meditation on knightly epics.

SANCHO P.: No, you haven't.

DON Q.: Haven't what?

SANCHO P.: Missed it.

DON Q.: That's absurd. How can you say that? It completely contradicts the antagonism going on here between us … Your position is "yes," mine is "no."

SANCHO P.: That doesn't matter one whit, you see, because right now we're living in the world of dreams, where there *are* no contradictions. The word "no" has no currency here. "Yes" is "no" and "no" is "yes." Fish is fowl, apples are oranges, and vice versa. But that doesn't mean there's no logic to it. There's a very subtle but powerful logic to it: Call it dynamic logic, or dialectical logic. It's a logic whereby things can turn into each other or evolve out of each other, as is the case with us, with you and me. You see, I am you and you are me: We represent two phases of the same consciousness. It's a little like the philosopher Hegel's example of the slave and the master. (That, by the way, is the Hegel who will not be born for another century and a half.) Over years of service, the slave becomes stronger, while the master, who is constantly waited on and lives a soft life, grows weak. Eventually the slave rebels, the master is overthrown and positions are reversed. Of course, in our case the violence of the rebellion is strictly metaphorical, you see, because my present superiority to you is the result of an evolutionary leap, not a grab for power. It's happened quite naturally in the course of the gradual awakening of the consciousness of the dreamer—you know, the guy "up there" who's dreaming us right now. So you see, I am you in a higher phase, and there's really no need for you anymore (nothing personal—literally). You are the ego, the raft the Buddha leaves on the bank of the river when he reaches the other shore. You served your purpose and served it well, but now it's time for me to take over. He, our dreamer, doesn't know it yet, but soon he will. Soon he will be me, and know it, and you'll be history ... And just who am I? I am nobody, nobody at all.

The barmaid comes back and looks at the Don, pointing at the two nearly empty mugs. The Don looks at Sancho, who nods yes to her.

DON Q.: So, Mr. Nobody At All, if you don't need me anymore, why do you continue to follow me around?

SANCHO P.: Because I have nothing better to do. And perhaps, having once actually *been* you, I feel a certain sense of responsibility for you. I love you the way a grown man continues to love a favorite stuffed toy, say, a raggedy raccoon, from childhood. There's this deep affection that never wanes.

He doesn't just throw the raccoon away; rather he preserves it, protects it from harm, maybe even puts it in a prominent place so he can look at it every once in a while. As I said, I have nothing better to do. I mean that literally: There's nothing better I could be doing.

DON Q.: I'm not sure what you mean by "better."

SANCHO P.: I'm using the word in two senses: First, I mean there's no greater fun for me to have than to follow you around on your whacky adventures. It's a supreme entertainment for me—entertainment in the sense that I just sit back and watch you engage in your antics and am perfectly free to intervene or stay out of them as I choose. (Remember the time in Salamanca when you got all tangled up in that garden hose that fell down over you from a tree branch. You took it as an attack by a giant basilisk. You flailed and flailed with your lance and only got yourself more entangled. Good thing I was nearby. What a hoot that was!) The other sense of "better" is harder to put into words. It's that you're my gateway to manifestation. As Self I'm free to dwell in nothingness—which is its own kind of fun—or to come into the world, i.e., manifest, and act upon it for one reason or another. But my channel for manifestation, at least during this lifetime, is you, i.e., the body/mind complex known as Don Q. Once you die, all bets are off. But as long as you're around, I, as Self, use your consciousness, as ego, to function here. So you see I have "nothing better to do" than that.

DON Q.: But if you *have to* manifest through me, isn't that a limitation of your vaunted freedom?

SANCHO P.: Excellent question, my man. Shows you're paying attention. The answer is, not really. You see, there's nothing more liberating than the experience of being cut loose from a necessity, which is what happens when, in a given instance, I finish acting through you and wish to return to the unmanifest. Just the very thought does it! In a paradoxical sense, it even gives being bound to you as my body/mind channel the most exquisite frisson of freedom since I know I can rescind the bond whenever I want to. It's sort of like the idea of a prison without a prisoner. Since I have realized myself as nothing, I can enter any prison I like and experience it as a glorious summer breeze high on a hill.

DON Q.: So let me get this straight. What you're saying is, ultimately, there's nothing at all.

SANCHO P.: No, not at all.

DON Q.: How confusing you are! You're bandying words with me.

SANCHO P.: Look, obviously there are things all around us, in the world, in the universe. They're *there* in some sense. Call it "materiality" or "physicality," if you like. Call it "particularity" or "discreteness" or "differentiation," if you want to include mental content or ideas as "things." What we don't see is the nothingness that is the other side of the coin. Nothing is also there. Always! Something and nothing need each other exactly the way you and I do, or Self and ego, or truth and falsehood, or beauty and ugliness, and so on down the

250

line of all the pairs of opposites. They constitute each other, can't be conceived without each other. Which gives one pause to suspect they have no independent existence and therefore are, in a profound sense, not real. What I've done is to have gone beyond them, beyond the pairs of empty opposites, to the fertile void that is their source—though even the word "source" is dangerous and can only be used in the most provisional sense. So, strictly speaking, I'm not even *me*, in the sense of a Self that exists in contradistinction to an ego, or a "me" over against a "you." That would be just another definitive, binding identity and therefore less than the plenum. Ultimately, there is only the plenum, the fullness, which is totally empty.

DON Q.: I'm afraid my head is spinning. It's too much to take in all at once. Maybe the beer is making me muddleheaded.

SANCHO P.: Listen, don't worry about it. Don't even think about it. Just leave it alone and let it all marinade in your unconscious. What's important will get in and bear fruit in the fullness of time … Of course, I realize that telling a man like you, a man of books, an intellectual, not to think about something is like telling water over a fire not to boil. So, by all means, go ahead, think about it. But let your thinking remain light, airy, playful, and not become just another grim, jaw-clenched search for Truth. But then, that's precisely the way you operate, isn't it? So, go ahead, be all grim and jaw-clenched about it … Hm. Seems like you're all boxed in, doesn't it? You can't make a move that isn't binding, can you? That can be good, very good, when you realize that not a hair's breadth separates your imprisonment from your release. Freedom is nothing more than necessity conscious of itself.

DON Q.: Enough, Sanchanselmo, enough! I'm feeling unsteady on my chair here. Look, either we stop drinking and continue this, or we drop it and continue drinking.

Sanchanselmo nods to the barmaid to bring another round.

VIGIL 19

Later That Night

"How the hell did I wind up here?" he exclaimed. It was a moderately large hall, lit by bright florescent light, and he was walking along close to the walls. But the instant those words left his mouth, he was rocked by an even greater epiphany: He realized he was dreaming, and knew that he knew this. In the blink of an eye, his awareness shot up in an exponential transcendence of levels, like facing mirrors, causing him to swoon inwardly. All he knew clearly was that he had suddenly been empowered, and that he had been placed, in a lucid state, within precisely this dream in order to use this new-found power to work something out, some cosmic purpose upon which everything—i.e., the cosmos—depended. So he immediately dismissed the temptation to use his power to escape the dream entirely by waking up, which he certainly could have chosen to do, that being one of the perquisites of lucid dreaming, as he well knew. No, he was to remain right within the dream and solve the problem it was presenting him, which was that he was trapped inside this plain, ordinary room with no obvious way out. How to get out?

He resumed his preliminary survey of the room, noting that it was entirely bare except for the tubes of florescent light on the ceiling, which, though sharply illuminating the space, had in consequence of their intense whiteness a tiring effect on his eyes, and by extension, all of him. Except for his own body, there were no objects in the room to break up the light's tedious uniformity. It seemed, then, that he would have to carry on with a slight headache. He noted four doors, one in the middle of each of the walls. Three of them opened onto a dark, entombing rockface no more than a hand's breadth away. No way out there, for sure. Only one door was not an obvious dead-end, leading as it did to an adjoining room rich in the colors of royalty, red and gold, and decorated with several ceiling-high mirrors and a large glass chandelier.

He felt in his gut the importance of solving the problem but could not account for it logically. Why should so much depend on his finding a way out of this room using his own wits when he could just decide to wake up and be done with it? Use the easy deus ex machina solution, the old Get Out of Jail Free card. Because then you would have learned nothing, in fact, you would have missed learning the one thing in all existence it is necessary for man to know, some inner voice whispered. Oh, yeah, *that*, he grumbled, gritting his teeth and turning back momentarily to external concerns. Looking carefully around the room, he searched for something, anything, that gave even the barest promise of being useful. The florescent lights were of no value, he determined; they're part of what's "given" here, part of the problem itself. Their bland sameness, an irritating white without warmth, without nuance, probably concealed more than they revealed. Besides, they gave him headache, for which he resented them, needing, as he now felt, a clear head for the task at hand.

Wait a minute! he stopped short, getting his first inspiration. Maybe that's just it! Maybe the lights are bland and tedious for a very good reason. After all, everything in a dream is significant, isn't it, even an embroidered felt copy of "Dogs Playing

Poker" hanging on the wall. So too tedium, so too headache. Why does this light give headache? That's the question. Pay attention to the tedious, headachy quality of the light. What is that telling me? This led by association to the richly suggestive dream theories of Freud and Jung, which were part of his *Allgemeinbildung*, as the Germans would say. As a sort of side bar or corollary, he also realized in that moment that, since he was dreaming lucidly, he had all his acquired knowledge, including dream theory, available to him to use or not as he saw fit. Then it struck him that a lucid dream such as this, over which the dreamer has great control, was precisely the venue for the application of empirical knowledge, since one was operating from within the powerful precincts of the unconscious. Here the two—head and heart—went fluently together. Suddenly there was less blandness, less tedium. Then it dawned on him in turn that the blandness and tedium, the headachy quality of the light, signified that the light in the room was meant to show the futility of all efforts to solve our deepest problems by the "light" of intellect alone. That just gave you headache.

Taking a mental step back, he saw that all of this meant that the room itself was a symbol of the mind, the dreamer's mind, his own mind, and by extension all minds, a perfect little microcosm displaying the inherent limitations of unaided intellect to save man from the suffering that shadowed his life. He recalled his studies of depth psychology and psychoanalysis and the frequent assertion of Freud and Jung that the mind was often symbolized in dreams by some sort of enclosure containing the dreamer—usually a room, or a house or a car, the latter particularly when one's "life direction" was at issue. Do you see how much you've deciphered, almost without effort, he said to himself by way of encouragement. It's astonishing! And not only have you begun to understand the dream and, in so doing, begun appropriating its power, you've also understood that lucid dreaming itself, as an activity encompassing both waking and dreaming states, and therefore a psychic power of a higher order, is a tool par excellence for solving the problems that cause suffering ... Take heart, you're dreaming for all men now!

Buoyed by the rapidity of this series of illuminations, which seemed to cascade over each other in rushing to him, he pressed on with growing confidence. Now he was both observing and interpreting what he observed, in rapid-fire alternation. He scanned the room again, now allowing the florescent light to have its way with him. He soon noticed a significant rise in his threshold of pain, a consequence, he was sure, of his more accepting attitude towards the light. If he looked to the left, his left temple ached a bit more; so too for the right. Then he concentrated on the pain itself—its degree, its rhythm, its quality, its "taste." It was an ache, but an ache with what seemed to him to be a sharp, bitter sting at the center of it, largely hidden by the ache. Only the careful probing he was doing could have identified it. As he made his way into that sting psychically, proceeding slowly and with the utmost patience, he began to sense a gnawing despair at its root. And, without any calculation, he knew the despair sprang from the deep awareness that all his effort was useless; he was not going to solve the problem and get out of the trap. But, of course, he could not admit this to himself, it being psychologically too costly, and so he threw up headache as a screen to obscure his own insight, while yet continuing to act as though he were "hot on its trail."

So, even with his formidable arsenal of psychological theory, he was still victimized by the very tricks of self-deception he had read about in his books. And he sensed this too, because he was not only knowledgeable but clever, adroit, to a certain extent "onto himself." But this half-suppressed awareness only added a degree of exquisite pain to the ache. Then, as he was struggling just to "hold" the ache without flinching, another thought came to him, unbidden, unforced, and therefore of superior psychic value. He realized that if the dream as a whole were about the workings of his own mind, in particular its subtle mechanisms of deception and denial and how these entrap us, then the second room, which he had thus far only peered into from the fluorescently lit one, must support that interpretation, even amplify and enrich it. And so he now proceeded to apply his two-pronged attack of observation and interpretation to that mysterious sphere.

He stepped over to the threshold to stick his head in and have a good look. He saw that this room was even more self-contained than the first, with no windows and only the one door, but it was also much more diverting thanks to its full-length mirrors, its royal red walls with gold trim and its chandelier hanging from the ceiling's dead center. There were three mirrors, one centered on each wall, with the door standing in for a fourth mirror on the fourth wall. Almost instantly, he felt his mind being bombarded by ideas from Jungian psychology: The mirrors could be images representing self-inquiry, which for Jung was the business of analysis, the work of those who wished to follow the Socratic prescription of *gnothi seauton*, that is, to "know themselves." Or, they could just as easily be the precise opposite: mirrors of narcissistic self-delusion. The ambiguity meant that their true sense could only be determined within the context of neighboring images. One such image was the red and gold walls, colors of royal status or at least of some personage of high social rank, say, of the aristocracy of old. Here he thought of Freud's famous pronouncement on dreams, the primary source material of psychoanalysis, as being "the royal road to the unconscious." The very idea made him delightfully dizzy by its aptness, as well as by the fact that it was occurring to him *within the dream state itself*, a fact bordering on the exquisite frisson of Romantic irony, a rarefied state of consciousness in which one experiences freedom from the binary struggle of subject versus object, self versus other.

As he turned, finally, to the chandelier, a magnificent complexity of rococo circles of glass which hung suspended high above him, he felt instantly its symbolic significance as an ideal of self-realization, of self-perfection, perhaps beyond reach but nevertheless worthy of dedicated striving. Or at least, that was what he took from Jung. For it seems that just then, in that very moment of invoking the master's wisdom, he also felt the excitement of doubting a great mind's powerful pronouncement: Who knew what was possible? Might not the very conviction that the self was an "unreachable star" act as a self-fulfilling prophecy, in effect, barring us from its realization? For a second he felt the room disappear, melt away, as a vast space of limitless possibility opened out before his mind's eye. But it was just a flash, yet a flash of such intense delight as to leave a certain leavening effect on the fissures within his psychic structure, as if some divine hand were holding all his deepest inner conflicts in its palm, messaging them all with its fingers, giving hope of a panacea for human woe.

Then Freud's idea-image of a "royal road to the unconscious" struck him anew and he could barely contain his delight. It was almost too much to take in that the Viennese sage's lofty revelation on dreams was, all by itself, the perfect key to the meaning of *this particular dream*, which was still unfolding. This dream, he now saw, was a dream about dreams, a meta-dream, meant to reveal the intrinsically contradictory structure of the human mind that ends up trapping most of us: The conscious mind, where we all ordinarily live, operates on the sound, if bland, principle of reason and intellect. This is "the room" in which we largely spend our waking lives, secretly hoping for something better. This "something better" is suggested by the second, more colorful, more interesting, room: the space of the unconscious, the arena of dreams, the psychic land beyond the humdrum, the quotidian. It then struck Anselm that this is why he didn't actually enter the second room; that would have cost him the governing control exercised by the ego, casting him, in effect, into madness. He needed the ego in order to discriminate between conscious and unconsciousness worlds as well as to negotiate between inner and outer.

However, he reasoned, needing a principle to regulate a psychic function didn't mean we were defined by that principle. After all, it was just a principle, an object of consciousness like any other. But then, was there anything that *wasn't* an object, he wondered. And if there was, and it was *not* the ego, the very definition of "subject," what could it possibly be? And once again he felt the exhilaration of being at the dead-end of stern, honest intellectual inquiry, needing a higher power, a more bracing light, as it were, in order to take that final step off the cusp of ignorance to discovery.

His inability to locate or identify a subjective principle of experience, to answer the question, for example, *Who* is doing the thinking here? *Who* is it that cannot locate a subject to experience? *Who* does *anything*, for that matter? became for him one of those impasses he'd read about in Zen folklore where the master puts that question to a spiritually ripe student, then takes a flat-edged stick, whacks him on the back with it and grins broadly when he sees the light suddenly flash behind the student's eyes. Anselm, alas, had no Zen master to lead him carefully along the path, but masters are not indispensable. In his case, his own nimble mind, vastly empowered by the lucid dream state he was enjoying, was a more than adequate substitute.

In this dream on this night it worked like this: There seemed to be no answer to the question, Who is it that does anything, who walks, who talks, who eats, who shits. Is there a Who anywhere. His first answer, "Who cares?", was flip, but he turned it right around and asked, Who is it that either cares or doesn't care? *Who?* He stood before a spiritual brick wall, powerless to answer. Then, feeling humbled by his inability to answer such a simple question, he felt a lightning bolt of a thought go through him: Maybe there is no Who! Maybe nobody does anything. Better put: Maybe there's nobody around to do anything. Maybe things just happen on their own, set in motion by cause and effect. Deeds there are, but none who perform them. Actions there are, but none who carry them out. Is that it?

Then another flash: Wait! If that's true, then what's the point of my using Freudian and Jungian dream theory to try to decipher this dream? If there's no Who, no "Freud" or "Jung," doing the theorizing, why should I grant it authority? Is it possible this is what my dream is telling me? Is the dream, sans dreamer (just another Who), presenting itself to me, not as an endorsement of psychoanalysis as an interpretative strategy for escaping the mind-room, but as the very opposite of that: as a critique of analysis and by implication, of *any* theoretical framework, for getting to the truth of anything? Is the dream telling me to put aside the tools of intellect—logic, reason, assumption (such as that there are such things as discrete and separate ego entities)—if I seriously want to know the truth that reveals things as they *really* are?

He pressed on, relentlessly: Is the theory of an unconscious mind, "the second room," then, any more valid than the theory of the first, or conscious, mind? Is the mind, as psychoanalysis claims, a lifelong battlefield between the inner armies of light and darkness? Is the dream perhaps telling me to drop that picture, that map, and take a fresh look at the territory itself? Could the dream itself *be* this fresh look? But if so, what was "the territory itself?" All he could see was an image of entrapment, two half-minds radically alienated from each other. But wait! Hold on! If the dream was telling him that this picture was false, that there were no such antithetical minds, no battlefield, no conscious versus unconscious, and if he, as he just then noticed, was beginning to breathe in the heady air of freedom as he observed that very delusion of the two rooms, then that delusion—and by extension, *any* delusion—must be truth itself! In other words, the only thing one had to change to transform delusion into truth, and therefore bondage to freedom, was one's point of view. He recalled the only words of Karl Marx he had ever committed to memory: "Freedom is conscious necessity." Freedom was the utter enjoyment of the very chains we had draped over ourselves, one of the heavier ones being psychoanalysis.

So, then, what *was* the mind, if not a conflicted binary, a house divided? Could it be ... freedom itself? In other words, a mystery?

VIGIL 20

Armageddon Lite

Dear reader, I doubt very much that you have ever found yourself confined to a bottle—unless, perchance, it happened in the course of a nasty nightmare. If that is the case, then you can well empathize with the suffering of poor Anselm. But if you've never had such a dream, then, for Anselm's sake and mine, at least allow your vivid imagination to lock you up in this transparent prison for a few moments. You're totally surrounded by glass, trapped in its hardness and glare on all sides, feeling much like a Pleistocene fossilized fly encased in amber. You raise your hand to scratch your nose and find you have to slide the hand up the narrow space between nose and glass. It's almost not worth it. The glare is such as to bend and twist the objects in the room out of all recognizable shape, not to mention endowing them with all the colors of the rainbow. This is claustrophobic hell, worse even than being buried alive, since you're both present to and totally absent from whatever's going on around you. Everything sags and droops and swerves in the glassy distortion. The worst of it, though, is the air, or paucity of same. You sit there, knees drawn up, breathing in slightly fetid draughts of what smells and tastes like the air in a crowded subway car in August with the AC down. And how grateful you are for it! For you're almost in panic over the imminent exhaustion of even this shabby etheric sustenance. Your pulse is racing, your nerves are raw, you're on the verge of hysteria.

Have pity, dear reader, on poor Anselm, beset as he was by circumstances too terrible for most of us even to contemplate.

But wait! There came to him then a thought that laid a fresh layer of anguish over all the rest: He realized there would be no imminent death to release him from his glass prison, no welcoming *mors ex machina*. Had he not just been awakened from a night of restless dreams (of which, by the way, he recalled nothing), effluvia of the torpor into which he had fallen? Was the sun not shining brightly and amiably into the room, signaling a new twenty-four-hour cycle of hell, the first of God knew how many? He could barely move a body part to shift positions; even his own thoughts seemed only to mock him, ignoring translation into words and merely clanging in inchoate form against the suffocating glass like the strokes of a gong. Every move he made, whether internal or external, was more binding than the last. He felt himself on the brink of madness.

Feeling out of options, he momentarily surrendered to his impotence and cried out in despair, "Serpentina, O Serpentina! Please save me from this agony!" And as he began to release his grief in this way without condition or reservation, he could feel the jar he was locked in being bathed in barely audible sobs and sighs, and these were accompanied in turn by the sweetly dolorous strains of a violin, whose signature style he recognized instantly. And in that moment of recognition, the clanging of thoughts ceased, the distorting glare of the glass disappeared, and he could breathe more freely. "Oh, God! I have only myself to blame for my predicament. Have I not sinned grievously against you, dearest—*my own heart*? Did I not deliberately allow doubt, doubt of your reality, to overtake me? Did I not lose faith and, with it, everything that would have secured my happiness? – Now I've lost you, and deservedly so. You'll never be mine, the golden pot will never sit on my table, never again will I behold its wonders. – Oh, Serpentina, if only I could see your lovely face one more time, hear your sweet voice, drink in the honeyed tones that you alone can coax from that wooden box!"

Thus did our poor beleaguered hero lament aloud from within the confines of his vertical glass coffin, when all of a sudden he heard a coarse voice from right next to him say, "I don't know what's bothering you, pal, but I'd say you're about three quarters around the bend. What gives?" Turning his head left, Anselm could see a young fellow next to him sitting in the same kind of jar, and, as well as he could make out, three or four others beyond him. All were Stoneham graduate students, engineers in the making of one kind or another. "Ah! I see I'm not alone in this glass prison; I've got the company of others who are bearing the consequences of their own failure. – But I don't get it. Why are you all smiling and looking like the cat who ate the canary? You're all just as—pardon the expression—'bottled up' on this shelf as I am, totally cramped up in body and, I'm sure, no less in mind, unable to think a simple thought without having it clang against this damned glass like a wrecking ball and throw your mind into a fury of chaos and confusion … So, I take it you don't believe in the salamander or in the green snake?"

"What have you been smoking lately, dude?" his neighbor smirked. "We've never had it better than we do right now. We're living high on the hog! We've got plenty of green in our pockets, care of the Archivist who pays us so well for copying those ridiculous manuscripts of his. We cut the boring lectures and field trips and hang out at Mitzi's or some other watering hole, of which Hoboken has more per capita than just about anywhere. I'm telling you, you can't get a bad draft beer in this town. We flirt with the waitresses—and, now and then if we get lucky, more than that—and usually end up singing Irish or German folksongs, depending on who's there.

"My colleague's got it right," an electrical engineering student chimed in. "Like him, I have more money than I know what to do with. But I save mine and like to go on hikes around the city and beyond, free of charge; I enjoy checking out the cityscape, especially the features unique to this area, like the 14th Street pier on the Hudson in Hoboken where we are now, or the tunnels, those great tunnels—how they fascinate me. Would you believe I've managed to walk through both the Lincoln and Holland Tunnels—both ways!—without being stopped? It sure beats sitting between the four walls of my room putting class notes on my computer."

"What in God's name are you all talking about?" Anselm asked in great consternation. "Can't you see where you are? Are you somehow not aware that we're all sitting here in airless glass bottles on the Archivist's library shelf, that we can't move, can hardly even stir, much less take a stroll on the Hoboken pier?"

Immediately they all burst out laughing, the electrical engineering student the least generous in his assessment of the situation: "This guy's a first-class whacko: He thinks he's sitting in a glass bottle when he's actually standing here with us on the 14th St. pier just staring into the murky waters of the Hudson. Come on, guys, let's move on!"

"Oh, there's no use arguing with them," Anselm told himself dejectedly. "What more can I expect from those who have no acquaintance with Serpentina. They just don't know what it is to live life in freedom, to live a life grounded in faith and love. In fact, their ignorance of the higher life is the very reason they don't chafe in this glass prison, this unbearable claustrum to which the salamander has banished us all. But I, poor wretch that I am, have the double-edged gift of awareness of our common imprisonment. They have only exsight, while I have that plus insight as well. I am aware of the suffering of my confinement, while they think they are living the good life. They don't sense the glass membrane separating them from the world; its very transparency hides it from them, while I, who have tasted freedom, am condemned to suffer the consequences of losing it—and by my own foolish devices! – O Serpentina, can you hear me? Are you near or far? I love you beyond all measure, but I am doomed to perish in disgrace and agony if you do not save me! It's as simple as that!"

Immediately he could hear a low sighing and murmuring as it gradually pervaded the room, and soon enough he recognized Serpentina's voice: "Anselm—believe, hope, love!" Her enchanting breathy voice was accompanied, unobtrusively, by a love melody on the violin, one of her own making. It bore some resemblance to Franz Liszt's "Dream of Love," its runs eventually swelling to heights of almost unbearable ecstasy, its ending as tender as a rose petal dropped on a pond. With each phrase Anselm could feel his glass prison widening, allowing his chest room to expand and thus to feel the piercing darts of love she was sending him. To these the glass was no barrier. Gradually the agony of his condition diminished, and in inverse proportion his conviction grew that Serpentina still loved him, indeed, that it was she alone who was now making his confinement in the bottle tolerable. He took no further notice of his frivolous comrades in captivity on the shelf and focused all his thoughts, his entire awareness, on the lovely Serpentina.

Just then there arose from the other side of the room a muffled muttering. As he turned his head and sharpened his senses, he could tell the sound was coming from the water compartment of the Keurig coffeemaker sitting on a credenza against the wall. Suddenly the lid on the water tank was thrown off and up popped the head, dripping wet, of a grizzled old woman, bearing two parallel burn marks on the left side of her nose, her thinning gray hair pulled back severely. Anselm blinked several times in horror, and when his eyes opened, he saw standing before him, looking up at him with a hideous toothless grin, the chestnut lady from the Journal Square strip mall. "Oof!" she grunted, as she shook off the excess water like a dog. "No more coffeemakers for materializing purposes! I was sure the reservoir of this one was empty, but I guess my clairvoyant powers are not as sharp as they used to be." Then she gave out a hideous laugh that was indistinguishable from a shriek and began to rant at Anselm: "Hey there, *muchacho*, now you're in for it, no? Your ass behind glass! Your ass behind glass! Didn't I tell you that on that fateful afternoon last July 4th?"

"Go ahead, hag, you cursed sorceress! Laugh and mock all you want!" Anselm shouted at her through the glass, which somehow gave his voice the booming timbre of a basso profundo. "You're to blame for everything I've had to endure, but the salamander will take you down, you vile beet root!"

"Easy there, Pancho, easy! Don't be so huffy," the old lady replied. "You knocked over my chestnut stand and got my little ones all trampled on. Plus, you gave me these two ugly scars here," she said reproachfully, pointing to her left cheek with her crooked index finger. "But, even with all that, I'm inclined to go easy on you, *canalla*, because you're not such a bad sort otherwise, and besides, a certain young miss dear to me happens to be fond of you. Why that is, I couldn't tell you. I've tried to turn her interest towards other, more suitable, young men, men of superior means and greater prospects, but she's one of those 'no one else for me' types … You know, by the way, don't you, that there's no way you're getting out of that bottle without my help? Unfortunately, I can't reach you from here, but my old *amiga rata* is just now climbing down onto your shelf from the attic. She'll gnaw on that shelf until it breaks and you come tumbling down into my apron, which will break your fall, save you a broken nose and preserve that handsome face of yours for Miss Veronica. Then I'll carry you off to her, and you'll marry her as soon as you become a professor."

"Get away from me, you root—you *beet* root—of all evil. You … you spawn of Satan!" Anselm shouted down at her, gripped now by paroxysms of rage. "It was only by your infernal arts that I was moved to commit the offense that has landed me in this glass cell and that I now must expiate. You bitch goddess temptation! … You have turned me into a house divided! You use a sex kitten to get me to betray my true love, to forsake the one I would give my very life for! How fickle, how shallow and vapid I must be, to be so easily manipulated! How shallow all men—how shallow the world! – But no matter. I will sit here and patiently endure this death in life, since it is here, and only here, that I feel any connection with Serpentina at all. Even now, in your evil presence, I feel the soothing swells of her love. – Listen to me, you garbage bag, listen and despair! I reject your evil influence; I will always love Serpentina alone, her alone and forever! I will never become a professor at the community college! I will never cast another lustful glance at Veronica, the one who, with your help, has lured me over to the dark side! If the green snake cannot be mine, then I'm prepared to go down with the pain of a broken heart! Get out of my sight! Out of my sight, you treacherous hellcat!"

At this the old hag let out a peal of mocking laughter that verily rattled the rafters, after which she called up to Anselm in a dismissive tone, "Have it your own way then, fool! Sit there and rot, for all I care. Now it's time for me to get down to business anyway; the fact is, my main purpose in coming here has nothing to do with you." And with that she threw off her black cape and stood there in front of him in all her hideous nakedness. It gave her great pleasure to give him the opposite of a lustful experience, which he felt as a sort of global cringing of his body as it contracted concentrically around his fast-shrinking genitals. He turned away in a spasm of disgust that stoked the still smoldering embers of his anger. Turning back when he suddenly heard feet pounding on the rug, he was astonished to see the old woman running naked around the desk in the center. Round and round she went, and as she did, large folio volumes, old and dusty, toppled down to the floor from the uppermost bookshelves. As she passed these while jogging, she would grab one or another of them up and pull out some of the sturdy old parchment sheets. These she artfully joined together into a kind of scaly paper armor, slapping sections of it onto her withered brown body—in preparation, it seemed, for some sort of self-defense. – Then all at once the

3D printer sitting on the credenza came to life, its nozzle and build plate clattering away. Soon enough, a perfect replica of the crone's black cat sprang out of the printer's plastic housing onto the floor, spraying blistering fiery sparks all around him and adding his ghastly howl to the old hag's obscene shrieks in a duet straight from hell. (Was it *really* a copy of the cat, a "copycat" [!], or was it the original? Who knows? Such imponderable questions are what make modern fairy tales even more uncanny than those of tradition.)

Together the deranged duo stormed out of the room, and, from the racket they made opening doors in their mad haste, Anselm could tell they were headed for the blue room and, of course, the golden pot, its hallowed grail. By now a general uproar was in full swing, an earsplitting dysymphony of chirps and squawks and hisses coming from the greenhouse in reaction to the two intruders. Underneath the general clamor of the birds, Anselm could make out the gray parrot's raspy baritone as it sounded the alarm: "Close ranks, fellows! Close ranks! Thieves! Thieves!" A moment later the old woman, with an agility that belied her years, bounded back into the room carrying the golden pot in the crook of her elbow and gesticulating wildly with her free arm as she shouted to the cat, "Now's the time, my little son! Now's the time! Go get the green snake! *Kill her!*" As if released at long last from an eternity of restraint, the cat scrambled out of the room in mad search of his deadly reptilian enemy. Before long a sound as of moaning reached Anselm's ears and played havoc with his fevered imagination: Was Serpentina being attacked? Wounded? Killed? Instinctively he hunkered down in the bottle, rotating as far as possible backward onto his spine while raising his legs into the air. Then, bending his legs, he rammed his feet straight into the glass as hard as he could, and kept on doing that. Each impact sent a resounding gong sound through the room, the rapid repetition of sounds creating a cascading echo that should have been heard halfway across the Hudson. Finally, in a mighty climactic thrust of his legs, Anselm's feet hit the glass exactly coincident with an external gong announcing the presence of the Archivist on the scene. When the tremendous echo faded, the old man was standing there in the doorway, looking twenty years younger, arrayed in his regal damask dressing gown with its white fox-fur collar. A formidable figure.

"Hey, hey! You verminous nuisances! You second-rate sorceress!" he called out boldly. "It's time I taught you a lesson!" At that the bruja's thinning gray hair stood up like so many brush bristles, her black eyes glowing like red-hot coals. Then she gnashed her teeth and growled at the cat, "Quick! Bare your fangs and hiss! Hiss at him!" Convulsed by hatred, she cackled and shrieked and whined hideously, all the while pressing the golden pot firmly to her flaccid bosom and furiously grabbing from it handfuls of earth, which she flung at the Archivist. However, the instant the soil touched his gown, it turned into flowers which fell to the floor. At the same time, the lilies decorating the Archivist's gown ignited and burst into flame, he then gathering them up and throwing them as they crackled at the paper-clad witch, who howled in pain. Yet, by frantically jumping up and down as she shook her parchment armor, she was able to extinguish the fire lilies, which fell to the floor in ashes.

"A second sally, my boy! Go for it!" she screamed, and the cat, with a running start, ventured a tremendous leap in the air to get past the Archivist by jumping over him, but the gray parrot intercepted him, grabbing him with his curved beak with such force that fire-red blood spurted from his throat. The cat let out a piercing howl and Serpentina's voice could be heard to shout "Victory is ours!" This infuriated the bruja, who flung the pot behind her and lunged at the Archivist, all ten boney fingers splayed in a desperate attempt to claw at any part of him she could reach. But her foe was far too nimble for this and gracefully stepped aside like a matador, letting the old hag crash into the credenza, which knocked both herself and the 3D printer to the floor, causing the latter to begin clattering once again, this time, however, with no issue, no "copycat"—a bad omen forecasting imminent defeat for the bruja. Which came seconds later when the Archivist removed his heavy gown and flung it over her as she struggled to get to her feet. This set off a welter of tiny explosions of crackling blue flames issuing from her armor of parchment sheets. At length, somehow succeeding in casting off the pyrophoric mantle, the witch stood up and howled in agony as she tried desperately to douse the flames by rubbing handfuls of earth from the golden pot over herself and by patting down the flaming armor sheets with new parchment torn from books lying open on the floor. But this was at best a holding action, for whenever she succeeded in extinguishing the fire in one section of armor, another flame would spring up in its place somewhere else. At this point, the Archivist saw that finishing the old hag off would be an act of mercy, so, reaching deep for his heaviest arsenal, he began bombarding her with whooshing beams of fire shot from his eyes. "That's it! There we go! Yes! Yes! Salamander 1, witch 0!" he boasted aloud, filling the room with his regal baritone and drowning out the shrieks of the witch, who soon found herself hopelessly surrounded by concentric rings of fire.

Meanwhile the battle of the second bananas raged on, the tomcat having survived the parrot's vicious first bite, but this survival turned out to be a poor man's Pyrrhic victory as the parrot in due course landed a hard right claw to the cat's jaw, knocking him senseless to the ground. Then, as the parrot held him fast with one claw while literally skewering him with the sharpest talon of the other, the cat in his death throes wailed a final wail of submission, and the parrot finished him off by hacking his glowing eyes out with his cleaver-sharp beak, the cat's eye sockets thereupon spewing up two mushrooming geysers of burning white foam.

Thick, dark plumes of smoke rose up from the dressing gown beneath which the witch now lay, defeated, her shrieks of anguish, muffled by the thick garment, gradually diminishing in volume and frequency down to the point of a barely audible whimper. The black smoke filled the room not only with itself but also with a horrible stench, which, thankfully, lasted only a few minutes. When the Archivist finally lifted the dressing gown, he found nothing more than an ugly beet root lying there. "This paltry scrap is all that is left of my worthy opponent," he said, perhaps to Anselm and the parrot, perhaps to no one, and with a faint note of regret in his voice. "Yes, 'worthy' I say, for she had her role to play in the drama and she played it well. Where, after all, would good be without evil? … It is as the devil Mephistopheles, my favorite character in *Faust*, says: 'I am a part of that power that always intends evil yet always creates good' … Without her we could never have arrived at this moment of triumph."

"Here, honorable sire," said the parrot, landing on the credenza, "I bring you my own defeated foe," and he extended his beak towards his master, who took from it a single black whisker, the modest remains of the tomcat.

"Excellent, my boy! Excellent!" the Archivist praised his trusty assistant, with a good deal more brio than usual. "Now please take the remains of both our adversaries and dispose of them properly. This evening you'll be given, as a token reward, six coconuts, along with a pair of new glasses to replace those the cat apparently broke during your joust."

"Your humble servant, sire," the parrot nodded gratefully, then fluttered down to the floor, picking the beet root up in his beak and flying with both scraps out the window, which the Archivist opened for him.

Then his master picked up the golden pot from the floor and pressed it to his bosom, calling out "Serpentina! Serpentina!" And when Anselm, who had remained a captive witness in his bottle during the entire melee and rejoiced at the stunning defeat of the hated witch, finally looked at the Archivist full-face, he saw, not his employer, but the tall, majestic figure of the Prince of Spirits, gazing up at him with an expression of indescribable grace and gravitas. "Anselm," spoke the Prince of Spirits, "It was not you who were responsible for your fall from grace but a hostile principle that strove to worm its way into the deepest reaches of your being and pit you against yourself … Still, that said, what happened to you had to happen, and happen in exactly the way that it did. Every detail, every blink of an eye, every breath was precisely as it was meant to be and could not have unfolded in any other way. – You have proven your faith. Be free and happy!"

And with that, Anselm suddenly felt lit up by a bolt of lightning, while the violin music he had first heard in the subway dungeon on July 4th rose up seemingly from nowhere and filled the room with the ache of lyrical loveliness. The more clarion and ravishing it waxed, the more his every nerve and fiber throbbed with desire and trembled with expectation. When the music reached a point of emotional intensity at which Anselm felt he could no longer bear it, the glass imprisoning him shattered and he tumbled down into the arms of his precious Serpentina.

VIGIL 21

An Engagement in Jersey City

"Branden, what in the name of Lucifer did you put in those drinks last night?" Paul Manheim groaned as he stumbled out of his bedroom into the living room the next morning without bothering to notice if his friend, who lay on the couch, was even conscious. His hair was mostly vertical and his bathrobe turned inside out and open, and he seemed to be looking for something without quite knowing what. What he found in any case was about a hundred shards of broken glass and ceramic intermingled with a gray ashen substance, all of it littering the hearth stone floor. In fact, he accidently stepped on an especially sharp shard that easily penetrated the leather sole of his left Ascot slipper and entered the tender, relatively fallen, arch of that foot. "Oh, ffffuhh!" he just barely contained himself.

"What in blazes happened here?" he asked, presumably rhetorically, as he surveyed the damage before slapping his forehead with his hand as the returning memory of the glass-throwing contest hit him hard and deep in the shame muscle. It seems that, after Anselm had made a hasty exit the previous evening, the two men continued their Dionysian orgy (sans sex, of course), running around the apartment, shouting, throwing things at each other, bumping into each other and finally collapsing in drunken exhaustion. Sally helped her father up from his easy chair and led him off to bed, while Branden lay sprawled on the couch with one shoe on and one off and would remain there paralyzed until his friend asked him what was in the drinks the next morning. His moustache was adroop and, most mysteriously, half shaved off. (It was a mystery that would never be explained to anyone's complete satisfaction.)

Despite a massive headache and profound lethargy caused by a hangover, Branden managed with great effort to swing his legs off the couch and onto the floor, come to a sitting position and lower his head gingerly into his hands where it felt like a bowling ball ready to explode. "Oh, come on, Paul!" he groused, reacting with stabs of pain to his own voice, "The drinks were heavy, I'll give you that, but they were hardly responsible for what happened last night, and you know it. It was that damned Anselm who caused all the trouble...." He ran his hand through his hair and then began touching the spot above his upper lip where he expected to find a full moustache but didn't. He squelched an impulse to run to the bathroom mirror to confirm his dreadful suspicion and pressed on with his point: "Surely you've noticed that he's become even more of an E.T. than he used to be. And we know now that some forms of madness can be contagious, do we not—at least temporarily? One fool makes a bunch, as it were. (Forgive me—an old saying.) You have a cognac or two and all of a sudden you're in La La Land being led around by the head La La. I mean, I *still* get the chills whenever I think about that gray parrot, don't you?"

"Stuff and nonsense!" Manheim replied, sitting down at the table and gently tweezing a piece of glass shaped like a tiny canoe out of his left arch. "That was no parrot; it was the Archivist's little old attendant wearing a gray coat who came looking for Anselm," he insisted, holding up the bloody crescent and staring at it with fascination, as if it were the Hope Diamond.

"You may be right," Branden conceded, "but I'm telling you, I had a terrible night. There was all this huffing and whistling and grunting keeping me awake."

"That was just me," the Assistant Principal clarified. "My girls tell me I snore to beat the band—right through the walls. I've probably got sleep apnea and should be on a CPAP machine. It's on my to-do list."

"Glad to hear it," Branden said supportively. "But the thing is, Paul, I didn't come here yesterday to test my alcohol capacity—nor yours, nor Ronnie's, for that matter. I was going to announce ..." Branden said, suddenly in a croaking voice, then tearing up as he raised his hand to his brow, obviously trying to hide a sudden rush of emotion. "But that damned Anselm ruined everything ..." And with that he jumped up from the sofa as though his pants were on fire, searched frantically for his jacket, found it, ran over to his dear friend sighing "Oh, Paul! Paul! Paul" without adding anything more enlightening, gave him a fairly crushing bear hug and was out the door, slamming it so hard that the chandelier over the dining-room table tinkled.

"That does it! That tears it!" Manheim grumbled as he limped to the bathroom, grabbed a tissue and, carefully wrapping the precious "diamond" in its folds, placed it in the locked drawer of his desk. "Never again will that cursed Anselm cross my threshold! Obviously even the best of us are vulnerable to his peculiar madness. Case in point: my ordinarily rock-solid friend, poor Branden. How easy it is for our thin veneer of rationality to give way to blathering lunacy. So long in evolving—eons!—this fragile empirical mindset of ours, and so quick, so easy, to slip away. One rotten apple spoils the barrel.

I just barely managed to avoid getting sucked into it myself last night—the devil was here luring me on in my besottedness—but how long can *even I* hold out? Two or three drinks and old Satan is already knocking on the door, waiting to unleash his chaos … So, get thee behind me, Satan! And you with him, Anselm!"

Veronica, who had come into the room and was sitting on the couch, said nothing. She sat in silence, looking lost in thought, almost brooding, only occasionally giving a faint smile. Her father looked at her and instantly molded her demeanor to fit the gist of his rant. Vindictively he raged, "Anselm has that girl's welfare—or lack of it—on his conscience! It's a good thing he hasn't showed up here this morning—I know he's afraid of me. I'm betting he'll make himself scarce. We won't be seeing him around here for quite a while, I'm guessing, if ever." This last was spoken by Manheim with such vitriol that Veronica was brought to tears and sobbed, "Oh God, is he even *able* to come here—or anywhere? It seems like he's been locked up in that glass bottle forever!"

"What the—!" Paul Manheim cried out in total befuddlement upon hearing this. "Oh God, she sounds even more demented than Branden! It's a *folie à deux* in the making! Soon it'll be a pandemic!" Then, shaking his fist, "Anselm, you misbegotten lout!"

After breakfast the concerned father drove his daughter over to the neighborhood walk-in clinic and had her looked at by the doctor on call, a Dr. Eckstein, a retired family physician who worked part-time "just to keep my hand in it." He was a portly man, portlier even than Manheim, had sparse gray hair and thick eyeglasses, and constantly made involuntary contortions with his lips, indicating he was on some heavy-duty drugs himself. More to the point, he had no training in psychiatry apart from the required three-week rotation in that field he had slept through in medical school. After listening to the father's presenting complaint of his daughter's fluctuating moods, bouts of weepiness and general listlessness, the good doctor took her pulse, checked her out with his stethoscope and looked deep into her mouth and ears before giving his diagnosis: "Nerves ... perhaps a touch of bipolar. Not to worry, II not I. I'll write a prescription for Xanax. Take her outdoors—fresh air—long walks, up and down the boulevard—go to the movies—Tom Hanks—highly therapeutic, his films."

Days, weeks and months passed and Anselm was nowhere to be seen; nor for that matter was Registrar Branden—that is, until the following February 4 when he showed up at his friend's apartment at high noon on Veronica's saint's day, dressed to the nines. Beneath a luxurious cashmere topcoat he had on a new navy blue blazer and under that a blue silk vest. His shoes were black loafers of the finest patent leather and normally would have topped off his appearance brilliantly, but, unfortunately, the piles of snow and slush just now clogging the streets had dimmed their luster down to a dull grayish brown. Typical for an academic, he had forgotten his rubbers. Most notable, however, about Harold Branden's total makeover was the full and complete restoration of his quasi Hitlerian moustache. This, in and of itself, announced the end of the old order of second bananahood and a ringing-in of the new order of taking charge.

After carefully removing his coat and fur-lined black leather gloves and placing them neatly over a chair, he walked right up to his friend, who was standing in the middle of the living room in robe and slippers, open-mouthed, struck dumb by the "new Branden," and gave him a bear hug that would have rivalled that of a grizzly in heat. He then proceeded to speak his piece: "Today, my good friend Paul, on the feast day of your lovely and charming daughter Veronica, I want to reveal to you everything that has long been on my mind and heart. Back on that ill-fated evening last Fall, when I arrived here with a bottle of Drambuie, never suspecting the lethality of mixing good scotch with good cognac, I had intended to share with all of you the good news that I'd been promoted to the position of Dean at the university—Dean of Exterior Space ... No, *seriously*, I am now— or will be, starting next Fall—responsible for the disposition of all outdoor space on the main campus: lawns, parking lots, walkways, roads, etc. Maintenance, use, functioning, and all the rest of it. Needless to say, the promotion comes with a substantial raise in salary—"

"—Oh, my goodness! ... Harold! ... Of all the! ... Who could've imagined! ... Dean of Outer Space!" Manheim stammered, staring off into some imagined version of same.

"*Exterior!*" Branden corrected, a bit miffed at his friend's obtuseness.

"Excuse me, I don't ..." Manheim blathered, confused.

"*Exterior* space," Branden repeated, emphasizing the words, trying, with only marginal success, not to sound annoyed by the dimwittedness of his probable future father-in-law.

"Oh, yes, yes, of course. Forgive me," Manheim fawned, beside himself with a surge of avarice and the hope against hope of finally entrusting the care and maintenance of the elder of his two daughters to a good man. Which is exactly what took place in the following exchange: "Paul, as you know, Ronnie and I have been fast friends for as long as you and I have known each other, and I can tell you that I have cherished a secret love for her for almost as long. Also, I have reason to believe that she is not ... ill-disposed towards me in the romance department." A poet Harold was not, but he soldiered on, "There have been numerous flirtations between us over the months and years, and even a stolen kiss or two, that is, up to the Night of the Rusty Nails when the world seemed to undergo some sort of seismic shift. – Now I know that, these days, young people don't bother so much with seeking parental blessing for marriage; they just run off and do it, or elope, or shack up, not even bothering with marriage at all. But I'm a little older, closer to you in age, and perhaps still something of a traditionalist. Above all, you're my dearest friend, so I wouldn't think of bypassing you in pursuit of my intentions towards your daughter. And so, Paul, let me say to you that you would make me a very happy man if you would consent to the marriage of your daughter and ... yours truly."

"Oh, my word! My dear Harold!" a euphoric Manheim clapped his hands together, unaware of thus enacting, through this very gesture, a manual symbol of marriage. "Such a surprise! So out of the blue! I mean, we've all been a bit gloomy around here since that cursed Night of the Rusty Nails. And now you've come, as it were, like a redeeming angel bent on delivering us from darkness. – *Of course*, I give you my blessing, on condition, naturally, that Veronica loves you and agrees to marry you ... Who knows, maybe her despondency of late has been merely the symptom of a concealed love for you. I wouldn't put it past her."

Just then Veronica walked into the room, slowly and with her eyes cast down, showing the pallor that had marked her complexion of late, an unearthly white that looked almost tubercular. It was a look that had actually characterized the facial beauty of women a century earlier. Branden rushed over to her, inquired about her health, congratulated her on her name day and handed her a small package wrapped in pretty purple paper and sporting a silver bow. She accepted the gift and wasted no time opening it. When she saw the earrings lying within—white gold zirconia to be sure, not diamonds— she came to life, color rushing into her cheeks and energy into her limbs. "Oh my goodness! I can't believe it! These are the very earrings I wore to midnight Mass on Christmas eve! I just love them!"

Somewhat confused and taken aback, Branden asked, "But how is that possible? I bought them at Macy's just this morning." Without bothering to answer him, which would have required her to focus on him long enough to clarify that she was familiar with the earrings from Macy's display window and had fantasized about wearing them, she ran over to the living room mirror, put the earrings on with practiced hands in no time and was promptly moved to an eruption of oohs and ahhs.

When his daughter finally quieted down, Manheim took the opportunity to inform her of Branden's elevation to the elect society of deans at Empyrean University. He was about to bring up the proposal when Veronica cut him off and said with a steady and serious mien, "No need to go on, Daddy, I heard everything said between you from my room." Then, turning to her suitor, she continued in the same firm, no-nonsense voice,

"Harold, I have sensed for a long time that you want to marry me. So be it. I give you my heart and my hand. But while we're discussing these serious matters and before we go any further, I must tell you—*both* of you, bridegroom and father—certain things that have lately weighed heavily on my mind, and I must tell them right now, without interruption, even at the risk of letting the soup get cold, which I see Sally is just now bringing to the table."

Without waiting for a response from either of them, as keen to respond as they were, Veronica continued: "As you know, Daddy, I loved Anselm with all my heart, and when Harold—or should I say in congratulation, *Dean* Branden—mentioned in a conversation one time that he thought Anselm could go far, I decided right then and there that he would be my husband. But after that it seemed that all these weird influences—alien forces—were trying to tear him away from me. Eventually I felt driven to seek help from Lisa—you remember, my old guardian—who these days is a practicing bruja and highly skilled in what some refer to as the dark arts. It took a bit of persuasion but she finally promised to send Anselm running into my arms … You won't believe this, but, on the night of the autumnal equinox, we drove to Weehawken, Lisa and I did, and parked at the football field that sits right on top of the Lincoln Tunnel. That field is the center of a circle—a magic circle—formed by the surrounding cloverleaf approach to the tunnel. And there, with the help of her black cat, Lisa conjured up the infernal spirits, imploring their aid in creating a cell phone made of silver for my exclusive use. Through the phone's automagical Skype-like spy application, I was able to keep track of Anselm and get into his head, exerting a high degree of control over his thoughts and desires. – But I now profoundly regret having done all that, and I hereby renounce all Satanic arts. The salamander has defeated the old woman—I heard her wailing but there was nothing I could do. The instant she was eaten by the parrot in beet form, my magic phone broke in two with a frightful crack." Veronica went to her room and fetched the two pieces of the silver phone along with a lock of her hair from her jewelry case, and, handing both to Branden, continued: "Here, Harold, please take these items. The lock you can keep somewhere close to you, preferably on your person, say, in a billfold or an amulet. The two pieces of silver—the phone—however, I'd like you to dispose of in the following way: On the evening of March 20, which marks the vernal equinox, I would like you to be standing on the outer edge of the 14th St. pier in Hoboken just before midnight. Then, on the stroke of twelve, you're to fling the pieces, one at a time, out into the river as far as you can ... Let them descend to a watery grave. – Once again, I swear off all the wiles and tactics of Satan and grant Anselm his happiness from the bottom of my heart, since he now lives in union with the green snake, who is far richer and more beautiful than I am. My only wish now, Harold, is to be a helpful and loving wife to you."

"Jesus, Mary and Joseph!" Paul Manheim cried out in despair. "She's totally bonkers! There's no way she could be the wife of an academic dean, much less a university chancellor! – I've got to get her over to Bellevue for treatment! – Electro-shock, maybe! They say it works wonders these days—no longer the Frankensteinian ordeal it once was."

"Nonsense!" the new Dean interjected, already feeling the confidence supplied by his new title. "I have not been oblivious to the fact that Veronica went through a phase of being smitten by young Anselm, whose charms are considerable, and that her ... fondness for him moved her to take steps she would not ordinarily have taken, such as appealing to this Mexican sorceress for help in securing his affection. – Now, there's no denying that there are strange forces—malevolent forces—at work in the universe, powers that remain utterly beyond the present purview of empirical science. Also, that there are individuals who are especially sensitive to these powers and who practice to gain a measure of control over them, alas, not always to the benefit of others. One reads of such cases even among the ancients. – Now, as far as this business of snakes and salamanders is concerned—the triumph of the salamander and Anselm's supposed marriage to the green snake, and so forth—I am prepared to regard it all as a sort of ... er, poetic allegory, an epic poem, so to speak, one in which the poet—correction: poetess—sings her farewell to an old flame."

"Take it any way you like, Harold," Veronica replied. "Perhaps as a silly dream or a fantasy," she suggested ever so slightly tongue-in-cheek, casting a sidelong glance at her father.

"Not at all, Ronnie. Not at all." Branden hastened to object. "I'm well aware that Anselm had fallen prey to certain, shall we say, paranormal forces that taunted him and drove him to traffic in all sorts of devilry."

By now Assistant Principal Manheim was beside himself and could no longer hold back: "In the name of all that's holy, will you two please stop sounding like paranormal forces yourselves! One would think we had taken another dip in the Rusty Nail pool. Or that Anselm's madness had fatally infected us.

I can't process what I'm hearing from the two of you. I can only conclude that love has addled your brain circuitry. But if that's the case, I am consoled by the fact that marriage will soon straighten all that out. If I weren't convinced of that, I would have grave concerns about your passing this malediction—whatever it is—on to the next generation. – Now, before things get any worse, let me give my paternal blessing to your joyous union ... Dean Branden, you may kiss your betrothed."

The kiss, sweet and tender, followed immediately, seemingly entirely unaffected by any malign preternatural powers that be, and the formal engagement was sealed even before the soup had time to get cold.

Not many months thereafter, on a brilliant Sunday morning in late Spring, what Veronica had always experienced only in fantasy at last became reality. She sat across from her husband in the second-floor bay window of her new home breakfasting on scones and coffee. Occasionally she waved greetings to the ladies passing by on their way to church or the local bakery. And since the window was open a crack to let in the fresh air, she could hear the admiring comments of the ladies below: "Such a splendid woman ... I'll bet she's wearing one of her own creations. How incredibly chic! ... Look at the two of them. Have you ever seen a more handsome couple? ... "

"Yummy!" Veronica thought to herself.

VIGIL 22

A Wedding in Atlantis

It is astonishing how deeply I was able to savor Anselm's exquisite happiness when, at last united with the lovely Serpentina, he travelled with her to that secluded land known as Atlantis. Upon arrival he instantly recognized it to be the land of his lifelong dreams. (Where is Atlantis, you ask? The fact is, no one really knows. Some say it's somewhere in the Greek Isles, possibly on the island of Corfu with its paradisiacal blue-green waters. Others regard it as a "movable" location, liable to be anywhere between, say, Myrtle Beach and Maui at any given time. Still others doubt it is a geographical location at all, viewing it rather as a condition of perfect integrity of mind and spirit.) Yet, however mightily I tried to rouse myself to paint for you, dear reader, a picture in words of the splendor, the wonder, the loveliness surrounding Anselm, I failed miserably. Nothing I scribbled down had the faintest pulse of life in it. Even the computer, with its vast arsenal of bells and whistles to aid composition, failed me utterly. I took to walking the city streets alone at night, lost in melancholy over my own creative impotence. In short, I found myself in the very same condition that beset Anselm just as I described it to you in vigil seven.

I would read the first twenty-one vigils of my story, which were a joy to write, over and over again, obsessively, and be tortured by the thought that there might never be a twenty-second vigil to cap off the grand structure. Indeed, every night when I forced myself to sit down in front of my computer screen in the dying hope of finishing my story, it was as if a pack of guileful spirits would hold up a highly polished rectangular slab of silver before my eyes, in which I would behold myself, pale, bleary-eyed and depressed (much like Registrar Branden after the Rusty Nail party, only without the half-moustache). I don't doubt that these spirits were relatives, first cousins perhaps, of the defeated witch, Lisa Ramirez. – Finally, I would turn off the computer in disgust, not excluding the surge protector on the floor, in the irrational hope that a sudden electrical storm during the night might destroy the hard drive and all documents it contained. Then I would go to bed, pathetically consoling myself with the thought that, if nothing else, I could at least *dream of* Anselm and Serpentina's happiness in Atlantis.

This wretched routine went on for several weeks, until, one morning, I received a totally unexpected e-mail from Archivist Lindhurst, in which he wrote as follows:

> My dear sir, a mutual friend informs me that you have written a biography of my former apprentice and now upstanding son-in-law, Anselm MacGregor, in twenty-one vigils, but that you have been unable to write the concluding twenty-second vigil describing his blissful life with my daughter in Atlantis, where they now live together on my capacious estate. Now, despite the fact that I am anything but happy over your revealing my true nature to the reading public, since it may well cause me a thousand unpleasantries in my service to the Stoneham Institute

as Special Collections Archivist—indeed, it may even give rise to a debate in the faculty council over the issue of whether and, if so, under what conditions a salamander may validly sign a contract of employment extended by the university, and, even if so, whether practical reason dictates the wisdom of entrusting important academic research functions to such a creature, especially in view of the grave doubts over the mental capacity of the so-called elemental spirits expressed by such esteemed Naturphilosophen (philosophers of nature) as Swedenborg and Carus, and, more recently, Sir Ethridge Danticott—and despite the fact that my closest friends and intimates may now strenuously avoid my hearty hugs and handshakes out of fear of my suddenly setting their moustaches and finely coiffed hairdos ablaze in my spontaneous ebullience—despite all that, I say, I would very much like to be of assistance to you in your completion of the work, since by all accounts it contains a good deal that speaks well of myself and my dear married daughter. So, seriously, if you are intent on completing the twenty-second and final vigil of your story, then step out of your wretched condo for a few hours and make your way over to my house here on campus. I'll sit you down in the blue-palm room, a room you're already familiar with. There you'll find the proper tools for composition, tools that will allow you to communicate directly and

concisely to your readers what you have yourself
seen, as opposed to offering them some vapidly
wordy description of something you know only
by hearsay.

Respectfully,
Salamander Lindhurst,
Special Collections Archivist
Stoneham Institute of Technology
Hoboken, New Jersey 07030

This somewhat gruff yet basically friendly e-mail pleased me no
end. I was certain that the old man was well aware of the, shall we
say, unusual manner in which the doings and destiny of his son-
in-law had become known to me—and which I cannot divulge
even to you, dear reader—but this didn't seem to bother him, as I
had feared it might. On the contrary, he even offered me a helping hand, from which I feel justified in concluding that he basically favored the project of my setting forth in print his fabulous
existence in the spirit world. Who knows, perhaps he knew of
other oddballs banished to our society from Atlantis with three
(or more!) daughters to marry off and hoped that some young
man, upon reading my story, might be moved to hear his own
"subway music" and find his way to his own Serpentina. (I've
been told that there is no overpopulation problem in Atlantis;
quite the contrary, it needs populating, always has.) Moreover, he
might hope that reading my story could possibly warn some candidate for Atlantis never to lose faith or relax vigilance during his
ordeal lest he suffer Anselm's fate of imprisonment in the bottle.

So, it was decided. At 11 p.m. sharp I left my condo and
drove over to the Stoneham campus, parking in front of the

manor house on the bluff overlooking the Hudson. The night was clear and the dark waters twinkled in the lights of the slow traffic of tugs and freighters crossing the river this way and that. The Archivist received me with warm greetings as I entered the vestibule: "Ah, so you've come, my good fellow! Wonderful! Wonderful! I feared the crusty tone of my e-mail might've scared you off. I'm afraid I've become quite the curmudgeon in my dotage. But clearly you see through all that to the good intentions that lie beneath. – So, let's get right to it, shall we?" And with that he led me quickly through the same series of rooms Anselm had traversed that first day, including the rotunda greenhouse and aviary (where, thank God, the birds ignored me entirely), finally coming into the blue-palm room with its astonishing fronded palm trunks arching up out of the walls. I felt a faint shudder wriggle up my back as I realized I was about to occupy the same seat from which Anselm had copied all those ancient folios.

Lindhurst excused himself momentarily, giving me time to get used to the chair and the air computer, and, hopefully, overcome my excessive awe before these—to me— hallowed surroundings. When he returned, he was carrying a silver goblet that exuded a blue flame. "Here," he said, "have a few sips of this. It was the preferred drink of a mutual idol of ours, the old gothic storyteller E.T.A. Hoffmann. Now *there* was an oddball! It's flaming arrack, a potent brandy made from coconut palm wine, rice and molasses. I do hope you like it. – Now, if you don't mind, I'll just slip out of my dressing gown here and take a little dip in your brandy. That's the best way for me to tune in to your creative process as you work."

"As you like, Professor," I said, "but as I drink this down, there'll be less and less brandy for you to … swim in, won't there?"

"Tut, tut, my boy! You just let me worry about that." And, tossing his dressing gown aside, he literally jumped, to my astonishment, right into the blue flames and disappeared deep down into the goblet. Having by now lost my shyness, I lightly blew the flames aside and sipped from the arcane concoction. It was exquisite!

Lo, it is the emerald palm fronds, is it not, that sigh and stir, as though caressed by the breath of the morning breeze? Roused from their sleep, they rise and flutter and whisper furtively of the wonders revealed in the lovely tones of the harp as though from far, far away. – The azure comes loose from the walls and mushrooms up like a cloud on steroids, filling the room with its blueness. But then blinding rays of light cut through the haze like a swift sword, causing it to swirl and spin in childlike joy, and, finally, to rise up to immeasurable heights, forming a grand arch above the palm trees. The rays of light increase in intensity and brilliance, until at last it is as though a curtain rises to present our Anselm standing in the middle of a forest grove bathed in sunlight. And is he a sight to behold! Dressed in beach wear, orange Hawaiian floral shirt, tan shorts and sandals, he stands on the lush green, waiting. He is not alone. He is surrounded by the community of nature, whose members are ecstatic to sing his praises. The flowers do it with their various fragrances, the rays of the sun with their light and warmth, the streams and brooks with their mirror-like surfaces of self-understanding, the birds with their jubilant chirping choruses, their Ur-music. All seem to say, "We are your friends and we will love you forever, for you have understood us. You possess the lily of insight that grows from the golden pot. You have reclaimed your birthright."

But, as delightful as this society of nature is to Anselm, he is only half attending, for his gaze is trained on the shaded space between two marble pillars fronting the temple that stands a stone's throw away in the grove's interior. Slowly he strolls up to the temple, his gaze now transfixed by the array of esoteric symbols adorning the classical pillars. At the same time, as he looks more closely at the pillars, they strike him as sturdy palms with carvings in their trunks. *Pillars or trees? Nature or culture? Must one decide? Can't we keep the intellectual distinction clearly in mind without losing the inward ambiguity, the agreeable ontological uncertainty? The deconstructionists in their wily way even take it a step further, insisting that culture precedes nature. What's that all about!* Then he looks down at the ancient steps leading up to the temple, now largely overgrown with moss, and smiles ironically at this perfect symbiosis of nature and culture, as though the mossy steps were responding to his ruminations right then and there.

"Oh, sweet lord of creation, she's not far off!" Anselm suddenly cries out, looking up in a swoon of bliss. And out of the inner temple she emerges, wearing the barest, minimalist, most diaphanous slip of a dress, her caramel locks framing her face seductively, the soft clatter of her shoes echoing crisply, rhythmically, off the marble floor. She walks straight up to Anselm and gives him a kiss, then smiles lovingly. She is carrying the golden pot, from whose soil a glorious fire lily has sprouted. "My love," she says sweetly, "the lily has opened its calyx. Forget your glass prison; a higher prophesy is here fulfilled! Is there anywhere else a happiness comparable to this?"

Just then, they hear another set of footsteps approaching from within. These have more of a staccato clatter, like sandals slapping a hard surface beneath. And lo, it is because the man approaching is, like Anselm, wearing sandals, along with matching beachwear. Anselm immediately senses the man's outfit as a gesture of solidarity and warms to him. Also, giving him the onceover and finding himself gripped by the peculiar intensity of his dark eyes and penetrating gaze, he cannot shake a vague sensation of familiarity. *Have I met him before? Where could it have been?* As if reading Anselm's thoughts, the man immediately relieves his uncertainty, saying as he extends his hand,

"Kafka, old boy. Franz Kafka. Call me 'Frank,' if you like, though you'd be the only one ... You remember, don't you, the South Sea island, the hill overlooking the deep blue sea where we chatted over Mai Tais? Marvelous afternoon, that."

"Yes, yes, of course," Anselm replied, intrigued but confused. "But that was ..."

"A dream?" Kafka said, filling in the blank. Totally befuddled, Anselm could say nothing. "Don't worry," Kafka reassured him, "You've just arrived here and it'll take you a while to revise—update—your pedestrian notions of so-called 'reality.' But, with Serpentina's help, the old view of things will fade away soon enough." Serpentina laughed as she put her arm affectionately around her beloved's waist.

"So, does that mean that I'm dreaming, or imagining, all of *this* right now? ... I seem to remember taking something," Anselm said, his voice trailing off as he placed his palm on his forehead in an effort to recall. Kafka placed his hand amiably on Anselm's shoulder while Serpentina pressed her head lovingly against his chest. Again, Kafka reassured him, "Don't worry, old bean, soon these distinctions between dream, imagination, fantasy, on the one hand, and so-called 'reality,' on the other, will no longer trouble you. Oh, to be sure, you'll still *have* them—the distinctions, I mean—they'll still be available to you, but they will no longer have *you*, and you'll no longer worry over which category applies to a given moment of experience. On the contrary, you will experience the joy of freedom from the pairs of opposites. That's because, as old Papa Hoffmann, a wise mentor of mine, and yours—and, apparently, Archivist Lindhurst's as well—once put it, you'll be living 'das Leben in der Poesie.' A life in poetry! You see, Anselm, a true poet need never write a line of verse. You yourself are a perfect example. It's your realization of your most intimate connection with the world around you, your total embeddedness in that world, that counts, that makes you a poet. Of course, you may at some point decide to celebrate that connection in verse; then you'll become a poet in the conventional sense as well ... Or you may just feel, say, like opening up a pizza shop—you know, you and Tina here having fun slinging dough together. The poetry of pizza! I like the sound of it.

Although Anselm was thoroughly enjoying his imaginary reunion—correction: strike 'imaginary'—with the man who helped launch him on his journey to deliverance, he was also getting a bit antsy about their main reason for being there: a wedding. Again, Kafka seemed to read his mind and responded accordingly: "Well then, shall we get on with it?" he said and looked at the happy couple expectantly. Once more Anselm felt confused and stammered, "I ... I don't know. I thought there would be someone here to perform the ceremony ..." Then, turning to Kafka, he barely managed to get the words out: "Could that be ... *you*? ... I don't know ... I mean, aren't you ...?"

"*Jewish*?" Kafka again filled in, emphasizing the point.

"Well, ... yes."

Kafka and Tina laughed. "Another distinction without a difference," the former clarified. "My religion, as indifferent to it as I was, belongs to my old Prague identity, my suffering identity. Here I'm just Franz, a witness. You yourselves perform the ceremony, such as it is, simply by announcing your total commitment to each other. That's all there is to it. Christian, Jew, Sikh? What's the difference? All love pizza." Then he added, upping the volume of his voice, "And by the way, lest I forget, there are other witnesses in attendance here," and, as if on cue, several faces and figures instantly recognizable to Anselm stepped out from behind various and sundry trees and bushes. Among them a goateed, uniformed doorkeeper; an imperial figure in his armor but without his horse; and a corpulent Sancho in his peasant's hat. These three were joined by others, including a tiger that bounded onto the green seemingly from nowhere and immediately lay down in perfect docility, three tiny ladies with bird bodies sitting on a tree branch humming a trio and a green dragon who was as much Barney as basilisk. Anselm nodded to each one in gratitude.

"They're all here to honor you, Anselm, for you have successfully negotiated man's last, greatest adventure, that of the spirit." Then, unable to resist a final quip, the sage of Prague concluded, "As for me personally, Mr. Mac-*Gregor*, it is already enough that you are the namesake of my most infamous literary character."

"Well, I'll be damned!" Anselm said, delighted.

"A*u contraire,* my love, *au contraire,*" Tina happily contradicted.

I am grateful to Professor Lindhurst for the wondrous vision I beheld of Anselm and his bride in Atlantis, a vision expertly conjured by the potion he concocted through his hermetic arts, and I must tell you that, when I came to and the mental fog cleared, I was astonished to see a copy of vigil twenty-two already printed out and lying on the desk in front of me. It was full and complete and provided the perfect capstone to my story, as you, dear reader, have just read for yourself in these pages. It only remains for me to say, for the sake of the genre, that they lived happily ever after.

THE END

Selected Books from PalmArtPress

Dennis McCort
A Kafkaesque Memoir - *Confessions from the Analytic Coach*
ISBN: 978-3-941524-94-1
474 Pages, English

Sibylle Princess of Prussia, Frederick William Prince of Prussia
The King's Love – *Frederick the Great, His Gentle Dogs and Other Passions*
ISBN: 978-3-96258-047-6
168 Pages, Biography, Softcover/flaps, English Translation Dennis McCort

Reinhard Knodt
Pain / Schmerz
ISBN: 978-3-96258-052-0
200 Pages, Philosophical Poetic Prose, English Translation Dennis McCort

Carmen-Francesca Banciu
Fleeing Father
ISBN: 978-3-941524-83-4
156 Pages, English

Kevin McAleer
POSTDOC
ISBN: 978-3-96258-088-9
220 Pages, Novel, English

Berndt Wilde
MY NY *Berndt Wilde – Drawings / New York*
ISBN: 978-3-96258-077-3
160 Pages, English

Jakob van Hoddis
Strong Wind over the Pale City / Starker Wind über der bleichen Stadt
ISBN: 978-3-96258-033-9
150 Pages, Poetry, Hardcover, English/German

Kevin McAleer
Berlin Tango
ISBN: 978-3-96258-051-3
274 Pages, Novel, English

Carmen-Francesca Banciu
Berlin Is My Paris – *Stories from the Capital*
ISBN: 978-3-941524-66-8
204 Pages, English

John Berger / Liane Birnberg
garden on my cheek
ISBN: 978-3-941524-77-4
60 Pages, Poetry/Art, Softcover/flaps, English

Rüdiger Görner
The Marble Song
ISBN: 978-3-96258-079-7
280 Pages, Novel, Softcover/flaps, English

Carmen-Francesca Banciu
Mother's Day - *Song of a Sad Mother*
ISBN: 978-3-941524-47-7
244 Pages, Novel, English

Jörg Rubbert
Beach Lovers
ISBN: 978-3-96258-046-9
176 Pages, Photobook, Hardcover, English/German

Kevin McAleer
Surferboy
ISBN: 978-3-96258-020-9
244 Pages, Novel, English

Robert Brandts
As We Drifted, Als wir dahin trieben
ISBN: 978-3-96258-056-8
100 Pages, Poetry, Hardcover, English/German

Matéi Visniec
MIGRAAAAANTS! – *There's Too Many People on This Damn Boat*
ISBN: 978-3-96258-002-5
220 Pages, Theatre Play, English/German

Carmen-Francesca Banciu
Light Breeze in Paradise
ISBN: 978-3-941524-95-8
360 Pages, English/Greek

Sara Ehsan
Bestimmung / Calling
ISBN: 978-3-96258-065-0
160 Pages, Poetry, Hardcover, English/German